Deat

Honour

Death or Honour

Michael Patterson

Crescent books

First published in the United Kingdom in 2017 by
Crescent Books Publishing

ISBN 978-0-9569798-6-5

Produced by
The Choir Press, Gloucester

The greater the power, the more dangerous the abuse.
Edmund Burke

Chapter 1

'Hello, David. What are you doing here?'

Before he could reply, Mary started to answer her own question, although this time with increased concern in her voice. 'It's Tom, isn't it? Has something happened to him?'

'Can I come in?' asked DS Milner, trying to remain as calm as possible. 'It would be better.'

This simply added to Mary's already high anxiety level. With some effort she replied, 'Let's go through to the kitchen.'

Mary and DS Milner had known one another for over a year now and, during that time, there had developed a strong bond between them. In fact, almost the type of relationship which might exist between a mother and son. What was slightly unusual, however, was that Mary was the partner of his boss, DCI Tom Stone.

'What is it?' asked Mary.

Milner could see the hint of a tremble on her lips, but he himself was feeling equally anxious, especially given what he was just about to tell her.

'I'm afraid Tom has been shot.'

On the way to Mary's house, he'd thought long and hard about what he would say. When it came to it, however, it was those few words which just tumbled out.

'Oh my God,' said Mary, her hands shaking and the first tears now starting to roll down her cheeks. 'Is he ... ? Is he dead?' she asked, struggling to get her words out.

'To be honest, Mary, I really don't know.' His voice now began to betray his own emotions. 'The last information I had was that he was with the medical team. DC Bennett was on duty when the call came in. He went straight to the hospital and then called me.'

'But he was alive then?' asked Mary, almost pleading with Milner.

'Yes, he was, but, as I say, that was a little while ago.'

'What happened? Who did it?' she managed to ask between her sobs.

'We are not too sure. It looks like he answered the door to someone at around 8pm. It was then he was shot.'

'I was there earlier this evening,' she suddenly said. 'I told him that I couldn't carry on with our relationship and how it was probably best if we didn't see each other again.'

Milner couldn't hide his astonishment at what Mary had just said. 'Really? I thought you were both very happy together.'

'We were, but his work just started to get in the way. The incident with James Grace was just the final straw for me.' This was a reference to a major investigation in which DCI Stone and DS Milner had recently been involved. Mary had become an innocent victim as Grace had tried to discredit and blackmail Tom by setting her up as a drug user.

Mary, when she next spoke, had regained a semblance of composure. 'Where is he? Can I see him?'

'He's at the West London Hospital. I'll take you there myself now, although I can't guarantee you'll be allowed to see him.'

'Who do you think did it? I bet it was Grace. It's the sort of thing he would be more than capable of doing. After all, he has made threats to both Tom and me.' By now anger had begun to replace her earlier emotion.

'I'm sure that he would be capable. The problem, though, is that he was already in custody when Tom was shot.' Milner paused, took hold of Mary's hands and in his most determined voice said, 'I promise you that whoever it was, they will be found and brought to justice.'

With a false laugh she said, 'You sounded just like Tom then.'

Chapter 2

'Are you DCI Stone's wife?' asked Joanne Grey. Mrs Grey was the senior hospital administration manager. Recognising the potential for a major news story, she had been contacted and immediately made her way to the hospital.

'No, I'm ... I'm his partner. How is he?' Mary asked in a hesitant voice, clearly betraying her anxiety.

'He's still in surgery,' answered Mrs Grey, in a tone of voice which sounded as positive as possible, given the circumstances.

Despite Mrs Grey's best efforts, her use of the word *surgery* had the effect of, once again, raising Mary's anxiety levels. 'Oh my God. Surgery? How long is he likely to be in surgery?'

Mrs Grey's voice was reassuringly calm when she replied. 'I'm afraid I can't say at the moment. I promise, though, that as soon as I know anything specific you will be the first to know. At the moment, he's in the best place.'

There followed a brief silence whilst Mary and Milner tried to take on board what they had just been told.

'Look,' said Mrs Grey, recognising their continued concern, 'why don't we go into the room there?' She looked towards one of the small rooms close to the main reception area. 'It's more private and I suspect you might be in for quite a wait. As I said, I promise I will let you know as soon as I know something.' She led both of them to the small room, in which there was a wood laminate desk and four uncomfortable-looking plastic chairs. 'If you'll excuse me, I'll go and see if I can find out what the latest news is on DCI Stone.'

Almost as soon as she had left, the door opened and DC Bennett walked into the room. Both Mary and Milner immediately stood up.

'Do you have any update?' asked Milner.

'Not really,' Bennett answered. 'Everyone I've spoken with just says it's too early to say.'

Before he could add anything else, though, Mary said, 'But you must know something. You've been here all of the time.'

'When I got here DCI Stone was still being examined by the doctors. I understand, not long after that, he was taken into surgery. I spoke to a couple of doctors but, as I said, they couldn't, or wouldn't, tell me anything other than that it's still too early.'

'That's what the hospital manager just said,' replied a now subdued Mary.

A brief period of silence followed and they all remained standing. Eventually it was Mary herself who broke the silence.

'I'm sorry I was so sharp with you,' she said, looking towards DC Bennett. 'It's just that I was hoping to hear that he was not in any danger.'

'I totally understand,' answered DC Bennett. 'I felt exactly the same.' Although he had only recently become part of Tom's team, DC Gary Bennett had known Tom for many years. Recently Tom had helped Bennett to revive his police career, after a difficult personal period of his life, and so Bennett felt a strong loyalty to him.

'Look, why don't we sit down?' suggested Milner. 'As Mrs Grey just said, we could be in for a bit of a wait, so we might as well try to make ourselves as comfortable as possible.'

After they were all seated, Milner, looking directly at DC Bennett, said, 'Do we have any more information about who might have done it?'

'No, not yet,' he answered. 'It was one of the neighbours who made the call. Apparently they heard two shots, came out to investigate, found DCI Stone on the floor, in his hallway, and then called 999.'

Suddenly Mary started to cry. Between sobs she said, 'I can't believe we are talking about Tom being shot, particularly today.'

DC Bennett, a slightly puzzled expression on his face, looked at Milner, who almost imperceptibly shook his head. Milner put his arm around Mary's shoulders, although he couldn't think of anything to say.

'Why don't I go and try again to see if I can find out what's happening?' said DC Bennett, recognising that any form of activity was probably better than doing nothing.

After he had left the room Mary said, 'I'm sorry. I know you have to do your job. You don't have to stay here. I'm sure you have got lots of things to do.'

'I'd rather stay here with you, if that's okay,' Milner replied.

There then followed what seemed like an extended period of silence, as both Mary and Milner were unable to think of anything more to say. In reality it was barely a minute before there was a knock on the door and Mrs Grey entered. There was a big smile on her face.

'I've got some great news for you. DCI Stone is not in any danger. Although he was shot twice, one turned out to be a flesh wound in his left arm whilst the other one went straight in and out of his right thigh. Thankfully it missed a main artery. I've just spoken with the surgeon who says that, although he might be in a bit of pain for a while yet, he should make a full recovery.'

'Where is he now?' asked Mary.

'He's out of surgery and has just been taken to one of the recovery wards. The doctor knows you are keen to speak with him about the attack, but is insisting you wait for a few hours more until the anaesthetic has worn off.'

The sheer relief in Mary's voice was obvious. 'Thank you so much,' she said, before, once more, starting to cry.

Chapter 3

Whilst they were still waiting to see Tom, and despite the fact that it was now the early hours of the morning, his immediate line manager, DCS Small, had arrived at the hospital. Although Tom's official rank was Detective Chief Inspector, he had, for the past few weeks, taken on the temporary responsibility of Station Superintendent, and it was in this capacity he had found himself reporting to DCS Small.

'It's Milner, isn't it?' asked DCS Small. They were both standing in the reception area.

'That's right, sir,' replied Milner. 'I'm DCI Stone's DS.'

'Do we know how he is?' asked DCS Small, with genuine concern in his voice.

'Yes, sir. The medical staff here have been great and regularly updated us. Although he was shot twice, one turned out to be a flesh wound in his left arm whilst the other one went straight in and out of his right thigh,' Milner answered, repeating Mrs Grey's earlier words. 'Hopefully we should be able to speak with him soon once the anaesthetic has worn off and they have been able to assess him.'

'That's wonderful news,' DCS Small said, clearly relieved. 'I got here as soon as I heard what had happened. Your mind plays tricks with you when you have the very basic informa-tion. I must admit, I was starting to steel myself for the worst.' After a brief pause he asked, 'Are any of DCI Stone's family here?'

'Not family as such,' answered Milner. 'His partner Mary is here, though. She's in one of the rooms down the corridor, and is obviously desperate to see him.'

'Yes, of course. She should see him first. I think that I should go and speak with her. Down the corridor, you said?'

'I'll show you where she is,' said Milner, deciding it might be better if he was there with her. 'I should warn you that, not surprisingly, she is very upset.'

6

'Thank you. Her name is Mary, you said, didn't you?' Before Milner could answer, though, DCS Small continued. 'Yes, I remember now. She was the person involved in the Grace case. Wasn't she accused of dealing drugs?'

Milner suddenly found himself getting angry, and this was evident when he replied. 'She was set up by James Grace to make it appear as though she was purchasing drugs. It was Grace's attempt to blackmail and discredit DCI Stone and so get the case dropped. As you know, though, DCI Stone carried on with the investigation and Grace, together with one of his sons, is currently in custody awaiting trial for a whole range of serious offences.' He drew in a breath. 'So, sir, you can see, after all of that, and now with the shooting, just how much Mary has gone through over the past couple of weeks.'

DCS Small didn't immediately respond, but eventually he said, 'Yes, I can see that. You make it sound as though you know the lady quite well. Would that be correct?'

'I have met her a few times over the past year or so and, I have to admit, I've come to like her more and more during that time.' Now slightly emboldened, he added, almost defiantly, 'Is there a problem with that, sir?'

'Not at all,' answered DCS Small. 'I just wanted to know the lie of the land before I met her.'

By now they were both outside the room. Milner knocked on the door and entered. Mary was seated and talking to Mrs Grey.

'Mary,' said Milner, 'this is Detective Chief Superintendent Small. He asked if he could meet you.'

DCS Small held out his hand. 'I apologise for meeting you in such circumstances. It must have been a terrible shock for you.'

'It still is, I can assure you,' replied Mary, now sounding more like her normal self.

'Yes, of course, I'm sure it is,' answered DCS Small. 'I understand DCI ... Tom ... will soon be well enough to see visitors. I'm sure you must be looking forward to seeing him.'

Before Mary could answer, however, Mrs Grey spoke. 'I'm Joanne Grey, Senior Administration Officer here at the hospital. I was just explaining to Mary that, whilst Tom is now much more comfortable, and in less pain, he will still be very tired. It's my experience that such patients take longer than you would imagine to fully recover from the effects of the anaesthetic. I understand that you will need to speak with him, but please be conscious of this.'

'Of course,' replied DCS Small. 'Whilst we will need to spend some time with him, we will make sure that it is as brief as possible.'

Turning once again to face Mary, he added, 'First of all I'd like to say that if there is anything the force can do for you, please just ask. I understand you already know DS Milner and so it makes sense that he should be your main contact with us.'

This was news to Milner although, in truth, he would have taken the role anyway.

DCS Small continued. 'Would you be okay if I made a statement to the press? I expect it won't be long before we have press and television people outside the hospital.' He then added, as if for reassurance, 'I've found over the years that it's best to issue a statement as soon as is practically possible. The longer one waits, the more the press start to suspect that things are happening which the police feel they shouldn't know about.'

'What would you say?' asked Mary, not unreasonably.

'Just how a senior police officer earlier sustained gunshot wounds but that his injuries are not considered life-threatening. Investigations are currently ongoing, and we would appeal to any members of the public who might have any information to come forward. It's fairly bland, I know, but it's more important we make some statement. Police shootings always generate a lot of press interest.'

Mary looked towards Milner. Picking up on this, he said, 'DCS Small is correct and, anyway, it might help obtain more information as to who did this.'

Suddenly a concerned expression appeared on her face. 'You don't want me to be there, do you? I'm not sure, right now, I could cope with that.'

'Not if you don't want to be,' DCS Small said. 'It's entirely your decision. I'm happy to talk with them if you are okay for me to do it.'

'Thank you,' replied Mary. 'I think that would be the best thing to do.'

'If you'll excuse me, then I'd like to go and make the

arrangements.' DCS Small stopped and, once again, faced Mary. 'And please remember what I said earlier. If there is anything you need, please just ask.'

DCS Small then left the room, leaving Mary and Mrs Grey seated whilst Milner remained standing.

'I was explaining to Mary,' said Mrs Grey, 'that we are hopeful she will shortly be able to see Tom. Normally, as I explained to DCS Small, we'd like the patient to have a bit more rest, especially given the time of day, but I think, under the circumstances, it wouldn't do any harm for you to be together for a few minutes. Anyway, he's asleep at the moment, but when he next wakes, and provided all of his observations are still normal, I'll come and get you.'

'That's great,' replied Milner, sounding as cheerful as he could be without it coming across as a little false. 'I'm sure he will be really pleased to see you.'

'I hope so,' Mary murmured to no one in particular, before repeating, 'I hope so.'

Chapter 4

Mary was seated by the side of Tom's bed and holding his hand. Despite being pre-warned that Tom still had numerous medical monitoring devices attached to his body she was, nonetheless, visibly shocked when she entered his room and saw just how helpless he seemed lying in the bed. There was an oxygen mask hanging down from the side of the bed and Tom had promised the nurse that he would use it if he began to feel breathless.

'How are you feeling?' she asked, not quite sure exactly what to say.

'Surprisingly good, considering,' he replied, quietly and in a slightly husky voice.

'I'm so sorry,' said a tearful Mary. 'If I hadn't walked out on you this probably wouldn't have happened.'

The previous evening, Mary had gone to see Tom at his house and told him she couldn't carry on with their relationship. It was only about twelve hours ago, and Mary suddenly couldn't quite believe how much had happened during that brief period. Tom's work, and especially the situation where she had been dragged into the Grace case, had driven home to her the growing conviction that she would always remain a distant second behind his job.

It had come as a real shock to him and he had found himself almost pleading with her not to leave. In fact, he had promised he would retire from the force so they could spend more time together. Mary knew, though, that this would probably just make things worse. She was convinced that, if she didn't end it there and then, their relationship would only deteriorate further until they both started to openly resent and blame each other. She still loved him, and she was sure he, at least in his own way, felt the same. Part of the problem, she knew, was that they were different personalities. She was outgoing and prone to bouts of impulsiveness, whilst Tom found it difficult to show his emotions and rarely did anything without first thinking through the consequences. That's why his offer to retire was too far out of character.

'Mary, please don't apologise,' replied Tom. 'It had nothing to do with you. It was just a coincidence.'

'But haven't you always said you don't believe in coincidences?'

'Trust you to remember that,' he said, with just a hint of a laugh.

'I'm sorry,' she replied, 'but I can't help thinking that way.'

'Look,' he said, after a brief silence, 'we can't undo what has already happened. Anyway, let's look on the bright side. It could have been a lot worse. If I had been shot by someone who knew what they were doing, for one thing. Fortunately, the person who fired at me was the world's most incompetent shot.'

Mary was not impressed by Tom's attempt at humour. 'Why do you always trivialise something which is very serious? You could have been killed.'

She began to cry as the sudden realisation of what she had just said hit home.

Tom squeezed her hand a little tighter. 'But I wasn't, was I?' he said quietly. 'Let's try and be grateful for that.'

She pulled her hand away from his and started to wipe away her tears with a handkerchief she took from her handbag. 'You're right,' she eventually said, albeit not too convincingly. She then asked the question which both of them knew was coming. 'What are you going to do now?'

'I thought you had already decided that we should split,' answered Tom, not meaning for it to come out quite in the way in which it did.

'Is that want you want?'

'You know it's not. I want us to stay together. I told you that yesterday.'

'I know, but ...'

Before Mary could carry on there was a knock at the door and Mrs Grey, together with one of the doctors and a nurse, entered the room.

'I think it would be best if DCI Stone was allowed to rest now,' the doctor said, addressing Mary. 'It really is important he does not get overtired, otherwise there's a chance that his recovery will be set back. And anyway, there are some other people ... police officers, I understand ... who would also like to speak to him.'

'When will I be able to speak to him again?' asked Mary.

'Why don't you go home and try and get some rest?' suggested Mrs Grey. 'It will be much better for his recovery if you have also had some sleep.'

'She's right,' said Tom. 'You look exhausted.'

The truth was, although Mary did feel physically and emotionally drained, she still felt her place was here, in the hospital. Even if she couldn't see him, at least she would be close by.

'I promise we'll look after him and not let him try to run away,' added Mrs Grey, 'and, anyway, there's that nice young police officer here to help me.'

'I assume that's Milner,' said Tom.

'Yes, he came to the house to tell me and then brought me here. I'm glad it was him who broke the news.' Mary leant towards Tom and gently kissed him. 'I'll be back soon,' she said, and then, with Mrs Grey alongside her, she walked out of the room.

A few minutes after Mary had left, DCS Small and Milner were allowed to see Tom, albeit under a strict time limit of just five minutes.

'First of all, Tom, I wanted you to know just how relieved we all are that you are not in any danger. I've just come off the phone from updating Commander Jenkins. He sends his best wishes, by the way, and looks forward to you making a speedy recovery.'

'That's nice of him,' replied Tom, in a voice tinged with sarcasm. This wasn't lost on either DCS Small or Milner, but both chose to ignore it.

Instead it was Milner who got straight to the point. 'Did you recognise who it was?'

'I'm not one hundred percent certain, but I'd still put my money on Billy Grace.'

'I thought they were all in custody?' asked DCS Small.

Milner shook his head. 'No, just William Grace, the father, and his son Brendan. Billy is the youngest son. We arrested him when he assaulted us – well, he mainly went for DCI

Stone – when we went to arrest Grace, but had to release him ahead of the court case.'

'Well, let's bring him in,' said DCS Small. 'We can't have an armed thug loose on the streets.'

'What makes you think it's him?' asked Milner.

'Although he was wearing a mask to cover his face,' answered Tom, 'he was wearing the same brand of trainers he wore when he attacked me at their house. The build was the same and I recognised his voice.'

'So he said something, did he?' asked DCS Small.

'He did. His exact words were … "This is from the Grace family, you bastard." Not the sort of thing you easily forget.'

'Did you notice anything else?' asked Milner.

DCI Stone looked up at Milner and said, 'Well, I didn't have time to make any notes. I was too busy trying to dodge the bullets which were being fired towards me.'

'Sorry, sir,' replied Milner, a thin smile appearing on his face, as he mentally welcomed back his old boss.

'Are the scene of crime team at the house yet?' asked Tom.

'Yes. They've been there for a while. We've also been carrying out house-to-house. Is there any CCTV in the area?' asked Milner hopefully.

'Not on any of the houses as far as I know. There's a small parade of shops partway down the street. I know at least one of the shops does have CCTV, so send someone to get the footage. You never know.' After a brief pause Tom added, 'I'm sure it was Grace, but without any hard evidence it's just his word against mine and, no doubt, he won't be slow to play the vendetta card, just like his old man.'

'But,' said DCS Small, 'in the meantime, let's pull this Grace character in.'

'I agree,' said Tom, 'but remember he's armed and desperate. So make sure you have the necessary resources and back-up.'

'I'll get on to it straight away,' replied Milner, before suddenly adding, 'I think we should have some security here until he's in custody.'

'I agree,' said DCS Small. 'As you yourself said, he's armed and desperate. The last thing we want is for him to start shooting here in the hospital. Leave that to me. I'll make the necessary arrangements. In fact, if you'll excuse me, I'll get onto that immediately.' He paused briefly. 'Milner. I think we should leave DCI Stone alone now to get some rest. I think he's had enough excitement for one day and, anyway,' he added, with a slight laugh, 'he'll soon start taking over the investigation.'

Just as they were both about to leave, though, Tom said, 'Milner. Can you stay behind for a short while? I might be able to give you a bit more information.'

'You heard what the doctor said, Milner. DCI Stone needs to rest, so don't let him keep you too long,' ordered DCS Small.

Chapter 5

After DCS Small had left the room, Tom said, 'I wanted to thank you for taking care of Mary. It was very kind of you.'

'It was not a problem. I just thought it would help if someone she knew told her.'

'But thank you anyway.'

'What was it that you wanted to tell me?' asked Milner, moving to a line of conversation he was more comfortable with. 'Have you remembered something else about the shooting?'

When Tom replied, it was not what Milner had been expecting. 'Do you still have the file which I gave to you?'

This was a reference to another case which Tom had been working on. A case which involved two deaths and their subsequent cover-up, behind which were senior people within both the government and the Metropolitan Police. Charles Cope was a government minister in charge of UK security, whilst the other perpetrator was, in fact, Commander Jenkins, DCS Small's immediate superior. Tom had, just a day or so earlier, confronted the two people involved with his evidence. Evidence which Tom had copied, placed in a file and given to Milner for safe keeping with the specific instruction to pass it to a named person within the media in the event of anything happening to him. Given the seriousness of his evidence, Tom had had to consider the possibility that someone might try to prevent him from disclosing it. His subsequent shooting had, however, complicated the matter in ways which even he had not anticipated.

'Sir, what is this all about? Is it connected to the shooting?' Milner had not been told about the contents of the file, nor had he, at least until now, asked about them.

'It's not,' answered Tom, and then he added, as an afterthought and almost to himself, 'Well, I don't think it is, although it's probably wise, right now, not to rule out anything.'

Milner, even more confused now, simply asked, 'Sir, are you going to tell me what's happening?'

'I will, Milner,' said Tom, 'but not at the moment. As I said to you when I gave you the file, it's best if you don't know. That way, if anything does happen to me, you can truthfully say you were not aware of the contents. I'm afraid you will just have to trust me on this.'

'If anything happens to you?' repeated Milner. 'What can be worse than being shot?'

Tom looked intently at Milner, who, for a fleeting moment, thought he was about to be told what it was all about. But that moment soon passed, and this was confirmed when Tom said, 'I can understand your concerns, but this is not the right time. If you are not happy with this, I understand that as well. If you want to return the file to me, then I will totally respect your decision.'

Although Milner had worked with DCI Stone for less than two years, he nonetheless knew when the DCI had made up his mind about something and had decided not to share any information which he felt was better not shared. In such circumstances it was usually best, however frustrating, to accept that decision. This time, though, things seemed different. It's not often that being shot isn't considered the worst-case scenario. For that reason he decided to try one last time.

'I didn't say I wouldn't do what we agreed,' Milner said. 'All I'm asking is that you give me some background information, so that I can at least know why you've asked me to do it.' He paused for a moment. 'After all, you never know, but I may be able to help.'

'Do you still have the file?' Tom asked, slightly tetchily.

'I do. It's still at home.'

'Good. My suggestion is that when you are next here, you bring it with you and hand it back to me.'

Once again, Milner's reading of his boss stood him in good stead. Even though he wanted to pursue the question, he knew that to do so would be counterproductive and would only harden DCI Stone's stance. So instead he decided to change the subject completely.

'I'll get on and follow up on the Billy Grace leads. With a bit of luck we should have him in custody shortly. I'll let you know when we have him. In the meantime, sir, I suggest, as the doctor said, you get some rest.'

Chapter 6

Milner suddenly started to feel tired. He hadn't had any sleep, and now the adrenaline that had kept him going was quickly starting to wear off. After he had left DCI Stone he headed back to the station. He had already spoken with DC Bennett and asked him to start making arrangements to assemble the team that would carry out the arrest of Billy Grace.

Despite this, on his way back, he kept returning to his conversation with DCI Stone regarding the mysterious file. On the one hand he was angry with DCI Stone for not sharing its contents with him. He'd even offered DCI Stone the opportunity to give him the scantiest of information, but even this offer was unceremoniously rejected. On the other hand, he had a grudging respect for DCI Stone's insistence that Milner should not be told anything.

What was genuinely worrying, however, was DCI Stone's continued references to the possibility that something might happen to him as a result of what the file contained. It wasn't in DCI Stone's nature to exaggerate things, so the secrecy simply added to Milner's increasing concern that the file contained information which was potentially very dangerous.

By the time Milner arrived at the station DC Bennett had already managed to assemble most of the team. Whilst Milner had been involved in a number of similar briefings over the past year or so, his role had usually been a supportive one to DCI Stone. So this would be the first time he had led the briefing and, as he walked into the briefing room, he started to feel a bit nervous. Not because he would have to communicate the details of his plan, but more because he knew he was about to be judged by his colleagues. Although, over the past year or so, his fellow officers had seen how he could technically fulfil the role of detective sergeant, he knew it would take considerably longer to gain their full respect. Rightly or wrongly, this was what really mattered most and, ultimately, would decide how he would be judged.

In many ways Milner was still seen as being in the shadow of DCI Stone. In fact, it wasn't that long ago, recognising how he was always going to be perceived, that Milner had applied for a DS role elsewhere, within the Brighton force. It was the logical thing to do. Make a complete break and develop his career without the guiding hand of DCI Stone. But his heart had overruled his head and he had decided, on balance, there was still a lot to be learned from him.

The other reason for Milner's decision was that he too had suddenly, and most unexpectedly, found himself in a relationship. They had met when she had started work, albeit initially in a temporary capacity, as DCI Stone's PA, and Milner's close working relationship with him had inevitably also brought him into contact with Jenny. It was still very early days but he had developed real feelings for her.

As Milner prepared to open the briefing, his doubts suddenly disappeared and he saw this as a perfect opportunity to win the respect of his colleagues.

'Okay, first of all, thanks for all getting here so promptly, especially given the short notice. I understand, for a few of you, it was your day off,' said Milner to the group of a dozen or so officers standing in front of him. 'You all know now that DCI Stone was shot twice last night when he opened his front door. We believe the gun was fired by our friend Billy Grace. The good news is that it's not life-threatening and it looks like he will make a full recovery.'

He paused for a moment before continuing. 'The bad news, though, is that this means he's likely to be back at work a bit sooner than I expected when I first heard he'd been shot.'

'Trust him to dodge not just one but two bullets,' one of the officers shouted. 'He'd do anything for a bit of a lie-down.'

'I bet he's on overtime rates as well,' someone else shouted out.

This generated a few more comments of a similar nature. Tom was considered to be of the old school when it came to policing, and he had often repeated the old adage about the importance of motive, means and opportunity when it came to solving a crime. What he also always added, however, was that, whilst these might get a suspect into court, it was unambiguous evidence which would ultimately obtain a conviction.

Over the past couple of years, DCI Stone's career had gone through a dramatic resurgence, to the extent that he was now seen as being at the top of his game. Although he had recently celebrated his fifty-fourth birthday, a time when most senior police officers were thinking about retirement, he had, most unexpectedly, found himself beginning a new chapter in his career.

This was in dramatic contrast with the time, not too long ago, when he couldn't wait for his own retirement to begin. It had coincided with a time when his old-school policing methods had been considered, at least by the top brass, to be too outdated for a modern police force. This was most clearly demonstrated by the way in which he was increasingly excluded from any of the major crime investigations. This point was not lost on his colleagues, as well as the younger officers, and they had almost begun to feel sorry for him. Of course he could see what was happening and had, even himself, started to count down the days when he could retire. Looking back, this was undoubtedly the lowest point of his life, both professionally and personally. What changed the situation dramatically, however, was a series of totally unexpected events.

Probably in an attempt to kill a bit of time ahead of his retirement, as well as keeping him away from the station, he had been assigned to help out on a case being handled by the North London force. This involved a series of unusual murders and it was DCI Stone, assisted by the fresh-faced new Detective Constable Milner, who had made the breakthrough in solving the case. The murders were headline, nationwide news, with extensive media coverage, and so his involvement had significantly increased his personal profile amongst the public. This was less appreciated by his immediate superiors, who nonetheless allowed him to return to the station and work on other cases. One such case not only resulted in the arrest of a gang of drug-dealing criminals but also exposed a hidden secret within the station itself, the outcome of which was the dismissal of the station's superintendent. It was for this reason DCI Stone had now suddenly, and most unexpectedly, found himself in the role of Acting Superintendent for the West London police force.

But there had also been another major turning point in his life: one which, in many ways, was even more unexpected than what had happened in his career. It was during the period when he had seemed to have lots of spare time that he had first met Mary. Totally out of character, he had registered on a dating website for older people and, after the occasional disappointment, it was through this that he and Mary had met. She was widowed and lived not too far away from him in Bagshot, where she had her own flower shop business. They had immediately hit it off and both felt increasingly comfortable in each other's company, to such an extent that, recently, they had discussed the possibility of moving in together. But this was before the ongoing James Grace case. Whilst Mary had always said that she recognised Tom's job would often have to come first, she had had little idea of just how much it could, and would, get in the way of their relationship. When Grace had used her in his attempt to blackmail Tom, the whole issue of relationship versus career had come to an emotional head and it was then she had told Tom that she was not able to carry on with their relationship any longer. But that was before Tom had been shot.

'Do we know if Billy Grace is still armed?' asked one of the officers.

'We should assume he is,' Milner said. 'So let's make sure that we do everything by the book. No heroics. Any possibility things might turn nasty and we back off. We will have armed officers in place, but I'd like to get this done as quickly and painlessly as possible.'

'Why do we think he'll have gone back home rather than done a runner?' asked someone else.

'Good question. We are not absolutely certain, but it would be the logical thing for him to do. Grace was wearing a mask and so probably thinks he was not recognised. Also, of course, he probably thinks DCI Stone is dead. So that's another reason why we need to move fast. Later today DS Small will hold a press conference, and it's better for us to make a move while Grace still believes DCI Stone is dead.' He turned towards DC Bennett. 'Have you been able to get a search warrant? As I say, by the book. We don't want to give any opportunity for Grace's lawyer to claim we have cut a few legal corners.'

'Expecting it any time soon, sir,' answered DC Bennett.

'Good. We need to make a thorough search of the place, outbuildings as well as the house. Evidence is what will send him down, so let's not miss anything.'

Milner then addressed the other officers. 'Most of you were there when we pulled in James Grace and his other son, Brendan, so you know the layout of the place. As far as we know there should just be him and his mother there. I seem to remember she can get a bit volatile, so, Constable Gilbert,' he said, looking towards one of the female officers present, 'if you could be prepared that might be advisable.'

He paused briefly before asking, 'Any questions?' When none came he simply said, 'Okay, let's go.'

Chapter 7

'Thank you very much for coming here today. I just want to make a very brief statement regarding the shooting of a police officer which occurred yesterday evening. I'm happy to take a few questions afterwards but please bear in mind I might not be in a position to answer every single question, as this is an ongoing investigation.'

DCS Small began reading his prepared statement.

'Yesterday evening, at around 8pm, Acting Superintendent Tom Stone of the West London force was shot twice when he opened the door at his home in Staines. Fortunately, although he suffered serious injuries, they are not considered to be life-threatening and, over time, he is expected to make a full recovery. Although a person is currently being held in custody I must stress that, at this stage, no charges have been brought. I would therefore like to take this opportunity to ask anyone who thinks they might have seen or heard something, however seemingly trivial, to contact the police.'

DCS Small then read out the police contact number before continuing,

'We take all shootings extremely seriously. Fortunately, they are still very infrequent and so it is especially shocking when a serving police officer is a victim. Acting Superintendent Stone has asked me to pass on his thanks to the paramedics who initially attended to him, as well as all of the medical staff at the West London Hospital. That concludes my brief statement.'

Immediately he had finished reading his statement, questions were being shouted at him from all directions.

'Please. I'll try and answer your questions, but I can only do that one at a time.' He pointed towards one particularly vociferous reporter. 'Yes. You, sir.'

'Is it true that the officer involved is the same officer who was all over the papers a year or so ago and recently involved in the arrest of the head of a criminal gang?'

'We have lots of officers who get media coverage and so I can't really comment on that. As far as your second point is concerned, yes, Acting Superintendent Stone did lead that particular investigation.'

DCS Small's reply simply prompted a burst of even more questions. Eventually one reporter, who seemed to shout the loudest, got DCS Small's attention. 'We have information that the person you are holding is one of the other Grace family members. Is that correct?' he asked.

'I'm sorry, I can't comment on that,' replied DCS Small.

'So are you still looking for anyone else?' the reporter added, as a follow-up question.

'Once again, I can't comment on that,' repeated DCS Small.

'So this is probably some sort of revenge shooting,' shouted someone else.

'I most certainly did not say that. Until we have completed all of our investigations it's important, in my experience, we continue to keep an open mind. I would also advise everyone here to do the same.'

'What information did you have which resulted in the arrest of your suspect? Was Superintendent Stone able to recognise the shooter?'

'I'm sorry, but you are asking operational questions which, as I keep telling you, I am currently unable to answer for obvious reasons.'

When it became clear that DCS Small was not about to share any operational information with anyone, the volume fell appreciably, and eventually DCS Small brought the press conference to an end.

Earlier, Milner and his team had arrested Billy Grace at his house in Essex. Although there had been some initial physical resistance, the arrest, as arrests of this particular nature go, was surprisingly straightforward. In fact, as Milner had anticipated, it was Grace's mother, Angie, who had proved to be more difficult and she too was currently in custody, charged with the assault of a police officer.

Not surprisingly, Billy Grace, backed up by his mother, said he had been at home in Essex all of the previous evening, watching television, and so could not have been the person who shot Tom. He did, however, add that whoever had shot him deserved a medal.

A quick search of the house and other buildings had, as yet, revealed nothing which could link Grace to Tom's shooting. But it was still early days and Milner remained hopeful they would find something. Nonetheless the clock was ticking and, unless they did find something fairly soon, then, in the absence of any incriminatory evidence, they would have to release him. As all of these thoughts swirled around his head Milner suddenly took comfort from one of DCI Stone's many adages: 'Absence of evidence is not necessarily evidence of absence.'

Chapter 8

It was later the same evening and Mary was back at the hospital. Fortunately, her shop didn't open on this particular day and so at least she didn't have to worry about that, although, considering everything else that was happening in her life, it was very much the least of her problems. She had tried to get some sleep, but whatever sleep she had got was restless. Eventually she had given up on the idea of being able to sleep and had got up, showered and then made herself a bowl of soup. She had no appetite but realised she did need to try and eat something.

Afterwards, deciding her place was back at the hospital, she had picked up her car keys and headed back there. On her arrival she had been told Tom had been moved to a different recovery room. When she found it, however, she was shocked to see an armed officer standing outside his room.

'It was something which DCS Small insisted upon,' explained Mrs Grey, who was still there on duty. Mary noticed that she was wearing the same clothes as earlier in the day and so quickly realised that she had remained at the hospital all day. 'This area is much more private because it's the furthest away from the main wards.'

If this was meant as some sort of reassurance it was, for the moment at least, lost on Mary. In fact, it simply increased her level of anxiety. 'How long has he been here?' she asked, looking towards the armed officer.

'Since about lunchtime,' Mrs Grey simply replied.

'How is Tom?' asked Mary.

'He's doing really well. In fact, he's been able to eat some toast already. The doctor is really pleased with his progress. Anyway, why don't you see for yourself?'

With that they both entered Tom's new room. Mary could immediately see how much better Tom looked. He was sitting up with a tray in front of him on which was placed a plate and a small toast rack as well as a small pot of coffee alongside a cup. Although he was still attached to the blood pressure and pulse monitors, the drip that had been attached to him when she had last seen him had now been removed.

'I'll leave you alone,' said Mrs Grey. 'But if you do need anything just press that.' She pointed towards a small buzzer by the side of the bed.

Mary quickly walked towards Tom and kissed him. 'You look so much better,' she said, as she took hold of his hand. 'How are you feeling, though?'

'I'm a bit sore, especially on my leg. It's throbbing like hell.'

'Have you told the doctor? I'm sure he would give you something for the pain.'

'I've already had some painkillers and so apparently can't take anything else for another couple of hours. Anyway, I'm sure the pain will soon wear off.'

Mary looked at Tom suspiciously. She was sure he was in more pain than he was admitting to, and she decided to mention it to Mrs Grey.

'Do you know there is an armed police officer standing right outside your room?' she asked.

'Yes. DCS Small insisted on it. A bit dramatic, in my opinion, but he was insistent. Anyway, I understand Billy Grace has now been arrested.'

'Billy Grace?' Mary asked. 'I thought he had been arrested already.'

From the look that flashed across Tom's face, she wondered whether he regretted mentioning it. 'No. That was his father and older brother. Anyway, they are all in custody now including, apparently, even the mother.'

The mention of the Grace family name suddenly made Mary very angry as it revived all of the feelings which the case had generated, and her subsequent decision to inform Tom that she no longer wanted to see him. Nonetheless, she decided now was not the right time to show those feelings and so, as normally as possible, she simply said, 'That's good news. At least they won't now be able to do us any more harm.'

The use of the word 'us' was not lost on Tom. He resisted the temptation to say, 'Let's hope so.' Instead he made do with, 'Yes, the courts will be busy dealing with the Grace family.'

An uneasy silence followed as both thought about the real issue which had still to be discussed. Eventually it was Mary who chose to raise it. 'Tom. I've been thinking about what I said to you last night before you were ...' Mary's voice trailed off as she struggled to find the most appropriate words.

'You mean before I was shot,' interjected Tom. 'You can say it, you know. I'm not going to fall to pieces every time it's mentioned.'

'I know, but it really upsets me just thinking about it.' She took hold of his other hand. 'Anyway, I suppose the only good thing to come out of all of this is, during all of the time that I thought you might be dead, I couldn't help thinking how much I love you and would miss you.' A few tears had, by now, started to emerge on her cheek. Nonetheless, she went on, 'I now realise that I can't live without you. I'm truly sorry for everything that I said last night.'

'Mary. I told you earlier you have nothing to apologise for. It should be me who is apologising. It was only because of my work that you had to go through all of this. If it hadn't been Grace then it might have been someone else. Who knows? It might happen again in the future. Of course I hope not, but I just can't guarantee it won't. That's why I told you I would be willing to retire if that's what it took for us to stay together. I still mean it.'

Whilst he genuinely believed what he had just said, he also knew, even if he did retire, there would still be a lot of baggage which would always be with him and was likely to impact on their relationship. The turn of events that had resulted in him being here in hospital did have one benefit: it had given him time to think about the future. A future which he hoped would still include Mary.

Chapter 9

At around the same time Mary was visiting Tom, Milner and DC Bennett were holding their first interview with Billy Grace. The Grace family lawyer was once again in attendance. He had become almost a permanent fixture over the past few weeks, representing the interests of James and Brendan Grace. Now he was back again to represent Billy Grace and using, predictably, the same tactics he had employed on all of the previous occasions.

'You don't have a shred of evidence to link my client to this shooting. This is outrageous and confirms this police force is engaged in a personal vendetta against the Grace family. Unless you can produce evidence then I insist that you immediately release my client. My client's reputation has been grossly impugned and so I will also be seeking a full and public apology on his behalf.'

Apart from confirming his name, Billy Grace had simply replied 'no comment' to every question which had been put to him.

'Where were you last night between 7pm and 9pm?'

This did prompt a reply. 'I've already told you when you came to arrest me. I was at home watching telly. I know you are stupid, but are you deaf as well?'

Grace's lawyer immediately turned to face his client, a look of sudden concern on his face. 'Just answer the questions, Billy,' he said, clearly trying to prevent Grace from losing his temper.

'What did you watch?' asked DC Bennett.

'I can't remember,' Grace answered. 'It's all crap anyway.'

'Do you, or any other family member, own a gun, Mr Grace?' asked Milner.

'No comment,' said Grace.

'So, just for clarification, you don't deny owning a gun?' asked Milner.

Grace's lawyer, once again, interjected. 'My client has already answered that particular question. What you are now doing is trying to put words into his mouth. For the record, I would like that to be noted.'

Both Milner and DC Bennett remained silent, which, intentionally or not, further increased the tension in the room.

Finally, Milner spoke again. 'What if I told you we had found a handgun at your house? Would that make you reconsider the answer you've just given?'

Earlier, whilst searching Grace's house, an officer had found a handgun hidden under a loose floorboard in his bedroom.

'You've planted it. I know all about you cops. If you can't get a result you'll just stitch me up. Just like you done with Dad and Brendan. You're just losers. Both of you.'

'We found it in your bedroom. Not the cleverest place to hide something like a gun. I thought you would at least make it difficult for us.'

Grace suddenly lunged forward and grabbed Milner around the neck. 'You bastard,' he shouted, before a combination of DC Bennett, the uniformed officer in attendance and Grace's own lawyer managed to pull him away from Milner.

'You lot will do anything to get a result,' Grace shouted. 'You'd better not hurt Mum, otherwise I'll do some serious damage to you both. Are you listening to what I'm saying?'

'For the record,' said DC Bennett, 'William Grace has just assaulted DS Milner and made additional serious threats against both myself and DS Milner.'

'Also, for the record, it is clear my client simply reacted to intentional provocation made by DS Milner.'

Milner had by now regained his composure. 'Your prints are all over the gun. How can we have done that?'

'I've told you already. I wouldn't put anything past you lot,' Grace answered calmly.

'We also have a witness who can remember seeing a small van parked a short distance from DCI Stone's house. Your van.'

'What evidence do you have to support that statement?' asked the lawyer. 'It could have been anyone's van.'

'We have officers, right now, who are going through CCTV footage. Fortunately, for us at least, the camera points along the street. So we should be able to see the registration number.' Milner glanced at his watch. 'It's now 7.26pm and this interview is ending.'

A short while later, Milner and DC Bennett were back in the incident room.

'I didn't know that the CCTV camera pointed towards where we think Grace's van was parked,' said DC Bennett. 'That was a bit of luck.'

'Nor do I,' replied Milner. 'Let's hope it does and that it's working. In the meantime, let him think about the evidence we have. You never know, it might persuade him to be more cooperative.'

Chapter 10

Tom was sitting up in bed, eating toast and drinking coffee, reading about himself in a newspaper. The previous day's press conference had generated quite a lot of media coverage. This was partly due to his personal involvement in the Grace case but mainly, he suspected, because of his increased profile resulting from the multiple murders investigation of a year or so ago.

He had always made a point, on previous occasions when his investigations had received media coverage, of not reading the papers. It was only now, when he had more time, that he began to realise just how big that particular murder investigation had been. Apparently, he was now considered to be one of the Met's top officers, tipped to go all the way to the very top. As he read this he couldn't help smiling to himself. He knew, if ever there was a police officer who was unsuited to joining the ranks of the 'top brass', it was him.

According to what he was reading he had come perilously close to death. That much, he supposed, was true, although the report made no reference to his assailant's total incompetence when it came to firing a gun. What descended, however, into the realms of pure fantasy was how, apparently, he was, even as he read this, still fighting for his life, when he was in reality enjoying his cup of coffee. Another paper stated, quite categorically, and based upon the expertise of a consultant surgeon whom he had never met, that he would almost certainly be incapacitated for life and that there was a real danger he would have to have a leg amputated.

He suddenly thought about his son, Paul, and whether or not this story had made its way to Australia. When Tom and his wife Ann had divorced after just a few years of marriage, she had emigrated to Australia and taken their young son,

Paul, with her. Apart from the occasional birthday or Christmas card in the early years, Tom had, to his great shame, entirely lost contact with him.

As Tom lay here in bed, unexpectedly having time to do so, he couldn't help but reflect on his life, the mistakes he had made, the opportunities missed as well as his plans for the future. Part of that future, he knew now for certain, was with Mary. But he also hoped that, somehow, he could regain contact with Paul.

The realisation he knew nothing about his own son came as a genuine shock to him. He suspected that, in the past, he had used his career and work to block out any such thoughts. But, during that time, Paul would have developed a life of his own. What did he do? Was he married? Were there any children? The thought that Tom might have grandchildren simply added to this sudden sense of loss and his determination to try to do something about it.

His reflective mood was suddenly broken when there was a knock on the door and Mrs Grey entered.

'Good morning, Tom,' she said. 'Did you have a good night?'

'I did, actually. It's amazing what a good night's sleep can do for you,' he answered cheerfully. This was in contrast to his darkest days, when his career and personal life were at their lowest points. During that time he had found it almost impossible to sleep and had often lain awake for what seemed like most of the night, when all he could think about were the negatives in his life. But that, thanks to Mary, now seemed like an age ago. 'Don't you ever go home? It seems as though you're here all of the time.'

'I do manage to get home sometimes. Fortunately I have an understanding husband, although I suspect the truth is he's just got used to it over the years.'

Tom wondered about his own situation with Mary and whether or not she would ever get used to it. 'Anyway, thank you very much for all of your help. Mary says you have been so kind and supportive. We both really appreciate it.'

'You really don't have to thank me. It's what I'm paid to do,' she said modestly.

'Well, thank you anyway.'

'You have a visitor,' she said.

Tom and Mary had agreed she would visit him later in the day, so he knew it was unlikely to be her.

Before he could speculate as to who it might be she provided the answer. 'It's a Commander Jenkins.'

Chapter 11

The last time Tom had spoken with Commander Jenkins was the day before he had been shot. Commander Jenkins, together with Charles Cope, had arrived at Tom's house in Staines in order to make Tom an offer. In return for handing over all of the information he had accumulated against them both, he would be allowed to take early retirement, based upon his current salary of Acting Superintendent, and at a time of his choosing. Trying to buy a bit more time, Tom had deliberately stalled. This would be, undoubtedly, the biggest professional decision of his life.

Despite knowing about Commander Jenkins, Tom could count on the fingers of one hand the number of times they had actually met and spoken. Commander Jenkins was too far up the pecking order for their professional paths to cross regularly. It was only recently they had met and spoken together at length, and their conversation hadn't turned out to be the most friendly, leaving a growing tension between them. A tension which would soon change into outright hostility, explode and lead to their professional paths crossing in a way which neither had anticipated.

But now, here Commander Jenkins was again, immaculately dressed in his commander's uniform, standing right in front of him.

'I have to say,' Commander Jenkins said, 'you look considerably better than I was led to believe by DCS Small.'

'You sound almost disappointed,' answered Tom, thinking about the threats that Commander Jenkins had made when they had last met.

He could see, from the slight facial change, his reply was not lost on Commander Jenkins. But he apparently chose to ignore Tom's confrontational reply. 'Perhaps I should have said how pleased I am to see you looking so well, especially for someone who was only recently shot.'

Tom didn't respond. In truth, Commander Jenkins was the very last person he had expected or, indeed, wanted to see right now.

'I'm sure that you will be delighted to know I've just been informed by DCS Small that Grace has now been formally charged with your attempted murder. There was CCTV footage, near your home, which clearly put him outside it around the time you were shot. That, together with all of the other evidence, ought to bring a conviction.'

Although Tom already knew that Grace had been arrested, he hadn't, until now, known about the CCTV evidence.

When he still didn't reply, Commander Jenkins continued. 'I wanted to come here to thank you for all of the work you *personally* put into the Grace family case. I suspect that, when we go through all of their activities in more detail, we will find much more criminality committed by that family.'

Tom's attention was on Commander Jenkins' use of the word 'personally'. By that, Tom suspected he meant Tom first being assaulted at the Grace family home, then having Mary, his partner, threatened and later accused of being a heavy drug user, in a way which resulted in their breakup. As if that wasn't enough, he had then been shot twice on his own doorstep. 'Personally' was probably the perfect description.

Given what had happened to him, as well as those dearest to him, Tom wasn't in the right frame of mind for any false flattery and, anyway, he suspected the real reason Commander Jenkins was here was still to be discussed. So he decided to raise it. 'Does that mean I now won't have an armed officer standing guard outside my room?'

They both knew Tom was not thinking of any potential danger from Grace. Commander Jenkins simply said, 'Do you still believe you need him there?'

'I didn't make the request in the first place, but, now that you ask, under the circumstances, it might be a sensible precaution.'

'What circumstances?'

'Well, let's start with the threats which you and Charles Cope made against me. I seem to remember how your parting words were along the lines that, unless I agreed to what you suggested, the matter would be taken out of your hands. The clear impression I got was that the decision would then be made for me. One way or another.'

'That's simply ludicrous,' Commander Jenkins replied, now suddenly in an agitated manner. 'Do you think we are going to have you killed while you are asleep here in your hospital bed?'

'It wasn't ludicrous when two innocent people were murdered directly as a result of your actions. What am I supposed to think?'

Commander Jenkins didn't, or wouldn't, answer Tom's questions, conveniently treating them as rhetorical. Instead he simply said, 'Our offer still applies.' This was a reference to their offer of early retirement. 'Given your current situation, it might be a more attractive option now. I don't expect you to answer right now, but please think again about the offer.'

Commander Jenkins seemed to hesitate momentarily before adding, 'There is something else that I am willing to do.' He continued without giving Tom the option of asking what that was. 'I would also retire from the force. It wouldn't be immediate, as I have some projects which still need my input. But it would certainly be within the next six months.'

'And what about Charles Cope?' Tom asked. 'Would he also retire? It doesn't seem much of a trade-off. Two people unnecessarily murdered compared to the promise of retirement with an index-linked pension.'

'The offer does not include Charles. Well, at least not at the moment. He told you about his current position. This country already owes Charles a huge debt of gratitude for the work which he has been involved in. Work which means our citizens can carry on with their normal, everyday lives without the threat of being murdered on the streets by terrorists. That threat is increasing daily. If Charles was not there then there would be a real chance that any future terrorist attack would be successful. That is not being melodramatic; it is being realistic. Charles is, right now, involved in many counter-terrorist operations. Removing Charles from those operations could have catastrophic consequences for this country. Is that what you want?'

Tom's increasing anger suddenly boiled over. 'If you are trying to emotionally blackmail me, then it won't work. What I want is for two dead people, murdered because of your and

Charles Cope's actions, to finally get justice. I would have thought you, of all people, would be true to that principle, or does reaching the position of a Met Commander suddenly disqualify you from having such principles?'

Tom's raised voice had obviously travelled beyond his room, as the door suddenly opened and a clearly concerned Mrs Grey entered.

'Is there a problem? Tom, do you need any help?' she asked, still a bit unsure as to what had caused Tom to raise his voice.

'There's no problem, Mrs Grey,' he answered as calmly as possible. 'I'm perfectly fine. Commander Jenkins is just leaving.'

After Commander Jenkins had left, Mrs Grey, who had remained in the room, said, 'Are you sure you are okay? You sounded as though there was something wrong.'

'There's nothing to worry about. Everything is fine,' Tom repeated. Even to Mrs Grey's ears his answer sounded far from convincing.

Chapter 12

DCS Small had earlier arrived unannounced at the station and was now seated in the room allocated to the station superintendent. Standing alongside him was DCI Richard Shaw, one of the other DCIs based at the same station as Tom.

If anyone epitomised everything which Tom found unacceptable about the modern police force, Milner reflected, it was DCI Shaw. He seemed to encapsulate the way in which the force had changed recently. His rise to DCI had been little short of meteoric, helped, Tom suspected, by an expensive education and privileged background as well as some very good connections. Tom felt that this fast-tracked rise within the force was at the expense of the experience to be gained by having put in the hard miles, over the years, based on good, solid police work. A natural instinct was something which couldn't be taught in the classroom. It could only come from making, and learning from, mistakes.

In Tom's view any shortcut to the top was seriously flawed. Unfortunately his view was not shared by the top brass. A new generation of senior police officers were now setting policy, and it was a policy which involved sweeping away a lot of the old policing ways in favour of more modern, technically savvy policing. Tom was most definitely considered a relic of the 'old ways', whilst DCI Shaw was considered to be the future.

What made it worse, at least for Tom, was the fact that DCI Shaw's rise had coincided with Tom's own career low point when his self-esteem was rapidly disappearing. Their differences were further highlighted as Tom, and other officers, began to realise that Tom was being increasingly excluded from any of the major investigations taking place, with DCI Shaw now becoming the default investigative officer. Not surprisingly, the two of them had taken an instant dislike to one another.

But it was then that fate intervened and Tom's interim posting to assist the North London force in their murder investigation was to change the dynamic completely. Apart from the positive effect that investigation had on Tom's own immediate career prospects, it had also subsequently brought him into contact with DCI Shaw on a different investigation. This was an extremely sensitive one, which, had it gone wrong, would have resulted in both of them being instantly and unceremoniously dismissed from the force. It wasn't lost on Tom that DCI Shaw had been willing to risk his own, still embryonic, career by putting his trust and faith in Tom. It was not surprising, therefore, that, whilst working together on this case, they had both come to realise that the two of them had different but complementary skills. Whilst it remained the case that they would never be natural friends, a genuine mutual respect had subsequently developed.

'I just wanted to congratulate you on a first-class job with the Grace arrest,' DCS Small said. 'Quick and without any major dramas. That's the way it should be done.'

'Thank you, sir,' replied Milner. 'The CCTV footage helped. The real clincher, however, was supplied by Grace himself. When we analysed his phone messages they showed he had been very close to DCI Stone's house, a few minutes after the time of the shooting. It's not often you get such weight of evidence. Of course, he still denies that it was him, but we are confident – well, as confident as you can ever be with this type of thing – we will get a conviction.'

'I think you are being far too modest,' said DCS Small. 'But, be that as it may, it was still a good result.' He changed the subject. 'You know DCI Shaw, of course.'

Milner had also worked alongside DCI Shaw on the investigation which Tom had led, and had come to both like and respect him.

'Yes, sir,' answered Milner. 'We worked together recently on the Superintendent Peters' – he hesitated briefly – 'situation.'

Superintendent Peters had been the station superintendent. He had been having an affair with his PA, who, unbeknown to him, was the relative of the head of a well-known criminal gang, shot dead years previously by police officers. Tom had been involved in that particular operation, and Superintendent Peters' PA had become obsessed with seeking revenge on the officers involved. It was due to Tom's tenacity and investigative skills, assisted by DCI Shaw and DS Milner, that she was finally exposed and brought to justice. A consequence of this was that, unsurprisingly, Superintendent Peters had resigned from the force, with Tom then being asked to fulfil his role, albeit on a temporary basis.

'Yes, how could we forget that particular ... situation?' replied DCS Small, more to himself than to the other two. 'I'll get straight to the point. I've asked DCI Shaw to take over all of DCI Stone's cases until he is fit to return to work. So, during that period, you and your team will report directly to him. None of us are sure, at this stage, how long this will be for, but I suspect it's likely to be a few months.' He paused momentarily before adding, 'That's always assuming, of course, DCI Stone does actually return.'

'Has DCI Stone indicated, then, he might not come back?' asked a now concerned Milner.

'Absolutely not, but you just never know what the final outcome might be in situations such as DCI Stone has just experienced. Anyway, we will work on the basis that he will return unless, and until, we hear anything to the contrary. In the meantime I want you to work closely with DCI Shaw. Hopefully you will not have a problem with that.'

Milner wasn't quite sure whether this was meant as a statement or a question, deliberately designed to force a reaction. In the event he simply said, 'No problem at all, sir.'

'Good. That's agreed, then. I'll be based here for a few days, until the situation has settled down. If there is anything you would like to discuss, then just make an appointment through my PA. I believe her name is Jenny.'

Milner chose not to reply, not least because, for the past few weeks, he and Jenny had become increasingly close. Although they had both tried to keep their growing relationship as discreet as possible, a few of the more perceptive people at the station, including DCI Stone, had spotted the subtle changes in their behaviour towards each other, and had, correctly, put two and two together.

It was DCI Shaw who next spoke, looking directly at Milner. 'I'm looking forward to working with you again, although hopefully it won't be for too long before DCI Stone

41

is back again. It won't be easy to step into his shoes. But if there are times when you think I'm charging down the wrong path, I hope you will let me know.'

Chapter 13

It was the following morning and Milner was standing by the side of Tom's bed.

'You don't have to come here so often, you know. I'm sure you've got better things to do than keep checking up on me.'

After the last time Milner had visited there had been an air of tension between the two of them, caused by the mysterious file which Tom had left with him. This time Milner was determined he would not be the first person to raise the subject.

When Milner had entered his room he had been really surprised to see just how much better DCI Stone looked. When DCI Stone spoke it was also in a much clearer voice rather than his previous rasping voice. Milner knew, however, that DCI Stone was now entering another difficult period. He had a notoriously low boredom threshold and lying here in his bed, waiting for his body to fully recover, would undoubtedly and quickly add to this already increasing level of impatience.

'I just wanted to fill you in on the Grace case, that's all,' Milner said. 'I thought you might be interested. But I can see you need your rest and so I'll come back when you are feeling less tired.'

Tom looked suspiciously at Milner before smiling and saying, in a far more conciliatory tone, 'Please sit down and tell me what happened.'

Milner didn't immediately sit down, but began to recount all of the events leading up to the arrest and subsequent charging of Billy Grace. After he had finished, Tom simply said, 'Well done. That's great work.'

Those few words meant a great deal to Milner. DCI Stone was not one to throw around compliments, so, when he paid them, they usually had a greater impact.

'Thank you, sir,' Milner replied. 'That's what DCS Small said.'

'You're being far too modest,' replied Tom, choosing not to rise to Milner's slightly mischievous reference to DCS Small.

'That's also what DCS Small said,' replied Milner, now enjoying their verbal sparring. It wasn't often he had the upper hand, and so he was determined to take full advantage.

'Okay, you've had your fun,' said Tom. 'Now that you are here you might as well fill me in on what happened. Please sit down, though. You are making me nervous.'

Milner, now seated, spent the next few minutes taking Tom through all of the main points relating to Grace's arrest, his subsequent interview and, finally, the evidence which had led to him being formally charged with attempted murder.

Tom didn't immediately reply, and when he did next speak it was in quite a reflective tone. 'No doubt his lawyers will try everything possible to reduce it to something less than attempted murder, but, I suppose, a conviction is still a conviction. Anyway, when did you see DCS Small? Did he summon you to his office at HQ?'

'No, sir. Actually it was at the station. He's planning to move in for a few days until things are back on an even keel.'

'I didn't think that they were on an uneven keel,' Tom said quickly.

Realising that his words had not come out as he had intended, Milner added, with slight exaggeration, 'He said how you would be missed and so he wanted to ensure that the station kept running smoothly during your absence.'

'Hmm,' said Tom. 'That doesn't sound too much like the DCS Small I know. Still, there's not too much I can do anyway whilst I'm lying here.'

Taking this as a good opportunity to change the subject, Milner quickly asked, 'So, have they mentioned how long you are likely to remain here?'

'The stitches need to be removed first. They then need to make sure that I don't get any infections. After that I'll need some physiotherapy on my arm and leg but, hopefully, that's something which can happen at home. Don't worry, I'll soon be back, if that's what you are worried about.'

'DCS Small did mention the possibility of you taking retirement. If you don't mind me asking, sir, is that something that you are thinking about?'

'Did he, now?' replied Tom. 'Well, I'm sorry to disappoint

you, Milner, but I have no plans to retire just yet. So I suggest you start getting used to the idea that you will still have me as your boss for a while longer.'

'Actually, that's the other thing I wanted to tell you,' said Milner, with a slight laugh. 'I've already got a new boss. Well, at least until you do return.'

'And who is that?' asked Tom, a discernible hint of concern in his voice.

'DCI Shaw,' replied Milner in as matter-of-fact a way as possible. 'It's the other reason why DCS Small spoke to me yesterday. He was there with DCI Shaw.'

Tom didn't immediately respond but, when he did, it was in an unexpected manner. 'That makes sense. In fact, you can learn a lot from Richard. He's got all of the hallmarks of making a good cop.'

It hadn't been that long since DCI Stone had said to him that DCI Shaw would *never* make a good cop, but Milner decided not to bring that up. 'Yes, we had a good meeting. Whilst he made it clear he was my boss he also said that, as long as I kept him informed, he would always back me.'

'Just what I would have said,' Tom answered. 'I told you he was a good cop.'

Once again there followed a brief silence before Tom continued. 'Anyway, it looks like I'm going to be laid low for a while yet, but if there's any aspect of a case you ever want to run by me then feel free to do so. I suspect, before too long, I'm going to get a bit stir-crazy.'

As Milner made his way back to the station he kept coming back to the less-than-enthusiastic remarks which DCI Stone had made about DCS Small. These, combined with the similar unflattering asides he had made about Commander Jenkins recently, had begun to puzzle Milner. Whilst it was certainly true that DCI Stone had never been a fan of those people who inhabited the upper echelons of the police force, something here felt different. And he had not mentioned the file.

Chapter 14

A week later Tom had been allowed to leave hospital. Although his speedy recovery had surprised everyone, his leg in particular still felt sore and weak. In addition to the physiotherapy he had also been encouraged to do a little walking, albeit with the help of a walking stick. Mary had insisted he stay with her and had made arrangements for her staff to run the shop whilst she was looking after Tom. He hadn't objected as even he knew, at the moment, he would not be able to manage by himself if he was alone in his own home. The question of whether or not this would ever become a more permanent arrangement was left unsaid.

Due to the necessity for him to take more exercise, he and Mary had found themselves spending a lot of time together. In fact, it was probably the longest period of time that they had spent together since they had met. This simply reinforced his feelings for her.

Slowly but surely, Tom's recuperation started to achieve results and, a few weeks later, he had permanently discarded his walking stick as the benefits of the continued period of exercise were felt. Regular meals, increased exercise and Mary's care had all resulted in him feeling even fitter than he had been prior to the shooting. His recovery was going so well that Mary felt able to, occasionally, go back into work.

Milner continued to visit him but, initially at least, only under Mary's strict supervision. To begin with, police talk was strictly banned, but eventually even Mary realised this was unrealistic and, anyway, she had to admit that it seemed to have a beneficial effect on Tom's recovery and sense of well-being. Tom would quiz Milner about the investigations he was working on and, if Milner asked, would offer some advice.

Apart from Milner, Tom also had other visitors during this time. His old nemesis DCI Shaw came to see him a couple of times, something which Tom particularly appreciated. After the last visit Tom suddenly realised how much he now actually enjoyed DCI Shaw's company. It was strange how what had started as mutual loathing had developed first into a sort of grudging respect and now this.

The most surprising visitor, however, had been DCS Small. He had appeared, unannounced, one afternoon. Initially, his visit had been hard work, with the conversation quite stilted, almost as if both of them were being deliberately guarded. Eventually, though, they both seemed to relax and their conversation became much more natural and, to Tom's great surprise, quite enjoyable.

DCS Small had, of course, raised the question about Tom returning to work. That was understandable and Tom knew he would have done exactly the same if their roles were reversed. When Tom confirmed that it was his intention to return to work as soon as he was fit enough to do so, DCS Small appeared to be genuinely pleased with his answer. To Tom this confirmed that DCS Small still had no idea about the file which Tom had compiled relating to Commander Jenkins. For a moment it did cross Tom's mind to tell him about the contents. But it was only a fleeting moment. That might have to be for another day.

Tom continued with his physiotherapy sessions and, much to his surprise, even started to look forward to his daily walk. He could, though, feel himself becoming increasingly impatient to return to work. Physically, he felt, with care, he could return. This wasn't lost on Mary, who, sensing Tom's growing impatience, and after advice from his doctor, realised that any resistance would be counterproductive. They both agreed that, if he continued with his recovery, he might soon be fit enough to return to work, albeit initially on a part-time basis. Part-time work, however, does not necessarily equate to an easy, gentle reintroduction. And so it was to prove for Tom.

Chapter 15

Tom arrived at the station, for his first day back, at about 8 am and was surprised to see just how full the car park was. Normally there were plenty of spare spaces, but today there was just the one. There was a handwritten sign which read, *Reserved for DCI Stone (aka Hopalong)*.

When he entered the station he could see why the car park was so full. Just inside the station's entrance were two lines of officers, with each line containing uniformed detectives as well as non-police staff. He had worked with many of them over the years, but there, in line, were also some of the newcomers whom he didn't know that well. As soon as he walked through the main entrance, all of them instantly burst into applause. He noticed that DCS Small had positioned himself at the end of the line, his hand outstretched, waiting to greet him.

To Tom's ears the applause seemed to continue for an embarrassingly long time, but it eventually started to subside and finally stopped completely.

'DCI Stone ... Tom ... welcome back,' said DCS Small, a big smile appearing on his face. 'We all know how much you like a lot of fuss and attention. Hopefully, this hasn't disappointed you.'

Most of the people there knew about Tom's aversion to attention, and so DCS Small's comment had generated laughter amongst them.

'Seriously, though, it is great to have you back,' said DCS Small. 'The station hasn't been the same whilst you've been away. You have a lot of friends here who were rooting for you.'

'Thank you, sir,' was all that Tom could immediately think to say.

Tom then turned around to look at all of the other people who were there. 'I have to say it feels genuinely good to be back amongst friends. There were quite a few things which I didn't miss – the disgusting machine coffee, for example – but you lot were not among them. I really appreciated all of your visits, letters, emails and texts. They kept my spirits up when ...' He hesitated briefly. 'Well, let's just say when I wasn't feeling too positive about things. It's a cliché, I know, but it's only in difficult times that you realise just how many friends you actually have.'

He hadn't meant to sound quite so sentimental, but the occasion had clearly affected him. He didn't feel comfortable with this and so made a concerted effort to move away from it. 'From now on, though, I will expect not to have to pay for any of my coffee.'

'You never did anyway,' someone shouted. This quickly became the trigger for other comments.

'The last time you bought anybody else a drink was when we all had Panda cars.'

'He still tries to use up his old pennies in the drinks machine.'

'When someone says to him, "Your round," he thinks they're referring to his shape.'

Eventually, all of the ribbing stopped.

'Yes, thank you very much. Very funny,' Tom said, holding up both of his hands in acknowledgement of their perceptiveness. He knew how coppers often resorted to humour in situations such as this. He himself had used it many times over the years, usually to alleviate a serious situation. 'Anyway, I'm sure crime hasn't stopped whilst we've been here. So thank you all again. I really appreciate it.'

For the second time there was a burst of applause before it ended and everyone made their way back to their own place of work.

'Tom. Let's have a few minutes together,' said DCS Small.

Whilst DCS Small seated himself at the large table in what had been the station's superintendent's office, Tom remained standing and looked out of the window. The office was located on the fifth floor and had an impressive panoramic view over west London. The buildings at Canary Wharf, together with their flashing warning lights, were all visible. When the weather conditions were especially favourable the River Thames estuary could also be seen, but today there were patches of low cloud which restricted the view. This simply, however, resulted in even more dramatic sights as all of the planes, on their descent towards Heathrow airport, emerged from the clouds, sudden and ghost-like. Despite the fact he had seen this hundreds of times, it still had an almost mesmeric effect on Tom.

Suddenly, these thoughts were interrupted as DCS Small spoke. 'Why don't you sit down? I've asked for some tea and coffee to be brought in.'

Almost on cue there was a knock on the door and Tom's PA, Jenny, entered holding a tray on which were two pots, together with all of the related accessories. After she had placed the tray on the table, looking directly at Tom, she said, 'It's wonderful to see you again, sir. We've all missed you.'

Jenny had still only been in this position for about three months, but during that time she had made a very favourable impression on Tom.

'It's good to see you as well, Jenny. I hope things are still good with you personally.' This was a not-so-veiled reference to her relationship with Milner.

If Jenny was embarrassed by Tom's comment, she certainly didn't show it. 'Things are very good there as well, sir. Thank you for asking,' she replied, an even bigger smile lighting up her face.

After she had left, DCS Small immediately spoke. 'I'm genuinely delighted you are back. I know we haven't always seen eye to eye on things, and perhaps our *modus operandi* is sometimes different, but that doesn't mean that I don't have the utmost respect for you.'

Tom resisted the urge to remind him how it wasn't too long ago that DCS Small had intimated that, due to his perceived dated policing methods, Tom should perhaps consider taking early retirement. Under the circumstances, it would have been churlish to do so. Instead he simply said, as graciously as possible, 'Thank you, sir. I really appreciate that.'

'Anyway, I wanted to inform you that we have now completed the process of appointing a station superintendent. I believe you may already know Howard Birch.'

'Howard? Yes, I've met him many times over the years. He's a DCI in south London, isn't he?'

'Yes, that's right.'

'So, when is he due to start?'

'Immediately. Well, next week, to be exact.'

Tom didn't appear to be too disappointed when he replied. 'That's very good news. Howard is a good man and, anyway, the station needs certainty. I've enjoyed my time as Acting Superintendent, but it also confirmed that it's not a role which suits my character.'

'That's very honest of you,' said DCS Small. 'I must say, during my brief time here, I have been impressed by both the commitment and the team spirit shown by all of the officers. I have to commend you on grasping the reins so effectively after the departure of Superintendent Peters. It's to your credit that the station continued to run so efficiently.'

'Thank you, sir,' replied Tom, still struggling to come to terms with DCS Small's bonhomie. By now, he was beginning to get a bit embarrassed by continually having to thank DCS Small for his generous comments. And anyway, Tom's natural defence had, more times than not, stood him in good stead. He knew there would come a time when things would not go quite as smoothly. They always did. It was just a question of when.

Chapter 16

'It's just like old times, isn't it, sir?'

Milner was standing in front of Tom, who was now seated in his old office. After his meeting with DCS Small, he had collected his personal items from the fifth-floor office and taken the lift back down to his old office on the second floor.

'What is like old times?' asked Tom.

'Well, me briefing you on what has happened recently, crime-wise,' Milner answered.

'This is not like the "good old days", Milner. It's not entertainment. It's criminality. For every crime committed there is inevitably a victim. I suggest, in future, you remember that.'

'Yes, sir, I will try and remember that,' Milner answered, a little too quickly for Tom's liking.

Milner had, during his time working with DCI Stone, come to realise that these occasional admonitions were all part of his character. When they had first started working together Milner had taken them as personal criticisms, but now he actually enjoyed them. In fact, sometimes he would deliberately say something just in the hope it would provoke DCI Stone into regaling him with one of his homilies. He had also learnt that it was always dangerous to assume anything when it came to DCI Stone's behaviour, especially if he felt their relationship might be getting a little too close. Milner knew the professional line between the two of them could only ever be crossed in exceptional circumstances. What was undoubtedly true, however, was that DCI Stone could be incredibly loyal towards his subordinates, sometimes to the possible detriment of his own career. Yes, DCI Stone was a truly contradictory person.

'Just tell me what has been happening,' said Tom.

Milner opened the file that he always seemed to be carrying, took out a single A4 sheet of paper and proceeded to read from it. 'A few car thefts. Three reported burglaries and a couple of muggings. Fortunately, all in all, a pretty quiet night.'

'Where were the burglaries?' asked Tom.

Milner took a different single A4 sheet from his file. 'One was in Hillingdon and the other two in Uxbridge. All of the victims had been away on holiday and so it was only when they returned they found out there had been a burglary.'

'Any sign of forced entry?'

'No obvious signs but officers are there at the moment, along with the fingerprint people.'

'And what was taken?'

'Any spare cash that was visible. Jewellery. Pieces of porcelain. A laptop, a couple of mobile phones and an iPad. In one case it also looks as though the burglars helped themselves to a few bottles of alcohol.'

'So, stuff that could be reasonably quickly sold.' Tom paused briefly as though he were about to say something else. Instead, he just said, 'Okay. Let me know if the house investigations reveal anything. You also mentioned a couple of muggings. Anything unusual about them?'

'They don't appear to be particularly unusual. One of the victims was a young man, who had been at a night club in Uxbridge until the early hours. It seems he had been drinking quite heavily. The doorman at the club remembered him leaving and, as he was clearly inebriated, tried to get him a cab. But the young man just started walking away. Anyway, he was set upon a few minutes later by a group of youths. It was only when they were disturbed by a road sweeper that they ran off. His wallet, phone and some cash were all taken. He took a bit of a beating and so is currently still in hospital, although he is expected to recover.' He paused briefly, allowing Tom to ask any questions. When none came he said, 'Uniform are currently following up.'

'And what about the second one?' asked Tom.

'All we know is that a man in late middle-age was found unconscious in a lay-by near Ealing. It appears he had been attacked as there was some bruising to his face. The paramedics were called by a local resident who had been walking his dog. The victim was taken to hospital and officers are currently investigating.'

'Okay,' said Tom. 'Keep me informed of developments. In

the meantime let me have a copy of your report on the burglaries. They all seem a bit too coincidental to me,' he added, now getting back into his stride.

Before Tom could continue, though, he was interrupted by Milner. 'And you don't believe in coincidences, do you, sir?'

'Have I mentioned that before?' asked Tom. 'Anyway, they might just be what I need to ease myself back into things.'

Chapter 17

Tom had left early for the day. He was under strict instructions from Mary not to try and do too much too soon. As he drove back to Mary's house in Bagshot, he suddenly started to feel quite tired. Even he had to admit that Mary was probably right to insist on his phased return to work. Whilst his visible wounds were slowly healing and, due to the regular physiotherapy and exercise, his mobility was definitely improving, he still was prone to bouts of sudden tiredness. Not the sort of tiredness a person might experience after exercise, but a more general lethargy. Even though he had been warned by the doctors that this might happen, he still found it difficult to come to terms with. Notwithstanding this, he had still got a real buzz from returning to work.

The extended period of time which he and Mary had been able to spend together had been extremely enjoyable. In fact, he had been surprised by just how enjoyable it had been. Despite this, however, it had become obvious to both of them that it would never work as a permanent option. Well, certainly not at the moment. Whilst they had not openly discussed it, as the weeks had gone by, there had been a growing assumption that it would make for a more healthy relationship if they continued with their own careers. For this reason there had been no discussion about the possibility of Tom taking retirement. Mary's only comment was a suggestion to him that a return to work would benefit both his sense of well-being and their personal relationship.

Mary was astute enough to know Tom was the type of person who needed to stay occupied. He didn't like gardening, and golf was not something which had ever interested him. Ironically, given the job he did, he was not a naturally sociable person and didn't like what he considered to be meaningless chit-chat, and so he had always found it very difficult to initiate any new friendships. That was why it seemed odd to him that he and Mary got on so well. Whilst he felt slightly uncomfortable outside police company, she seemed to thrive on interaction. She had been an active member of the North-West Surrey Players Amateur Dramatics Society for a number of years now. Even here, though, her involvement had been affected by Tom's job and, due to unforeseen circumstances, she had missed participating in their last production. This was another thing which Tom felt guilty about and demonstrated, as clearly as anything, how a police officer's work could impact on all aspects of one's home life.

As he continued his drive home, he tried to put these thoughts behind him and recalled his conversation with Milner. It was an area he felt more comfortable with.

He couldn't help but suspect how the burglaries all seemed to have a similarity in terms of their *modus operandi*. Either there was a common denominator or they were all just coincidental. And, as Milner had already highlighted, when it related to crime, Tom had never believed in coincidences. Milner had provided him with a copy of his report and, he promised himself, if he got the opportunity, would read through it later that evening.

When he arrived home, Mary was already there and waiting. 'So, how was your first day back?'

Tom made a point of looking at his watch. 'Well, half-day, to be exact. You told me to come back early and so here I am.'

Mary laughed. 'I must admit I didn't expect you to be back at this time. You always said that crime doesn't just happen on weekdays between nine and five.'

'Well, actually, today, at least, it looks as though that's exactly what's happened.'

'How was it, anyway?' asked Mary.

'To be honest, it was almost as though I had never been away. Milner was there to meet me carrying a few files and the machine coffee was as undrinkable as ever.' He chose not to mention the welcoming reception.

Mary looked at him closely and then said, in a more serious tone of voice, 'You look tired, Tom.'

'Actually, I do feel a bit tired. If you don't mind, I think I might go and have a lie down for a couple of hours.'

Mary continued to look closely at him. 'Do you want me to come and lie down with you?'

'That sounds like a good idea,' said Tom. 'After all, it would be selfish of me if I didn't share my free time with you. I thought you were out tonight, though. Don't you have a rehearsal?'

'I do' she replied, 'but that's not until later. If you want, I can always take back my offer,' she added, with a slight laugh.

Tom made a face, as though he were giving this serious consideration, and then, in an exaggerated way, looked at his watch. 'I think we might have time. And, anyway, to refuse would just be impolite.'

*

It was later the same evening and Mary was busy preparing dinner, so Tom decided he would take the opportunity to read Milner's report. Before he did that, however, he switched his mobile phone back on. Immediately he could see a number of missed calls, coincidentally from Milner, and so pressed the 'call back' button.

'Sir, thanks for getting back. I've been trying to contact you as you did say to let you know immediately if there were any further developments in the cases we discussed earlier.' As there was no immediate reply, Milner carried on. 'The man who was found unconscious near Ealing died earlier this afternoon. So we are now talking about the possibility of murder.'

'Yes, I do understand that,' replied Tom, a little tetchily. Instantly realising that he had been a bit too sharp with him, he then added, in a more conciliatory tone, 'You are quite right. I did ask you to let me know. Anyway, where are you? Still at the station?'

'Yes, sir. As soon as I heard, I began to pull together more information about the deceased. We could go through it tomorrow, if you like. I'm quite happy, though, in the meantime, to follow up on it. That's not a problem.'

'I'll be with you in about thirty minutes,' answered Tom.

*

Milner was waiting for Tom when he walked back into his office. He was holding the ubiquitous file. 'You didn't need to come back, sir.'

'Well, I'm here now,' replied Tom, 'so what do we know about the victim?'

'The deceased is Benjamin Green. Sixty-two years old, from

57

Ealing. He never recovered full consciousness and died at approximately four forty-five this afternoon. Officers are right now informing his family. What we do know is that Mr Green comes from a well-respected local Jewish family and so his death is likely to generate a lot of interest amongst the community.'

'Was there anything to suggest a racial motive?' asked Tom.

'Nothing obvious. But it's too early to say for sure. Anyway, officers are, right now, at the scene carrying out a forensic investigation.'

'Did anyone see anything?' Tom asked, as much to himself as to Milner, and almost as though he were reminding himself about the normal procedures to be followed in such situations. 'What about CCTV? Was anything taken? Where had Mr Green been, or where was he going? Who had he met?'

'We are on those questions already,' replied Milner. 'We are also carrying out house-to-house in the area, close to where he was found.'

'Good. Let me know when you get anything back. You also mentioned how Mr Green never recovered *full* consciousness. Does that mean he was conscious at some point?'

'I'm not too sure,' admitted Milner. 'Why do you ask?'

'Well, it could be, if he was, he might have managed to say something to the officers or the paramedics, or, indeed, any medical staff at the hospital.'

Milner, for once, showed some annoyance in his voice when he answered. 'Sorry, sir. I didn't think about that. I'll get DC Bennett onto it straight away.'

'Don't worry. It's only a couple of hours since you found out he had died. One person can't be expected to do everything. That's why we work as a team.'

Milner considered this to be slightly strange, not least because DCI Stone was not averse to working alone when it suited him. The mysterious file was a good example of that.

Milner's thoughts, however, were interrupted when Tom continued. 'Is there a Mrs Green? If there is, I suggest tomorrow we go and visit her. Perhaps she can answer some of those questions.'

Chapter 18

It was almost ten o'clock in the evening and Tom had arrived back to an empty house. Mary was with her amateur dramatics group and not expected back until after eleven. He walked into the kitchen and immediately spotted a handwritten note stuck to the microwave door. *Just reheat for 2 minutes,* the message read. *See you later. XXXX*

Tom opened the microwave door and saw a bowl of risotto. He had not eaten anything since lunchtime and suddenly realised just how hungry he was. He set the microwave timer for two minutes and then pressed the start button. Whilst the risotto was heating he poured himself a glass of red wine from an already opened bottle. The microwave pinged and he took out the bowl of food, tasted it, decided that it was at the right temperature, put it down on the kitchen table and then started to eat.

Although he had spent most of his adult life eating alone in his kitchen, he suddenly realised how this felt different. For the past few weeks, whilst he had been staying at Mary's, they had usually eaten together and he had really enjoyed those occasions. It was a little worrying, he thought, as he sat alone, how on his very first day back at work he had slipped into his old solitary eating habits.

Notwithstanding this, and while he waited for Mary to return, he decided to finally read Milner's reports relating to the recent burglaries. As per his usual routine with such things, he read them and then reread them, this time whilst making a few notes. When he had finished he took another sip of his wine and studied the notes he had just written.

What immediately became apparent was the number of similarities between all three burglaries. No obvious forced entry. It was instantly disposable items which had been taken. None of the houses had any alarm fitted. The victims were all middle-aged, or more elderly, people, and, finally, all the burglaries had occurred when the victims had been away. These had been carried out either by a fiendishly clever person or by someone who hadn't really thought them through properly. As Tom hoped it had been the latter, his thoughts were interrupted by the noise of a key being inserted into the front door.

'Hi, it's me,' shouted Mary. She then appeared in the kitchen and, seeing Tom's empty bowl, said, 'Good. I see that you found your dinner. I hope it wasn't too bad.'

'It was delicious,' answered Tom, perhaps just a bit too quickly. He then added, although this time with genuine contrition. 'I'm really sorry about earlier. I felt as though I needed to be there.' He shook his head. 'It seems as though old habits never die. Milner seemed to have it all under control anyway.'

'Perhaps you need to trust him a bit more. How is he expected to make decisions for himself if you are always there making them for him?'

'I know. You're right,' he answered. 'I am trying, though. It's just sometimes easier to tell him rather than ask him.'

'Tom Stone,' said Mary, 'I can't believe you just admitted that. You really are starting to get mellow in your old age.'

'Old age? Do you mind? I'm a man at the peak of all his powers. You seem to have forgotten this afternoon.'

'Not really,' she replied with a laugh.

He decided, if only for his own self-esteem, he would not pursue this any further. Instead he said, 'How was the rehearsal?'

'A bit chaotic, as usual, but I'm sure it will all come together in the end. It usually does.'

'It's *Midsummer Night's Dream*, isn't it?' he asked. 'And aren't you playing Titania, Queen of the Fairies?'

'So, sometimes you do listen to what I'm saying,' she said, once again with a laugh. Before he could respond, she continued, looking at the written notes on the kitchen table, 'I see you've already started making your word charts.'

'I like to see things written down in front of me. It helps me to bring some order to events. It must be the way my brain works.'

'Are they related to the death of that man?' she asked.

'Actually, they relate to some burglaries which recently occurred. I was looking for a pattern.'

'And did you find one?' she asked, genuinely interested.

'I think so but, as I've often found with these things, it's always best to plan for the unexpected. That way you don't become too lazy and complacent.'

'Goodness. Famous detective, mentor, lover and now philosopher. I really am honoured to be sharing my life with you.'

Chapter 19

It was the following morning and Tom and Milner were seated in the front room of Mrs Green's house. She was immediately opposite them. She was crying quietly and had a tissue in her hand with which she regularly wiped her eyes. Also in the room were two other women, both of whom looked as though they were in their late thirties or early forties. Whilst one of them was holding Mrs Green's hand, the other one glared, almost menacingly, at Tom and Milner.

Although the house was near the busy North Circular Road, it was set back enough that the constant sound of traffic was surprisingly muted. It was a large, three-storey Victorian house. Although there was no garage, there was enough space on the gravel drive for at least three cars. On one side of the drive there was a neat flower border, whilst on the other side were a couple of small bushes. Behind the house, on the right-hand side, Tom had glimpsed what looked like a large garden. Clearly this was quite a substantial property.

'Thank you for seeing us,' said Tom, after the formal introductions. 'I know this must be an extremely traumatic time for you and your family.'

'How could you possibly know how we feel?' said one of the women, now fixing her glare on Tom alone. 'Have you ever had one of your parents killed? Of course not. So please don't just say things you think might make us feel better. You should be out there trying to find whoever did this to Papa.'

'Please Ruth,' said Mrs Green. 'They are only doing their job.'

Tom waited a while longer and then said, 'If it would help, we could always come back on another day.'

This time it was the other woman, the one holding Mrs Green's hand, who spoke. 'Let's just get this out of the way. I'm not sure Mum could cope with any more visits. Please tell us what it is you want to know.'

It was Milner, taking out his notebook, who responded. 'Are you also Mrs Green's daughter?'

'Yes. I'm Rebecca, and Ruth,' she said, now looking at the woman who had spoken earlier, 'is my sister.'

'Thank you. We'll try and keep this as brief as possible. Mrs Green, do you know where your husband had been?'

Mrs Green once again had to wipe away a few tears before she could answer. 'Benjamin had been to our synagogue. Well, at least, that was what he intended.' She was clearly struggling to keep speaking, and so her daughter put a supportive arm around her shoulder. After a while she carried on. 'He was due to meet with Samuel ... that's Rabbi Samuel Aphron. But, of course ...'

Ruth handed her another tissue. 'Mum, you really don't have to do this. They have already said they will come back when you are—'

This time it was her daughter who didn't have the opportunity to complete her sentence.

'Do you mean when I'm better?' said Mrs Green, her voice now rising in anger. 'I'm never going to be better, am I? How could I? My husband has just died.'

As they heard their mum's sudden emotional outburst, both daughters began to cry, and Tom and Milner maintained a respectful silence until their sobs had subsided.

'I offered to drive Papa there,' explained Rebecca, between the occasional sob, 'but it was a nice evening and, anyway, he said the walk would help him clear his head, as he needed some thinking time. He promised, though, to call after he had finished his meeting with Rabbi Aphron, and I'd then drive there to pick him up. When he didn't ring we just thought that either the meeting had gone on longer than he had expected or, more likely, he'd decided to walk back home. Eventually, Mum telephoned Rabbi Aphron, who said how Papa had never arrived for their planned meeting. Of course, it was then we started to become very worried. So I decided to drive along the route, expecting to see him walking back. I even drove past the spot where he was ...'

This time it was Mrs Green who tried to comfort her daughter, who, by now, was sobbing almost uncontrollably.

Milner patiently waited for her to regain some composure.

'Please take your time.' After a further short while he said. 'What time did Mr Green leave to walk to the synagogue?'

'It must have been about 9.45 pm,' answered Rebecca.

'Thank you,' replied Milner. He looked at Ruth. 'And were you here at the time?'

'I was, yes,' she answered tearfully. 'I had come round to see Mum before I picked up my son from the railway station. He had been in central London for the evening, with some friends, and I didn't want him to walk home at that late time of night.' She then began, once again, to cry as she undoubtedly realised the irony of the situation. Eventually she was able to resume. 'I picked him up at the station and got back home at about midnight.'

Now it was Tom who spoke. 'I understand Mr Green was a prominent member of the local Jewish community. Is that correct?'

'Why are you asking that? Do you think he was killed because he was Jewish?' asked Ruth, her previous aggression resurfacing.

'The truth is we just don't know. At this stage, it's best not to rule anything out. But, I repeat, we have no evidence either way,' answered Tom.

This appeared to placate Ruth, but before she could say anything else her mother said, 'We are a Jewish family and we live in a small Jewish area. Most of our friends are Jewish and we attend the local synagogue. Ruth is married to Rabbi Aphron's son. So, yes, I suppose we are quite well known, but no more so than most of our friends. As I said, it's a tightly knit community.'

Tom decided now the time was right to ask probably the most difficult question. 'Do you know of any reason why anyone would want to murder Mr Green?'

This time it was Rebecca's turn to become aggressive. 'Murder? No one has mentioned murder before. We were told that Papa had died as a result of a mugging. *Murder* suggests something far more sinister. What is it you are not telling us?'

'Absolutely nothing,' answered Tom, truthfully. 'It's just we treat any death that results from an assault as murder. At this stage, we don't think anything of value was taken. Your father's phone, wallet and credit cards were all still with him.

Usually, with a mugging, the main motive is theft. But, of course, whoever did it might have been disturbed and decided to leave quickly.'

'So you are *not* ruling out Papa's death being the result of a religiously motivated attack, then?' asked Rebecca, still fixed on this possible motive. 'Otherwise whoever did it would have taken as many valuables as they could get their hands on.'

Tom could see that this wasn't going too well. 'As I said, we can't rule anything out at this stage,' he repeated patiently. He then decided on a different tack. 'You mentioned Mr Green was due to meet with Rabbi Aphron and he had mentioned how the walk would help him clear his mind. Do you have any idea why he was planning to meet him? After all, that time at night was quite an odd hour for a meeting.'

'I assumed it might have something to do with the extension project for the synagogue, but, to be honest, I'm not too sure,' answered Mrs Green.

'Is that your husband there, in the photograph?' Tom asked, pointing towards a large, framed photo hanging on one of the walls.

'Yes,' replied Mrs Green. 'It was taken earlier this year on my father-in-law Jacob's ninetieth birthday. It's one of the few we have which includes all the family.'

Tom stood up and walked towards the photograph so that he could look at it more closely. 'Who is the man with his arm around your father-in-law?'

'That's our son, Daniel. He lives in America but came back for the birthday celebrations.' She suddenly started to cry again but eventually said, 'Ruth called him as soon as we found out. He's now on his way back.'

'Where does your father-in-law live?' asked Tom, once again looking at the photograph.

'He used to live here, with us, but suddenly died about two months ago,' answered Rebecca. 'After our grandmama, Magda, died about ten years ago, he began to lose heart, but then, after his friend Ethel also died, he suddenly became much more fragile, disoriented and forgetful. It was still a real shock when he died of a heart attack, though.'

'Do you mind me asking who Ethel was?' asked Tom.

'Ethel was a friend of Jacob's.' She hesitated briefly before saying, 'They had known one another for a very long time and had recently ... well, over the past few years ... begun to meet again. Unfortunately, Ethel died about three years ago.'

'Thank you,' said Tom. After a short pause he said, 'Ninety years old, you say. He must have been so proud of you all.'

This time it was Ruth who answered. 'It was us who were proud of him. The Nazis shipped him, along with his mother, father, two sisters and a brother, to Auschwitz in 1944, when all of the Jews in his town in Hungary were rounded up. He was the only one out of his entire family who survived. He was then shipped further west, into Germany, along with lots of other prisoners, just before the Russians arrived at Auschwitz in January 1945. Somehow he managed to survive until the Americans liberated Dachau concentration camp in April 1945. He and the others had been transferred there just a few weeks earlier. After that, somehow, he found his way to England. He had no family still left alive, no money, and could only speak one or two words of English. Despite this, he still managed to set up a small business, buying and selling all types of filing products. Eventually he bought a bomb site, which still had a couple of run-down huts on it, and started his own manufacturing operation. Over the years it got bigger and bigger and eventually he sold it to a much larger company. That's when he bought this house.'

'That's such an incredible story,' said Milner, with genuine admiration in his voice.

No one spoke for some time. Finally, it was Tom who said, 'Mrs Green. Your husband did say something to the paramedics.'

Milner had earlier checked with the paramedics who had been called to assist Mr Green. They had confirmed that, although he had never regained full consciousness, he had occasionally managed to mumble a few words. Although most of these were incomprehensible, he did say something which they were able to understand.

This clearly grabbed everyone's attention. 'What did he say?'

'Apparently they could only make out the one word: *Hannah*. Do you have any idea who Hannah might be and why he would say that?'

'Hannah?' repeated Mrs Green. Her voice suddenly tailed

off as she started to sob again and Ruth, not for the first time, put a consoling arm around her mum.

'My daughter, Papa's granddaughter, is called Hannah,' Ruth said. 'As Mum mentioned, I'm married to Rabbi Aphron's son, Emmanuel, and Hannah is our daughter.'

Mrs Green continued to sob quietly. Tom looked at Milner, as if to say that perhaps now was a good time to leave. But just as they were about to do this, Rebecca said, 'Isn't that what Grandpapa also said at Hannah's wedding ceremony? Don't you remember? He suddenly got quite upset and started shouting *Hannah*.'

'When was that?' asked Tom.

'It was earlier this year, about a month before Grandpapa died,' Rebecca said. 'When Hannah later appeared, after the formal ceremony, that's when he started shouting. At first we couldn't make out what he was saying, but then we realised he was calling out Hannah's name. It was his friend Yitzhak – they were in Auschwitz at the same time – who managed to calm him down. He said something to Grandpapa in Hungarian. Hannah said it didn't really matter, but it was a bit uncomfortable, especially as it was all being videoed at the time.'

'Did your grandfather say why he had been calling her name?' asked Tom.

'Not really,' answered Ruth. 'We just put it down to the occasion getting to him. And, anyway, as we told you earlier, by then he was clearly losing his faculties.'

'Thank you,' replied Tom. 'So, someone else your grandfather knew managed to survive Auschwitz? That's incredible.'

'Not incredible,' said Ruth. 'More like miraculous. 'My husband's grandpapa, Josef, and grandmama, Ethel – the lady who Grandpapa had become friendly with again – had also been there at the same time. Somehow they all managed to survive and stay in touch.'

'I see what you mean,' replied Tom, amazed that four survivors from Auschwitz, all of whom knew one another while in the camp, had lived so close together. 'One final question. Had your husband argued, or fallen out, with anyone lately?'

'He wasn't a teenager, you know,' said Rebecca, interjecting.

'I'm sorry,' Tom quickly replied. 'What I meant was, had your husband's behaviour changed at all recently?'

'Not especially,' replied Mrs Green. 'He had, I suppose, become a bit more ... how can I put it?'

'Agitated, I suppose,' said Rebecca.

'Yes, agitated,' agreed Mrs Green. 'He had spent quite a bit of time sorting out his father's things, will, estate, personal belongings. The type of job which you hope you will never have to do. Occasionally he did seem to get a bit angry, which was most unlike him, but the death of a parent would make us all think about our own mortality.' Her own words were the trigger for her, once again, to begin to cry.

Chapter 20

'What do you think, sir?' asked Milner as they drove back to the station. 'Do you think Mr Green's death might have been murder or was it just a random attack?'

'I've got no idea,' answered Tom. 'Anything else would be pure speculation and, as you know, speculation is not something I normally encourage. It is a bit odd, however, how his body was found in a lay-by, yet he had gone there on foot. Anyway, the only way we will know for sure is when we have evidence to support one or the other. I suggest we wait and see if house-to-house or forensics throw up anything. I also suggest you pay a visit to the synagogue, get a list of who was there that night and speak with the rabbi to see if he can tell us why Mr Green wanted to speak with him at such a late time. I must admit that does seem a bit odd, but, anyway, let's see what they come back with.'

As Milner continued to drive he could sense that DCI Stone was in one of his contemplative moods. In such situations, experience had told him it was better not to interrupt. When DCI Stone wanted to speak, he would. So, for the next five minutes or so, no one spoke until finally, and predictably, the silence was broken by DCI Stone.

'Do you have the address of the burglary victim who lives in Hillingdon?'

Another lesson learnt by Milner was not to reply to such requests by asking another question. So, instead of asking, 'Why?' he simply said, 'Yes, sir.'

'Right,' said Tom, in a way which suggested he had just made up his mind about it, 'let's go and visit the victims. We should almost be passing anyway. Do you also know their names?'

'It's a Mr and Mrs Rogers. They live at 124 Jenks Road,' replied Milner, without any hesitation.

*

A short while later they were both seated in Mr and Mrs Rogers' front room.

'Thank you for seeing us. I know our visit is unexpected, but we just wanted to ask a few questions concerning the burglary,' explained Tom.

'But we've already spoken with some other policemen,' replied Mr Rogers. 'What more do you want to know?'

'We'd just like to confirm a couple of points,' answered Tom. 'Also, it's sometimes best to have a different pair of eyes look at it.'

Mr Rogers looked as though he was not totally convinced. Nonetheless, he said, 'Well, I suppose it won't do any harm. And anyway, if it helps to get our things back ...'

His voice trailed off, allowing Tom to resume. 'Thank you. I understand you were on holiday when the burglary took place. Where had you been?'

'Well, not so much a holiday,' answered Mrs Rogers. 'But it was still a long way for us to drive. We had gone to Cornwall to visit our son and his family. It was when we returned we discovered we had been burgled.' The memory clearly affected her and suddenly she began to cry. Mr Rogers moved closer to his wife to put a consoling arm around her shoulder.

'Why do people do this sort of thing?' asked Mrs Rogers between sobs. 'We don't have much anyway. It's just horrible. The house now feels dirty. I can't sleep at night and I don't want to stay in the house alone when Peter is out.'

Tom couldn't immediately think of anything to say and it was Milner who asked, 'Do you have any idea how they managed to get in?'

'I thought that was your job,' said a suddenly angry Mr Rogers.

'It is, but your thoughts are also important.'

'The other policemen said they didn't think whoever it was had forced their way in.' Mr Rogers paused before adding, his voice once again showing some anger, 'I know what you are thinking. Just because we are elderly, you all think we must have left the door open. Well, I can tell you that we didn't. I always make sure the house is properly locked up whenever we go out. Don't I, dear?'

'He does,' answered a still tearful Mrs Rogers.

'Did you leave a key with anyone? I see you have a cat. Who

looks after it when you go away?' asked Tom, having spotted a cat dozing in one of the other armchairs.

'Are you now saying it's Mrs White who did the burglary? She's in her seventies, for God's sake,' said Mr Rogers, still clearly angry.

Tom waited a while until his anger had abated. 'I'm sorry,' said Tom, not, he suddenly realised, for the first time today. 'I wasn't suggesting that. It just helps to rule things out.'

It was Mr Rogers' turn to apologise. 'I'm sorry. I know you are only doing your job. It's just that it's been so upsetting.' He paused for a moment. 'You don't know what it's like for us. First the burglars are in our house and then your people taking fingerprints of everything, and now you. I don't think we'll ever get over this.'

'If it's any consolation,' said Tom, 'my experience is that eventually things will return to normal.' He stood to hand Mr Rogers a card with his contact details. 'You've both been very helpful. If there is anything else you think might help, please don't hesitate to call me.'

Just as they were leaving, Mrs Rogers, who had not spoken since she had become upset, suddenly said, 'Please arrest whoever did this. I don't care any more about what they took. I just want to know they won't do it again to us.'

'I understand,' replied Tom. 'That's why I want to assure you that my officers and I will do everything possible to find out who did this.'

Although Mr Rogers did not reply, his body language clearly suggested he was far from convinced.

*

When they got back to the station, DC Bennett was waiting for them. He had the preliminary reports from the area where Mr Green had been attacked.

'I'm afraid house-to-house came back negative,' he said. 'The other bad news is that there is no CCTV in the immediate area. Although the area is quite built up, the road where Mr Green's body was found has sections which are quite secluded, and the lay-by is at such a point on the road. I have, though, asked for the area for any possible CCTV coverage to be widened. You never know; they might have captured something suspicious.'

As there was no response from either DCI Stone or Milner,

71

he continued, 'The search of the area resulted in the usual mixed assortment of items. They are all bagged and with forensics for further analysis, but I did make a list of them.' He took out his notebook, turned a couple of pages, and then started to read. 'A selection of empty drinks cans and bottles, a few cigarette butts, various bits of paper, what looks like a fancy hair clip, a blue biro, an old comb and a three-day-old newspaper. There were even a couple of coins. A pound coin and a twenty-pence piece. At the back of the lay-by was a pile of domestic refuse which had obviously been fly-tipped there.' He paused before adding, 'As I said, the usual selection of stuff. What was possibly more interesting, however, were the tyre tracks which were found very close to Mr Green's body. We are trying to match them to a make of car. There were some others, which seemed quite fresh, but they were some way from the body. There were also some footprints close to where the body lay, which might be interesting.'

He waited for a response but, again, when none was forthcoming, he went on. 'As I say, forensics have taken everything away for DNA and fingerprint analysis and are also taking a closer look at the tyre marks and footprints.'

'Good work,' said DCI Stone, before addressing Milner. 'It's possible Mr Green was followed from his home. I understand it's only about a fifteen-minute walk, so whoever did this could have followed him, knowing there was a lay-by on his route.'

'Wouldn't that suggest the killer knew where Mr Green was going?' asked DC Bennett.

'I guess it would,' admitted Tom. 'The alternative, of course, is that the killer was waiting there for him to pass.' He nodded to Milner. 'Anyway, the first thing is to go and see Rabbi Aphron. And don't forget to get a list of everyone who was at the synagogue that night.' Just as they were about to leave, he added, 'And check to see if there have been any recent racially motivated attacks or threats relating to the local Jewish community.'

'Is that it, sir?' asked Milner. 'Or will there be anything else? I was hoping to get away at a reasonable time tonight.'

'Anything to do with Jenny?' Tom asked.

Milner didn't answer and so Tom said, 'There are a couple of other things I'd like you to do, but I'm sure they can wait until the morning.'

Chapter 21

After Milner had left, Tom spent some time catching up on his emails. Whilst he had been recovering he had been removed from the station's mailing list. This was a huge relief to him as it meant he didn't have to work his way through hundreds and hundreds of 'for information' emails. Whilst he could see the benefits of using email he was also acutely aware of, at least to him, the drawbacks. And the proliferation of copying in seemingly everyone at the station was the biggest drawback. In his view it was almost invariably used simply to cover the sender's back so that, if necessary, they could claim that all recipients had been informed about any particular course of action. The irony, of course, was that any time saved by the use of emails was often wasted by having to read every single email, just because your name was on the distribution list.

During his time as Acting Superintendent this situation had become noticeably worse. It was amazing just what people thought he should know about. The redecorating of someone's office, a change in the weekly canteen menu and even, on one occasion, the date when a blocked toilet was going to be fixed were all, apparently, things so important that the most senior station officer should be aware of them.

His strategy in dealing with these emails had always been the same. He simply ignored them, his thinking being that, if they were so important he needed to know, then someone would come and talk to him. Most of the time this strategy worked and, even on the very few occasions when it was important he should know about something, it had never seriously affected the eventual outcome. So, scrolling down the list of emails, he felt an almost perverse pleasure as, without even opening them, he pressed the 'delete' button on his computer keyboard and instantly removed those emails he considered likely to be unimportant.

One particular email did, however, grab his attention. It

was from DCS Small and entitled *Private and Confidential.* He could also see, from the other names on the distribution list, it had been sent to a very select group of people indeed.

He clicked on the email and read through it.

Your invitation to Commander Jenkins' retirement dinner.

After almost 35 years of total dedication to the Met, Commander Jenkins has decided he would like to spend the next stage of his life doing something different and has, therefore, decided this is a good time to retire. He will be leaving the force at the end of this month.

I have the pleasure of arranging a special retirement dinner and cordially invite you to share in this momentous event.

Further details relating to the date, time and venue of the dinner were also included in the email. Tom read it for a second time and then looked away from his computer and focussed on some unspecified place in the distance. The whole issue of the incriminating file, and especially what to do with it, had been playing heavily on his mind ever since he had left hospital. DCS Small's invitation had now brought it into even sharper focus. In truth, and against his normal instincts of immediate action, he had been almost looking for excuses to delay his decision as to what to do next. He suddenly felt a sense of relief surging through his body. He now knew that the moment of decision could no longer be put off.

Chapter 22

'That's incredible,' said a clearly stunned and almost disbelieving DCS Small.

It was the following morning and Tom had, first thing, contacted DCS Small's PA to arrange a meeting. Although he had stressed the urgency of the meeting, the earliest date she had been able to give him was more than a week away. It was only when he had insisted she put him through to DCS Small personally and immediately that she had realised Tom was not going to take no for an answer. Amazingly, she then had found this opening in DCS Small's schedule.

Tom had spent the previous evening rereading all of the notes in his file as he knew it would be important to present a compelling, evidence-based summary of the facts to DCS Small. During his brief time as Acting Superintendent he had witnessed, at first hand, just how much mutual respect there was between Commander Jenkins and DCS Small. Not surprisingly he'd had a restless night's sleep as he had continued to rehearse his case. But, as he had often found in similar circumstances, the adrenaline flowing through his body had, for now at least, overcome any physical tiredness which the lack of sleep might normally have caused.

'You do know what you are suggesting, don't you?' DCS Small asked, still trying to fully comprehend what he had just heard from Tom. 'That a very senior Metropolitan Police officer, together with a current government minister, was involved in murder. If that wasn't incredible enough, they then conspired not only to cover up the murder, but also to knowingly allow an innocent man to be convicted of the crime.' He shook his head. 'If what you are suggesting is correct then this will have huge implications, not just for the Met but, conceivably, also for the government.'

'I have thought of little else since the facts became clear,' answered Tom, who was standing in front of a seated DCS Small. 'It's all here in the file.' He placed the file on the desk in front of him. 'Just to be clear, they were not the people who actually murdered the woman.' He paused briefly. 'Incidentally, she was called Susan Chambers. But they were involved in sending whoever did do it to her flat with the intention of finding the photograph. I'm certain they never expected her to be killed. Nonetheless, Susan did die, they did cover it up and they then allowed an innocent man to be sentenced for her murder. A man, incidentally, who himself was later killed by a cellmate. The obvious implication being, of course, that if he had not been incorrectly sentenced then he would still be alive today. Finally, both Commander Jenkins and Charles Cope are also guilty of perverting the course of justice. They might not have inflicted the blow which killed Susan, but they probably know who did and refuse to say who it was.'

DCS Small ignored the file. 'And you say you've already approached Commander Jenkins with all of this.'

'Yes, sir, as well as Charles Cope.'

'My God,' he replied, now even more exasperated. 'And what did they say?'

'They both eventually admitted it. Just so it didn't become my word against theirs, though, I recorded their admission. It's all in the file.'

Suddenly DCS Small became quite angry. 'Why didn't you bring all of this to me sooner? When you first suspected, or at least when you started to obtain evidence?'

Tom had anticipated DCS Small's question. It was perfectly logical and one, in fact, he would also have asked if their roles had been reversed. He had decided that a more proactive, unequivocal approach was needed. 'Would you have believed me, sir? And, anyway, I had to first make certain that you yourself weren't also involved.'

For a fleeting moment Tom thought DCS Small would explode with anger. But it was only fleeting because instead, and most unexpectedly, he started to laugh.

'I tell you, DCI Stone, you've certainly got some balls. I'm not sure how I would have reacted if I'd had your suspicions. You are certainly no respecter of seniority. First there was Superintendent Peters, and now Commander Jenkins and

Charles Cope. Who next? The Commissioner himself? Or what about the Prime Minister?'

'I was simply following the evidence. I'm sure you would have done exactly the same, sir.'

Just briefly, Tom thought that, once again, he could see a hint of anger on DCS Small's face. But, if there had been one, then, like before, it quickly disappeared.

'Well, yes,' DCS Small replied. 'The main priority right now, though, is what to do with all of this. Clearly, this is so sensitive that it's vital there are no leaks whatsoever. Does anyone else know about this?' he suddenly asked, clearly concerned.

'Just me,' replied Tom, suddenly grateful that he had resisted the temptation to bring Milner into the picture. 'Although I did take the precaution of copying the file and placing it in safe keeping just in case anything happened to me.'

'My God,' said DCS Small, for the second time. 'Did you really believe you were in danger?'

'Why not?' Tom asked, with an accompanying shrug of his shoulders.

'This is like some convoluted spy thriller. Any normal person would dismiss it as being just too unbelievable.'

There then followed an extended period of silence until, finally, DCS Small said, 'Right. This is what we will do. I will take your file and go and see the Commissioner. I'm sure he will, at some point, also want to see you. In fact, that is a certainty. In the meantime, tell no one – and I mean no one – about this.' He paused. 'Is there anything else you think I should do?'

'If I were you,' replied Tom, 'the first thing I would do would be to cancel Commander Jenkins' retirement dinner.'

Chapter 23

At that time of the day it didn't take Tom long before he was back at the station. The time felt especially short as it was one of those occasions when, in retrospect, you can remember very little about the journey itself. His mind, not surprisingly, had been fully occupied by his meeting with DCS Small and the likely consequences. On the one hand, he felt a huge sense of relief now he had finally made the decision to pass on the file. On the other hand, he felt a slight sense of guilt at having now, in effect, passed the problem over to DCS Small. He immediately, however, dismissed this thought on the basis that he had done his job and it was now up to others to do with the file as they saw fit.

His mind was still on all of this as he entered the station. For once there was no sign of Milner, although DC Bennett was in the office.

'Morning, sir,' DC Bennett said. 'Just to let you know, DS Milner has gone to visit the synagogue. When we got there last night there was no one about and so DS Milner called first thing this morning to arrange a meeting. Hopefully, he should be back soon.'

'Did you manage to walk the route?' asked Tom, referring to the route that Mr Green had taken on the night of his murder, from his home to the synagogue.

'We did. As you said, it didn't take too long to walk it. Whoever did it chose the location really well. It is set well back from the road and, because of the trees and a few overgrown bushes, there is plenty of cover from the road. I also spoke with the man who contacted us after he had found Mr Green's body.' He referred to his notebook. 'A Mr John Stephenson. He found the body – well, it was his dog which first alerted him – at about 10.30pm and he called us at 10.33 pm. He'd walked past the lay-by about ten minutes earlier, when he'd spotted a car pulling into it. Unfortunately he couldn't recall what make it was. But he was sure there were two people in it.'

'Both males? Male and female?' asked Tom.

'He doesn't know, I'm afraid,' answered DC Bennett. 'But he does think at least one of them was male.'

'It was a bit late for pulling into a lay-by,' suggested Tom, 'unless, of course, you are up to no good.'

'That's what I thought,' said DC Bennett, 'although Mr Stephenson did say there had recently been a bout of fly-tipping there. Given the time of night, he wasn't about to confront them.'

'Makes sense, I suppose,' admitted Tom.

'Anyway, I've got his statement and I told him we are likely to want to speak with him again. Regarding the possible racial motive, I checked and there has been no increase in attacks or threats reported at all.'

'Well, that's something, I suppose,' said Tom. 'The last thing we need are organised attacks on local Jewish people. There's still the fingerprint, DNA, tyre track and footprint analysis to come back. Hopefully, they might give us a lead.'

Just as DC Bennett was about to leave, Tom said, 'Do you have anything else you are working on at the moment?'

DC Bennett had known Tom much longer than Milner had, and so he immediately realised where this might be leading. 'I was planning to start writing up some reports, sir. That is, at least, until DS Milner returns. Why? Is there something you would like me to do?'

'There is. Unless, of course, you'd prefer to write up your reports instead.'

DC Bennett smiled as he said, 'Tough choice. What is it, sir?'

'You know about the recent break-ins where there was no obvious forced entry, don't you?'

'I do, sir. DS Milner mentioned to me, yesterday, how you had been to visit one set of victims.'

'That's right. So what I'd like you to do is to do the same with the victims in the other two cases. I believe they both live fairly locally in Uxbridge. I'm particularly interested to know where they had recently been on holiday, how they had got there, and if they had any pets.'

'Any pets?' asked a clearly puzzled DC Bennett.

'That's right, any pets,' repeated Tom.

'Any reason for that, sir?' DC Bennett asked, not unreasonably.

'Just a hunch, that's all. It might not be relevant, but find out anyway.'

*

It would be early afternoon before Milner returned, giving Tom the opportunity to complete the task, which had been interrupted by the receipt of DCS Small's retirement dinner email, of reviewing all of his outstanding emails.

Midway through, Tom went to the canteen and, whilst eating his lunch, spotted Jenny, who was just about to pay for her own lunch.

'Hi there,' he said. 'Fancy keeping me company?'

'That would be nice, sir.' She walked over to where he was sitting, placed her tray on the table and then sat down. 'How are you feeling now, sir? David ... sorry, DS Milner mentioned to me how he thought you were almost back to your old self.'

'Did he?' said Tom. 'And did he mean that as a compliment or as a criticism?'

'I'm sure he meant it as a compliment, sir,' she answered quickly.

'I'm sure he did. I was only teasing you.'

Jenny started to laugh. 'I never quite know when you are being serious.'

'I would have thought you had got used to me by now. Anyway, if you don't mind me asking, how are you and Milner getting on? I haven't had the chance to speak with you properly since I returned.'

Tom recognised the irony of the situation. Sometimes he found it easier to discuss quite personal things with someone who he had not known for that long than with someone who he had known for much longer or, as with Mary, who he had strong feelings for.

'So far, so good, sir,' she replied. 'Although I'm beginning to realise it's not that easy to plan ahead when your boyfriend is a policeman. Take last night, for example. We were planning to go out for dinner together but had to cancel.'

This was the first time Tom had heard the word 'boyfriend' mentioned, but he decided not to follow up on it. 'Yes, well,

86

that was my fault, I'm afraid,' he replied, before quickly adding, 'At least you have the advantage of also working for the police, so you know how unpredictable things can be. I'm not sure my partner has quite come to terms with that yet.'

'It's Mary, isn't it?' she asked. 'David has mentioned her a few times. I get the impression he's quite fond of her.'

It wasn't lost on Tom that she now was confident enough in his presence to use Milner's Christian name. 'The feeling is mutual. She ... and I, for that matter ... was extremely grateful for all of the support he gave her when I was shot.'

'I think I'd like to meet her. She seems a lovely woman. Perhaps we could all go out for dinner one night?'

Tom suddenly realised that this friendly conversation had rapidly moved onto dangerous ground. It had always been his style, rightly or wrongly, to keep his professional and private lives as separate as possible. Many years ago someone had said to him that being *friendly* with and being *friends* with someone were two totally different concepts. It was a principle which he had always tried to apply.

'I'm sure it would be possible at some time,' he answered as vaguely as possible, before changing the subject. 'But what about you? Are you looking forward to Superintendent Birch's arrival?'

Jenny, uncharacteristically, hesitated briefly before answering. 'Well, it would be nice to have a permanent boss again. I must admit it's been difficult whilst you have been away. I like DCI Shaw, but it's not the same as having you there.'

'I'm sure you will get on just fine with Superintendent Birch. I've met him a few times and he always struck me as very straightforward in all his dealings. You'll be fine,' he said. 'I can assure you he will be relying on you to help him until he gets properly settled in. It's a big step up from DCI to station superintendent. Even an experienced person like him is bound to be apprehensive. Anyway, I'm not going anywhere. If you feel you need to speak with me, then I'm always available.'

'That's very kind of you, sir,' she replied.

Chapter 24

Milner and DC Bennett had both returned and were now seated in Tom's office.

'Right, what have we got?' asked Tom, initiating the conversation. He looked towards DC Bennett. 'Why don't you go first?'

'Well, the first thing to say is that neither of the victims had any pets.'

Milner looked at him quizzically. 'Pets?'

'It was something DCI Stone asked me to find out,' he answered.

When Milner decided not to pursue it, DC Bennett, referring to his notes, continued. 'As we already knew, both had been away for a while. One had travelled to Yorkshire, to see some family members, whilst the other had travelled to Norfolk to stay with friends. It was only when they returned they discovered they had been burgled. No obvious sign of a forced break-in, although whoever did it had made a bit of a mess as they'd turned out drawers and cupboards. As we have seen many times before, it was this which upset the victims more than anything else.'

'Did they leave a key with anyone whilst they were away?' asked Tom.

'No, although they had both informed their immediate neighbours they would be away. They had stopped the papers and cancelled their normal milk deliveries. In fact, all of the things we would usually suggest when someone is going away for a while. I also spoke to a couple of the neighbours, who confirmed they had not seen or heard anything suspicious.'

Tom didn't immediately respond as he considered what he had just been told. Finally he spoke. 'How did they get to Yorkshire and Norfolk? Did they drive there, get the train or bus?'

'They both drove there.'

Tom's continued silence seemed to suggest DC Bennett's contribution was over, and this was confirmed when he turned his attention towards Milner. 'And what about you, Milner? Did you manage to see anyone at the synagogue, this time?'

'Yes, sir. I met with Rabbi Samuel Aphron. He was still extremely upset about Mr Green's death. In fact, as we found out when we met with Mrs Green and her daughters, their families are very close. You'll remember, sir, Rabbi Aphron's father and mother were in Auschwitz at the same time as Mr Green's father. And, of course, his son is married to Mr Green's daughter.'

As Milner said this Tom suddenly recalled his earlier, angry conversation with Ruth. 'And they are the parents of Hannah,' he said.

'That's right, sir,' answered Milner.

'Did you manage to get a list of everyone who was at the meeting on the night Mr Green was killed?' asked Tom.

Milner opened his file and took out a sheet of paper on which he had already typed a number of names. 'Yes. There were five people at the meeting.' He proceeded to read out the names. 'Rabbi Aphron, of course. Simon Weiss, Morris Kalb, Michael Rosen and, finally, Dominic Samuel. They were there to review progress on the fundraising campaign, so they can build an extension. They also had a discussion relating to the planning application.'

'But Mr Green was not expected to attend the meeting, correct?'

'That is correct, sir,' confirmed Milner. 'As we already know, he was heading there to speak with Rabbi Aphron privately.'

'Do we know what about?' asked Tom, more in hope than expectation.

'I asked Rabbi Aphron that, of course, and he did say Mr Green had called him earlier that evening and said he wanted to speak with him about a personal matter. All he said was that it was something to do with his granddaughter's wedding,'

'Did he give any indication at all what that might be?' asked Tom, already, once again, suspecting what the answer might be.

'No, none at all, other than it was a personal matter. Rabbi

Aphron gave me the impression he was as puzzled as we are.'

'He's right about that,' agreed Tom. 'This wedding keeps cropping up everywhere. What time did the meeting finish? We now know that Mr Green was attacked sometime between when he left home, at around 9.45pm, and when Mr Stephenson found his body at 10.30pm.'

'According to Rabbi Aphron it finished just after 10pm,' answered Milner.

For a short while Tom remained silent before finally saying, 'Okay, go and visit all of the others to see what they can remember about the meeting, and also if they have any idea why Mr Green wanted to speak so urgently with Rabbi Aphron. Chase up forensics and the pathology lab for the results, too. They may have something which would help us.'

Tom, once again, turned his attention towards DC Bennett. 'I'd like you to do something else for me.'

He then proceeded to tell him exactly what that was.

Chapter 25

Tom was standing just outside the Met Commissioner's office. He had received a call from DCS Small earlier the same afternoon asking him to attend the meeting. In fact, it was more than a polite request, as Tom had been told to drop everything that he might be working on and immediately drive over to Met HQ.

The reason he had been summoned was obvious, and totally expected. Nonetheless, as he stood there, he began to feel slightly nervous. He felt very confident about the strength of what he was alleging, based upon the evidence he had gathered to support his case. But he equally knew that what might be clear and unambiguous to him might become less so as it went up the chain of command. And, as far as the Met Police were concerned, there was no one higher than Sir Peter Westwood. Over the years Tom had, of course, seen Sir Peter many times, but never on a one-to-one basis. He suddenly started to smile to himself. At least if it all went bad he would go out at the top.

He was interrupted from these thoughts when a door opened and DCS Small appeared.

'Tom. Glad you could get here so quickly,' he said, making it sound as though Tom had actually had a choice in the matter. 'Please come through.'

He led Tom into a very spacious and well-appointed office. Sir Peter stood with his back to a huge window.

As soon as Tom appeared, Sir Peter walked towards him and offered his right hand in greeting. 'First of all, how are you? It must have been a very distressing time for you and your family when you were shot. DCS Small did, though, keep me informed about your situation, and I was hugely relieved when it became clear you were out of danger.'

'Thank you, sir,' answered Tom. 'It's certainly not something which I would recommend. The main thing, though, is that I'm almost fully recovered and it looks like we will get a result in the case against the Grace family.'

'Well, yes,' Sir Peter replied, 'but I believe you are being overly modest. In fact, I have to tell you DCS Small has recommended you receive a police gallantry medal.'

Tom's reaction was one of borderline shock and it was a while before he could say anything in reply. 'That's very kind of you, sir, but it's not something which I feel I either deserve or can accept. Yes, I was shot, but it took place in my own home, not trying to prevent a murderous villain from inflicting harm on the public.'

'Well, I see your point, but it's not always the most obvious actions which warrant such a commendation.'

Tom genuinely didn't understand the point which Sir Peter was making but decided not to pursue this conversation.

Sir Peter had clearly come to the same conclusion because, when he next spoke, he had moved away from the subject of a possible commendation. 'I don't think we have previously met, although, of course, I've heard so much about you recently. You seem to have a nose for ... well, let's say the more unusual cases.'

'After over thirty years in the force I suppose, eventually, it was my turn to have these types of cases,' Tom answered.

'Why don't we sit down?' suggested Sir Peter.

Tom noticed the two empty cups already on the table. He also noticed that there was no immediate sign of a third one appearing.

Once they were all seated, and with the introductory complimentary small talk seemingly over, Sir Peter said, 'Let me be frank. When DCS Small informed me about what you are alleging, I have to say I was very sceptical.' He paused for a moment before continuing. 'I believe in situations such as this, we all have to be as honest as possible. That way there is less chance of any ambiguity. The reason for my scepticism was because, and please bear with me here, I felt there was a danger you might have developed a taste for being in the public eye. After all, your profile has increased significantly recently. But, having now read your file, I'm certainly willing to change my mind.'

Tom laughed quietly. 'That's a relief. I appreciate your honesty, at least. In turn, I thought, due to the people involved, there would at worst be some sort of establishment cover-up and, at best, a watering down of the actual charges.'

'Do you still think that?' asked Sir Peter.

'I'll let you know after we've had our discussion,' answered Tom.

This time it was Sir Peter's turn to laugh. 'Good. At least we know where we are both coming from.'

Suddenly Sir Peter's previous joviality disappeared. 'As I said, I've now read your report,' which was lying on the table immediately in front of him, 'and studied the evidence you have compiled. I think that, on balance, what you are suggesting is extremely compelling, but ...' He opened the file to reveal the front page. 'There are one or two aspects which do concern me. More to the point, I believe they would concern a court of law.'

Tom remained silent, determined not to comment until Sir Peter had finished.

'The biggest problem I have is how, ultimately, it could come down to your word against theirs. No doubt you will say Commander Jenkins' admission is on tape. And that is my problem. Any lawyer worth their salt would claim that this part of the evidence is inadmissible. The fact is you did not seek, or receive, any official or legal approval to carry out the wire recording. It was carried out without any permission whatsoever, and using police equipment. Given the legal resources which would be available to Commander Jenkins and Charles Cope, it is my judgement the case would be thrown out almost instantly.'

Tom was stunned and, for what seemed like an eternity, could not think of anything to say in response. Eventually he found some words. 'So are you telling me you will not proceed with this?'

'I'm afraid so,' replied Sir Peter. 'Well, at least not in any formal, legal sense. I have already spoken with the Home Secretary and it is our considered opinion that not only would the case be thrown out, but it might also do irreparable damage to the standing and reputation of the force.'

'And, no doubt, to the standing and reputation of the government as well,' replied Tom, in a tone which clearly showed his anger.

'Well, yes. That as well, I suppose,' replied Sir Peter. 'But *my* sole priority is to protect the integrity of the Metropolitan Police Force.'

'So two innocent people are dead and, despite the fact we know who was responsible for those deaths, we cannot or, more precisely, will not do anything to bring them to justice. Is that what you are saying?'

Neither Sir Peter not DCS Small chose to answer Tom's question. Instead DCS Small said, 'Tom, you have every right to be angry. If I was in your shoes I'd feel the same.'

'Really?' replied Tom with undisguised sarcasm.

DCS Small chose to ignore Tom's outburst. 'What I can assure you of, though, is that both Commander Jenkins and Charles Cope will be resigning in due course.'

Sir Peter now joined in. 'They will be made aware that we know what they did and have the necessary supportive evidence. They will not be asked to serve on any future committees and there certainly won't be any fanfares or rewards coming their way. If I have my way, they will disappear completely from the public eye, never to be seen or heard from again.'

'But the truth is, sir, it's unlikely you will get your way,' said Tom, once again making clear his frustration. 'The reality is my file will be quietly put to one side and, before too long, long forgotten.' He added, with increasing anger, 'And what about Susan Chambers and Jimmy Griffiths? It's too late now for them to receive any fanfare or rewards.'

Once again, neither Sir Peter nor DCS Small responded to Tom's outburst and an uneasy silence followed.

Eventually, it was Tom who spoke, but this time in a more composed tone. 'So, when exactly will they be leaving their posts?'

'That has still to be finalised, but there are discussions taking place right now about that very subject,' answered Sir Peter. 'You have my assurance I won't let it drag on. It's clearly in everyone's interests for it to happen sooner rather than later.'

'I'd also suggest the same applies to anyone else who was involved in this,' replied Tom. 'There must have been a large degree of collusion for this to happen. And there's another thing,' he added, the increased tempo of his voice indicating, once again, a rising anger. 'There is still the small matter of who actually killed Susan Chambers. I don't doubt it was never the intention for Susan to die. But, for whatever reason, she did, and in my book that constitutes a major crime. Or is it policy now to be selective in which murders we investigate?'

Sir Peter answered. 'If it's any consolation to you, I also share your view. You have my guarantee that I, personally, will ensure all of those responsible will be tracked down.'

'And what about me?' asked Tom.

'I'm not sure I understand,' replied Sir Peter.

'Well, during my conversations with both Commander Jenkins and Charles Cope, not-so-veiled threats were made against me. I would like your assurance someone senior will confront both of them about this. I'd rather not spend the rest of my life having to look over my shoulder.'

Sir Peter was clearly shocked by what Tom had just said. 'Are you really suggesting they would try to do you harm?'

'Why not? Given what has already happened, and what is at stake, it could provide the logical solution to their problems.'

Both Sir Peter and DCS Small looked at Tom in disbelief.

'This situation gets more bizarre by the minute,' said Sir Peter, clearly still struggling to totally comprehend the implications of all of this. 'If this were in a murder novel, no one would believe it.'

Tom looked straight at him. 'Earlier, you asked me what I thought the outcome might be. To be frank, I have heard nothing that has changed my mind. In fact, I would go so far as to say that my worst fears have been fully realised, and I would like that to be put on the record.'

'That, of course, is your prerogative,' replied DCS Small, before adding, 'and equally I have to make the point that whatever is contained in your report, and whatever has been discussed here today, should be considered totally confidential. From now on we will handle this case. I know you'll be disappointed with this but, given its highly sensitive nature, it is the logical thing to do.'

Once Tom had left, and they were alone, Sir Peter turned to DCS Small and said, with a slight laugh, 'It seems as though it's true what people have said about DCI Stone. He's definitely a very awkward character. We could do with a few more officers like him in the force.' He quickly added, 'But, then again, perhaps not.'

Chapter 26

Tom thought about heading straight home but, as Mary was at a meeting of her amateur dramatics group, he decided to go back to the station. When he walked into his office, DC Bennett was waiting for him.

'Sir,' DC Bennett said, excitedly. 'You were right. There was a connection between all three burglaries.'

'Why don't you get me a cup of coffee first, and then you can tell me what the connection is? I haven't had a drink all afternoon,' Tom said, remembering the non-appearance of the third cup in Sir Peter's office. 'Right now, even a coffee from the machine would go down well.'

It wasn't long before DC Bennett returned, holding a plastic cup in each hand.

'Where's DS Milner?' asked Tom.

'He's gone to see some of the other people who attended the meeting at the synagogue. I'm not sure if he's planning to come back here today.'

'Okay, tell me what you found out.'

'There is a connection,' replied DC Bennett, a wide smile appearing on his face. 'And it's a garage. It seems all three people had recently had their cars serviced at the same garage. It's on the A40, just outside Uxbridge. The business name is 'Knights of the Road: Auto Services and Repairs'. As they were planning to drive a considerable distance, they wanted to make sure their cars were properly serviced and roadworthy. I asked each of them if they had left their cars there and later returned to collect them, or waited whilst the service had been done. All three waited. When I asked them about any conversation they might have had, only one could remember mentioning they needed their car serviced as they were shortly going away. In fact, he recalled how friendly the receptionist was and how interested she was in their planned trip. Where were they going and when were they going? That type of thing.'

'And was there a house key on the same key ring as the car keys?'

'There was, sir. On all three, in fact. And none of them removed the house key whilst their cars were being serviced.'

Tom remained silent whilst he considered what he had just been told. Finally, he said, 'It could, of course, just be a coincidence, but, if it is, it's a very big one. All three houses were burgled when the occupants, conveniently, were away. None of them had an alarm fitted. There was no obvious forced entry. All three had recently had their cars serviced at the very same garage. Their house keys were on the same key ring as their car key. And the garage had possession of the keys, including the key to the house, for a while.' He looked at DC Bennett. 'What do you think?'

'Well, in this particular case, I think I share your scepticism about coincidences.'

'Do a bit of digging into the people who work at the garage. You never know, it might throw up something interesting. Without any clear forensic evidence, though, it will be impossible to prove anything. So we might have to flush them out.'

'How do you propose to do that, sir?' asked DC Bennett.

So Tom told him.

Chapter 27

Milner was already at the station when, the next morning, Tom arrived.

'Did anything interesting come out of your discussions with the others who were there at the synagogue that night?' asked Tom, as soon as he entered his office.

'Not much, I'm afraid,' Milner replied. 'They all knew Mr Green, of course, and, like Rabbi Aphron, were really shocked about his death. One of them, Mr Weiss, did confirm that Mr Green had seemed preoccupied with something during the weeks leading up to his death. I asked him if he had any idea what it might be, but he didn't know. As I say, it was just a perception which he had.'

'Well, that's something useful, I suppose,' said Tom, 'because he was not the only person who thought that. Even Mr Green's own wife, who ought to be able to recognise these things, thought he had been preoccupied with something.'

Milner nodded. 'I've also now received a preliminary copy of the *post mortem* carried out on Mr Green.'

'That was quick,' said Tom.

'The Jewish faith calls for followers to be buried as quickly as possible after death. In fact, most Jewish people who have died do not have a *post mortem*. It was because of the nature of Mr Green's death that the coroner asked for a full PM.'

'And what were the main findings?' asked Tom.

'That Mr Green died as a result of a heart attack,' said Milner. 'Although it was the heart attack which killed him, it's highly likely it was brought on by severe head trauma. There was also some evidence that Mr Green had experienced some type of seizure.'

'So, had someone hit him on the head?' asked Tom.

'Either that or he had fallen and hit his head on something hard. There were also a few bruises on his face, almost certainly the result of being attacked. Based upon these injuries, the pathologist said the most likely explanation is that someone hit Mr Green, quite hard, in the face; he then fell backwards and hit his head. This, not too long afterwards, caused a seizure which then triggered the fatal heart attack.'

'At least we can be very specific about the time when the attack actually took place. Some time between 9.45pm and 10.30pm,' Tom said. 'Has anything come back yet regarding the DNA from the various items found near the crime scene?'

'Nothing yet, sir, but I'll chase it up straight away.'

'Good,' replied Tom.

'What do you suggest we do next?' asked Milner.

'A bit of drawing might help,' answered Tom. Before a slightly puzzled Milner could ask him what he meant, Tom helpfully provided the answer. 'I always find, when I've come to a bit of a dead end, it helps to put down what we do actually know on paper. Sometimes the eyes can see things which the brain can't.'

A while later and Tom and Milner were studying their work. In front of them was a large sheet of paper on which they had written lots of names. At the very top was Mr Green's name. Some of these names were joined together by solid lines, whilst in a few other cases they were linked by a dotted line. The former denoted where there was a direct connection, whilst the latter indicated a more tenuous link.

'So, what do you think?' asked Tom, directing his question at Milner.

'Well, nothing immediately stands out, apart from, of course, the most common connection, which is between the Green family and the Aphron family. Mr Green's daughter, Ruth, is married to Rabbi Aphron's son, Emmanuel. Plus there's the connection with the wedding, when their daughter Hannah was married.'

'Very good, Milner,' said Tom. 'Just what I was thinking.'

Milner didn't quite know whether to take this as a compliment or DCI Stone's attempt at mild sarcasm. In the event, he decided that silence was probably the wisest course to take.

'There's also, of course, another connection which we have missed completely,' added Tom, more to himself than to Milner. 'Mr Green's father, Jacob, and Rabbi Aphron's mother, Ethel, and father, Josef, were all held in Auschwitz at the same time and came over to England shortly after the war ended. I think we should add their names to the chart.'

'Wasn't there also a third man who was there with them?' asked Milner. 'Actually, I made a note of his name when we were at Mrs Green's house.'

He took out his notebook and flicked through a few pages until he found the one he was interested in. 'His name was Yitzhak. Yitzhak Sax. If you remember, he also attended the wedding and helped to calm down Jacob after he became upset.'

Whilst Milner was speaking Tom was already adding these new names to the chart. After he had done this they both stood back and, once again, studied the, now, updated chart.

'Do you think one of these,' said Milner, pointing at the chart, might be the murderer?'

'It's impossible to say, at the moment,' answered Tom. 'They could be, I suppose, but there are still a lot of gaps on the chart. Let's wait until we have a few more names on it.' He paused briefly before carrying on, 'I have though missed one other important thing.' He then proceeded to write the words 'Hannah's wedding' in the middle of the chart. 'You've said yourself how the wedding keeps cropping up in this. So, let's put it in.'

After he had done this he then drew a series of arrows towards the word 'wedding.' All of the arrows represented the people who had attended the wedding. Once again he stood back to take a closer look at his handiwork.

'Hmmm... All roads lead to the wedding,' he then said.

This appeared to give him an idea. 'I'd like to meet Rabbi Aphron. Perhaps he can provide us with some more names, as well as his recollections of what happened at the wedding.'

Chapter 28

It was later the same day and Tom and DS Milner were both seated in a small, cramped room, towards the back of the synagogue.

'Thank you very much for agreeing to see us at such short notice,' said Tom.

'I've already told your colleague everything I know,' Rabbi Aphron replied, glancing towards Milner.

'I understand that, but it would be very helpful if you could now tell me what you said earlier,' replied Tom. 'You mentioned to DS Milner that Mr Green wanted to speak with you privately. Do you know what he wanted to discuss with you?'

'Look,' answered Rabbi Aphron, slightly tetchily, 'I've had this conversation already with DS Milner.'

'I do understand that, but, as I said, I was hoping you would be able to now tell me.'

When Rabbi Aphron replied, his words were overemphasised and quite deliberate. 'When he called me earlier in the day, he wanted to meet immediately, but I suggested later in the evening, as it would be more convenient for me. I did ask him what it was about, but, as I've already told you, he simply replied that it related to our granddaughter's wedding and that he wanted to speak with me privately about it. So we agreed we would talk after my meeting here.' His previous tetchiness suddenly disappeared and he became visibly upset. 'If I had found time to speak with him when he suggested, it's likely he would still be alive today.'

'You can't blame yourself for what happened to Mr Green. Life is full of what-ifs. What happened to Mr Green was totally out of your control,' replied Tom as sympathetically as possible. He waited a while, until Rabbi Green had composed himself, before saying, 'Weren't you intrigued as to why Mr

Green needed to speak with you so urgently about your granddaughter's wedding?'

'Yes, I was; well, at least at the time. But, to be totally honest, I soon forgot about it as I had a lot to do in preparation for the meeting. We have ambitious plans to enlarge the building. As you see,' he said, looking around the room, 'we don't have much space here.' He hesitated fleetingly before adding, 'I should have realised something was not right when he didn't turn up.'

'So what time did your meeting finish?'

Rabbi Aphron once again looked towards Milner, this time with a hint of suspicion. For a brief moment it looked as though he was about to say something to Milner but, in the event, decided not to. 'It must have been about 10pm. I then had a few things to do and left just after 10.30pm.'

Tom followed up with another question. 'Did you have any conversations with Mr Green in the weeks before his death?'

'I'm sure we must have. After all, our families are very close and, anyway, the Green family have always been a major part of our community. The Jewish community in and around Ealing is a very close one. It's not like the ones in North London. We often see each other socially, as well as when we celebrate our faith. I can't remember any recent conversations about Hannah and Aaron's wedding, though, if that is what you are asking.'

'Aaron is the name of your granddaughter's husband. Is that correct?' asked Milner, notebook already in hand, now with another name to add to the chart.

'Yes, that's correct,' he answered.

'I understand, at your granddaughter's wedding, there was an incident involving Mr Green's father, Jacob. Can you remember it?' asked Tom.

'I think to call it an *incident* is, perhaps, a slight exaggeration. At one stage Jacob seemed to get a bit overcome, emotionally. At the time we put it down to the occasion being a bit overwhelming for him. Jewish weddings can take a long time and it must have been a very tiring day for him. But it really wasn't a problem and certainly didn't spoil the occasion.' He paused briefly before saying, 'Could I ask what all of this obsession with Hannah's wedding is about? Benjamin was murdered, wasn't he? What possible connection could there be between my granddaughter's wedding and Benjamin's murder?'

'Only that you have confirmed Mr Green was very keen to speak with you about something related to the wedding. As this was only a few hours before he was murdered, it could be significant. Most likely, however, there is no connection, but we are just trying to understand Mr Green's mindset in the time leading up to his death.'

This appeared to placate Rabbi Aphron and he didn't ask any follow-up question relating to the wedding. So Tom continued, 'Also, Mr Green mentioned the name *Hannah* to the paramedics when they were taking him to the hospital. Do you have any idea why he would say that?'

Rabbi Aphron looked genuinely surprised. 'Really? I've no idea why he would say that.'

Tom then began a new line of conversation. 'I understand both your father and mother were at Auschwitz at the same time as Mr Green's father. That would suggest your two families had already been very close, even before the marriage of your son and Mr Green's daughter.'

'That was true in the immediate years after the war had ended, but since then I wouldn't say we were especially close. Certainly, no closer than with some of our other friends. But, as you say, that did change when Emmanuel and Ruth were married, back in the mid-1990s, and then, of course, when their children ... our grandchildren ... came along. Children tend to be great bridges between families,' he added. 'Do you have any children, Detective Chief Inspector Stone?'

'Yes, I have a son,' he answered.

'And grandchildren?'

If Tom had been totally honest he might have said he wasn't sure, but, in the event, he made do with, 'No.'

'I'm sorry about that,' answered Rabbi Aphron. 'They are God's gift to us.'

Tom, with some difficulty, remained silent.

Fortunately this uncomfortable hiatus was broken as Rabbi Aphron suddenly appeared to remember something. 'Although it is true that Mother did start to meet up again with Jacob – that's Benjamin's father – occasionally, usually at the local coffee house, in the years before she died. It was actually really nice to see them both enjoying one another's company again, particularly after what they had both been through earlier in their lives.'

'Would you mind telling me when your mother died?' asked Tom.

'Not at all. Papa died way back in 1990 and Mother quite recently, in 2014,' he answered.

'I'm sorry to hear that,' replied Tom. 'It must have been such a loss for you and your family.'

'It was,' answered Rabbi Aphron reflectively, 'but after everything they had been through, each day was a sort of blessing.'

When there was no follow-up question from Tom, he carried on, almost as though he found discussing it therapeutic. 'Father, Jacob and Mother actually met in Auschwitz ... well, Auschwitz- Birkenau, to be more accurate. Somehow they managed to survive and, although they worked in different parts of the camp, incredibly, it was whilst they were there that I was actually conceived.' He fell silent momentarily and then said, 'I suppose when you don't think you are going to survive you just try and live for the day.'

'And it was there, you say, they met Jacob. Is that correct?' asked Tom.

'Yes, that's correct. He and Father were both allocated to the same part of the camp, doing the same job, and, not surprisingly, a real bond of friendship developed between them. Well, in fact, between Father, Jacob and Yitzhak Sax, who was also there and managed to survive.'

It was Milner who now spoke. 'Wasn't Mr Sax also at your granddaughter's wedding?'

'Yes, he was. Sadly, he is now the only one of the four who is still alive.'

'Were both your parents deeply religious people?' asked Tom.

'Do you mean "did they encourage me to become a rabbi"?' Rabbi Aphron asked.

'Yes, I suppose that's what I meant.'

'Yes, their Jewish faith was very important to them, especially as they got older, but, to be honest, no more so than most Jewish people of their age. Perhaps, though, their time in the camps had strengthened their faith?' He paused reflectively. 'You would have thought that those experiences would have destroyed any faith they might have had. But, strangely, they seemed to strengthen it.' He then continued, 'For me, though, I seemed to know from an early age that this was something which I wanted to do. This was particularly the case after I learnt more about the Holocaust and what people like Mother and Father, Jacob and Yitzhak had endured. Young people these days, Detective Chief Inspector Stone, tend to have very short memories. That's why I have made it my life's work to do everything possible to educate young people about our recent history, especially the Holocaust. Do you know,' he said, with a degree of anger now in his voice, 'that there are many people who not just don't know what happened in the camps, but don't actually believe it ever happened? People who claim that it is some kind of Jewish conspiracy? Of course, we can forgive, but we must never forget. That's why I will continue to tell the story until my dying breath.' He paused for a while, whilst he regained control of his emotions. 'Family is at the heart of our faith, and I hope, when I'm no longer around, my own children will pick up the baton.'

It was clear to Tom and Milner that Rabbi Aphron had become very moved by his own memories and words, and so, out of respect, neither immediately spoke. Eventually, however, Tom said, 'How did your parents make a living when they arrived here, after the war?'

'Well, as you can imagine, life initially was very difficult for them. I was just a baby, and so Mother looked after me whilst Father found work wherever he could. As the years went by, however, they started to make a better life for themselves and, by the 1950s, had enough money to buy their first house, here in Ealing. Anyway, I do remember, even as a child – I must have been about seven or eight at the time – just how excited my parents were to buy their very first house.'

'You must be very proud of them,' suggested Tom. 'That must have been such an achievement, given their back-grounds.'

'I owe them so much,' answered Rabbi Aphron, as tears suddenly and unexpectedly began to roll down his cheeks.

'I'm sorry. I didn't mean to upset you,' said Tom, now moved himself by Rabbi Aphron's burst of emotion.

'Please, you don't need to apologise. I always say to my own children it's sometimes good for the soul to show real human emotion. I see it as a sign of strength rather than weakness.'

'Did your father or mother ever talk about their experiences in Auschwitz?' asked Tom.

'Certainly Father didn't. He was a man who found it very difficult to speak about it and, despite what I just said about showing your emotions, he wasn't naturally one of those people. Perhaps his experiences were just too painful. If so, you couldn't really blame him. Of course, as I got older, I did ask him about that particular time, but he was never really forthcoming. Mother, though, was, in many ways, far stronger than Father and so was able to discuss her time there more easily.' He paused. 'Although I always suspected there were things that happened there which even she could not bring herself to talk about.'

'So they never wrote anything down about their time in Auschwitz?' asked Tom.

'If you mean writing a book or such like, then the answer would be "no". Mother was a prolific letter writer and, even up to the time of her death, she would still write the occasional letter to friends. But, as far as any book is concerned, then no.'

Tom now stood and said, 'Thank you for your time. If there is anything else which you remember, however trivial, please don't hesitate to contact me.' He handed Rabbi Aphron a small card, containing his contact details.

Just as they were about to leave, Tom hesitated and then turned around to face Rabbi Aphron. 'Actually, there was one other thing. I understand your granddaughter's wedding was filmed. Would you mind if I was to borrow the DVD for a short while? I'll make sure I return it to you as soon as possible.'

Rabbi Aphron, looking slightly perplexed by Tom's request, simply shrugged his shoulders and said, 'If you think it might help, then of course. Although, as I said earlier, I can't imagine what it might help you with.' He then added, helpfully, 'Actually, coincidentally, I have a copy in my car which you can take with you.'

Rabbi Aphron led Tom and Milner towards where his car was parked, unlocked the door and took out a DVD from the glove compartment. He handed it to Tom before asking, 'Do you think Benjamin's death might have been racially motivated?'

'I really don't know,' Tom answered truthfully. 'I hope not, but, at this stage, it can't be ruled out. Why do you ask? Do you have a particular reason to think it was?'

Both Tom and Milner noticed how Rabbi Aphron briefly hesitated before he replied. 'Well, there was one slightly disturbing thing which happened recently.'

'Do you mind telling us about it?' asked Tom.

'As you can imagine, we do occasionally suffer from what I would call low-level racial abuse. It's something, I'm afraid, we Jews have had to get used to. But this seemed different. A week or so ago I received a letter which stated, in no uncertain terms, how the extension to the synagogue was not welcomed and how there were too many Jews here as it was.'

'Do you still have the letter?' asked Milner.

'I was going to throw it away but, for some reason, decided to keep it. It's in a drawer back in the synagogue.'

'Do you mind if we take a look at it?' asked Tom.

'Not at all. I'll just go and get it for you.'

While they were waiting for Rabbi Aphron to return, Tom passed the DVD to Milner and said, 'Run off a couple of copies of this. It would be useful if we both took a look at it. I think two pairs of eyes might help with this one.'

It wasn't too long before Rabbi Aphron returned. He handed the envelope to Tom, who briefly examined it before taking out the typed letter and reading it out loud.

'Jews are not welcome here and we will do everything to make sure you don't get a larger synagogue. If you carry on with this then you will be next. You have been warned. No more Jews.'

Tom re-examined the details on the front of the envelope and could see, as Rabbi Aphron had suggested, it had a fairly recent postmark date. He then passed the letter over to Milner. 'Could I ask why you didn't take this to the police,' he asked, 'especially as you admitted it was quite unusual?'

'I did consider it. In fact I intended to do it, but, unfortunately ... well, events overtook me.'

'I understand,' said Tom sympathetically. 'So you received the letter prior to Mr Green's death, did you?'

'Yes, a day or two before,' he answered.

'Would you mind if we took this away with us?' asked Tom.

Rabbi Aphron sounded quite relieved when he replied. 'Please do.'

Chapter 29

'Hello, you're back early,' said Mary. It was just after 5pm and Tom had decided, rather than going back to the station, he would instead head home towards Bagshot.

'Am I?' he answered, looking at his watch, before adding, with a slight laugh, 'Why? Are you complaining?'

'You know I never complain about seeing you,' she said, now with her own slight laugh.

'Correct answer,' replied Tom.

Since the shooting, their relationship had undoubtedly grown stronger. Or, at least, it had as far as he was concerned. He now couldn't imagine his future without Mary. Although he knew she cared for him, and probably loved him, he had a nagging concern that she didn't feel quite the same way about their relationship as he did. Whilst she had never said as much, he did occasionally think her motivation was more about ensuring he got better rather than being part of a longer-term relationship plan. So far, there had been no discussions about him returning to his own home in Staines, but in his mind it was the thing which remained unsaid. For all of these reasons he had come to the conclusion that it couldn't remain unsaid any longer, even though there was always the possibility he might not like the outcome.

'Why don't we go out for dinner tonight?' suggested Tom. 'It seems ages since we did that.'

'That would be nice,' said Mary, in a tone which gave him some encouragement. 'Where do you have in mind?'

He hadn't really thought about this and the suggestion of dinner had actually been made on the spur of the moment. 'What about that small restaurant on the A30, where we first met?'

He was pleasantly surprised when Mary answered, 'That's a good idea. It seems a long time ago now that I first met that shy, nervous man.'

'You're right. I was nervous. In fact, as I've no doubt told you before, I very nearly didn't come. I seriously thought about cancelling.'

'Are you now glad you didn't?' asked Mary, suddenly becoming quite serious.

'Of course I am,' he answered quickly. 'You're the best thing that has happened to me.' He suddenly realised that, perhaps, now was as good a time as any to make known his feelings.

He took her hands in his and said, 'I don't know what I would have done without you. These last few months have simply confirmed I can't live without you and want to spend the rest of my life with you.' He hadn't intended for his words to come out in such a clichéd way but, now that they had, he actually had no regrets.

Mary pulled away from him. 'Wow,' she said. 'For someone who has difficulty in showing their true emotions, that was quite some speech.' She hesitated briefly before carrying on. 'Are you saying what I think you are saying?'

'I am,' he answered. 'Mary Parker, will you marry me?'

'You know I will,' she answered, as they embraced.

Chapter 30

Tom had arrived at the station, the next morning, a little later than he had intended. He and Mary had celebrated the momentous event of the previous evening. He still couldn't quite come to terms with what he had said to her. She had been quite right when she had alluded to his inability to show his true feelings. It wasn't something which he had deliberately set out to cultivate, rather just something which had developed in his personality as the years had gone by. No doubt a psychiatrist would be able to explain to him why this was the case. All he knew was that it seemed to have helped him to manage many of life's disappointments which had come his way over the years.

'Morning, sir,' said Milner. 'Did you have an enjoyable evening?'

'Yes, thank you, Milner, I did. However, if I hadn't, I wouldn't like someone reminding me of that.' As soon as he had said those words he regretted his ungracious response but, somehow, couldn't bring himself to say so. Instead, he asked, 'Have there been any developments in the Benjamin Green case?'

'Only that I have now received the lab reports on the items found close to Mr Green's body. Unfortunately the DNA on most of the items is not very clear, probably due to natural degrading. Even where there is some clear DNA it doesn't match with anyone known to us. So, a bit of a dead end there, I'm afraid.'

'Well, you never know. They might not be known to us now, but that might change in the future,' answered Tom. 'Anyway, thanks for getting the results so quickly. As I say, you never know.'

Whether this sudden and unexpected praise was an attempt to compensate for his earlier churlishness was difficult to say. Nonetheless, Milner saw it as his opportunity to raise another matter. 'DC Bennett has briefed me on what you are proposing with relation to the burglaries. Is there anything I can help with?'

'I'd like you to focus on the murder investigation. DC Bennett and I can, I'm sure, handle this. But thanks anyway.'

It wasn't lost on Milner how this was the second time in as many minutes that DCI Stone had thanked him. Given their less-than-satisfactory start to the day, this was yet another example of DCI Stone's unpredictable and quite complex nature.

'What do you think we should do next?' asked Tom.

'Well, I thought I would take a look at the DVD which Rabbi Aphron gave to us.' Milner handed Tom a DVD case. 'Here's the copy that you asked for.'

'Thanks,' replied Tom. 'It'll be interesting to see if there's anything in it which might help.'

After Milner had left, Tom fired up his computer and started to work his way through his emails. Just as he was completing this his phone rang. He immediately recognised Jenny's cheery voice.

'Morning, sir. It's Jenny. I hope that you are well.'

'Thanks, Jenny. Yes, I'm fine,' he replied in a similarly cheerful tone. 'How is it with Superintendent Birch? Are you helping him to settle in?' Superintendent Birch had recently taken up his appointment as head of the station, the role which Tom had previously carried out on a temporary basis.

'I hope I have,' she replied. 'He seems very nice.'

'That's good. Hopefully, it will help you decide to stay with us.'

'Well, let's see,' she answered, before quickly changing the subject. 'The reason for the call is that Superintendent Birch has asked if you are available to meet up with him this afternoon. He's trying to meet all of his senior team as quickly as possible, starting with you.' Somehow Jenny, impressively, made it sound as though his meeting with Tom was the most important.

'How about 2pm?' Tom suggested.

As soon as his conversation with Jenny had ended there was a knock on his door and DC Bennett entered. 'Is this a good time to discuss the burglaries?'

'Yes, no problem,' said Tom. 'Were you able to sort something out?'

'All done. We are good to go. It just needs your final okay,' answered DC Bennett.

'Good. So, what's the plan?' asked Tom.

For the next thirty minutes or so, DC Bennett took him through what he was proposing and, except for one or two minor changes, Tom was happy with the suggestion. All they needed to happen now was for the bait to be taken.

Chapter 31

'Good to see you again, Tom,' said Superintendent Birch. 'It's been a while.'

They were seated at the table in Tom's 'old' office on the fifth floor.

'It certainly has,' said Tom. 'And congratulations on your appointment. It's always good when talent is recognised.'

'Thank you, Tom,' Superintendent Birch replied. He hesitated briefly before saying, 'That means a lot to me, particularly as you must have had your eye on the job after standing in over the past few months.'

'To be honest, it wasn't the job for me. I never felt that comfortable anyway. I'm much more at home in my current comfort zone. I also think I tend to rub the top brass the wrong way.'

'That's not what DCS Small said. In fact, he was very complimentary about you.'

'Really?' Tom asked, genuinely surprised. 'I must have been doing something wrong, then,' he added, with a slight laugh.

Superintendent Birch then said, although this time in a much more serious tone, 'I know, of course, about the shooting. I understand at one point it was a bit touch and go.'

'Well, I don't want to understate the seriousness of being shot, but the truth is that I was never in any life-threatening condition and, as you can see, have made more or less a full recovery. These stories become a bit apocryphal over time. By this time next year, the story, no doubt, will include how I was given the last rites.'

'I know what you mean,' said Superintendent Birch. He then went on, 'I have read your report on the Grace family investigation. That was an excellent piece of police work. It's good to know such people are no longer able to ruin the lives of innocents.'

'Well, it's still got to go to court, of course, but the evidence is very compelling.'

'I also read how your own partner had been dragged into the case. I hadn't realised. That must have been very distressing for both of you.'

'It wasn't a pleasant time, that's for sure,' Tom replied, with considerable understatement, suddenly remembering the pressures it had placed on their relationship.

'Do you mind me asking how your partner is now?'

'She's ... well, both of us, really, are much better. You know how this job can get in the way of personal relationships, but in many ways it actually brought us closer together.' Before he could stop himself he added, 'In fact, we are planning to get married.' He wasn't sure why he had confided in Superintendent Birch and suddenly regretted his uncharacteristic openness.

'That's great news. Many congratulations,' Superintendent Birch said, shaking Tom's hand. 'When is the big day?'

'We haven't set one yet. In fact, you are the very first person I have told and so, for the time being, I'd appreciate it if you could keep it to yourself. You know what it's like when something like this happens in a station.'

'Yes, I'm sure your life would be hell for a while,' Superintendent Birch said, laughing. 'Rest assured I will keep it to myself.'

Superintendent Birch decided not to pursue this line of conversation. Instead he said, 'As you're my most experienced DCI, I will be relying on you, more than anyone else, over the next few months. I hope you feel you can speak with me at any time. I'm not one of those precious people who think they have to play up to their new role. That's not to say, of course, I will always agree with what you say, but I can guarantee, at least, I will always listen.'

'Thank you,' replied Tom. 'And equally, if you ever feel you just need to speak with anyone, then you know where I am. Even during my short time in the role I sometimes found it quite lonely.'

Superintendent Birch laughed again. 'Okay, that's the mutual love-in over. Why don't you tell me what you are currently working on?'

So Tom told him about the murder of Mr Green and the

status of their current investigation. He also told him about the recent burglaries and what they were proposing. Finally, he mentioned how Jenny had been such a great help when he had been in the role, and that, although it would be Superintendent Birch's decision, he could, nonetheless, strongly recommend her for the position of PA.

He didn't tell him about the file relating to Commander Jenkins and Charles Cope.

Chapter 32

After his meeting with Superintendent Birch, Tom immediately returned to his own office and there waiting for him were both Milner and DC Bennett.

'It looks like you two mean business. What is it?' asked Tom.

It was Milner who spoke first. 'Nothing earth-shattering, I'm afraid, but interesting nonetheless.'

'Well, sometimes it's the minor stuff which turns out to be the most important,' replied Tom as encouragement. 'Why don't you just tell me what you have?'

'I've now looked at the wedding DVD. Rabbi Aphron was certainly correct when he said that Jewish wedding ceremonies last a long time, so I fast-forwarded to the interesting bit, at the reception, when Mr Green's father, Jacob, became upset. In fact, he became very emotional, if not distraught, at one point.'

'And what was that point?' asked Tom.

'It was when the bride, Hannah, came over to where the rest of the Green family were all seated. When Hannah went towards Jacob and tried to kiss him, he began to almost ... well, wail. He held out both hands to her, and it was then he began to repeatedly call out her name. At first, Hannah seemed to quite enjoy this, but, after a while, you could clearly see how she was getting more and more uncomfortable with it. Eventually, Mr Green stepped in and tried to calm him down, but it was only when his friend Mr Sax came over that Jacob did finally calm down.'

'Could you make out what Mr Sax said or did to calm him down?'

'No, sir. The sound wasn't too good, and what I could make out I didn't understand anyway as he appeared to be speaking in a foreign language. Don't you remember, sir, when we were with Mrs Green and her family? They mentioned how Mr Sax had spoken to Jacob in Hungarian.'

'That's right. I do remember now,' answered Tom.

Milner remained quiet, anticipating a follow-up question from DCI Stone. When none came, he carried on. 'I think it might be useful if I went to speak with Mr Sax, if only to find out what he said.'

'Good idea,' agreed Tom. 'I'll come with you. Just set it up and let me know.' He turned to face DC Bennett. 'And what about the burglaries? Is everything set?'

'All set for Saturday night, sir. Hopefully, they've taken the bait. We have a bungalow in Hayes. The plan is to have four uniformed officers outside and two of us inside.'

'Does that include me?' asked Tom.

DC Bennett suddenly looked concerned. 'No, sir. It's me and DC Jones. I assumed you didn't want to be there.'

'Never assume,' replied Tom.

'So you would like to be there, sir?' DC Bennett asked.

'Of course I would,' answered Tom, slightly offended.

Before he could add anything further, though, Milner suddenly spoke. 'Are you sure it's wise to be there, sir? It's possible there will be some rough stuff. After all, it wasn't that long ago you were still in hospital. I'm sure DC Bennett and his team can handle it.'

Tom looked at Milner with a degree of suspicion before a smile, suddenly and unexpectedly, appeared on his face. 'I appreciate your concern, Milner. How about if I promise to stay out of any trouble? Would I be allowed to attend then?'

It was clear that Milner, despite the assurance, was not convinced. Eventually, though, and somewhat reluctantly, he simply said, 'I suppose so,'

Tom once again turned to face DC Bennett. 'So, tell me what will happen.'

'Your suggestion to ask Jim King has worked really well. When I spoke to him he was immediately up for it. In fact, he wanted to be there with us on Saturday night.'

'Who is Jim King?' asked Milner.

'He used to be the desk sergeant but retired a few years ago,' DC Bennett said. 'He and his wife have a bungalow in Hayes, so not too far away from where the garage is. He took his car in for a service yesterday and waited whilst it was being done. As we suggested, he mentioned to the receptionist that he and his wife would be away on Saturday night. Sure enough, she suddenly started to show some interest, asking him a few questions. Where was he going, what time was he leaving? That type of thing. Jim, I suppose being a naturally inquisitive ex-copper, even had the foresight to check his house key after they had returned the keys to him. He says there was definite evidence of some sort of resin or plastic on the key. So it looks like it was copied.'

'Good,' answered Tom. 'Let's hope they now play their part in the plan.'

Chapter 33

The following morning, Tom and Milner were seated in the front room of the house, in Wembley, where Yitzhak Sax lived with his daughter and son-in-law. At their side was a small rectangular wooden table on which had been placed a pot of tea, two cups, a small jug of milk and a bowl of sugar, all of which had earlier been prepared by Mr Sax's daughter. Mr Sax was seated immediately opposite them, where, alongside him, was a slightly smaller table on which were a pair of spectacles.

The first thing which surprised Tom was just how physically robust Mr Sax still was for a man of such advanced years. It wouldn't be too long before he would demonstrate to them that his mental powers were equally robust.

'Thank you for seeing us at such short notice,' said Tom. 'I'm Detective Chief Inspector Stone, from the West London police force, and this is my colleague, Detective Sergeant Milner.' Both Tom and Milner held out their identification cards for Mr Sax to examine.

Mr Sax put on his spectacles and examined both cards for what seemed like an age. Eventually, though, he removed his spectacles and placed them carefully back onto the table.

'You look a bit young for a detective sergeant,' he said, in a clear but distinct mid-European accent, as he handed Milner's ID back to him.

'Don't they say that all policemen look young these days?' asked Tom.

'They do when you are ninety years old,' replied Mr Sax, with a slight laugh. 'How can I help you? When I spoke to your sergeant on the phone, he said you wanted to speak with me about Jacob and Benjamin. I assume it's something to do with poor Benjamin's death. Would that be correct?'

'That *is* correct,' said Tom. 'We are speaking with everyone who came into contact with Mr Green in the weeks leading up to his death. It is standard procedure,' he added, slightly disingenuously.

Mr Sax looked at Tom in a quizzical way. 'But the last time I saw Benjamin was not weeks but months ago, at the wedding of his granddaughter, and even then it was only for a few minutes. I'm not too sure how that can help and why it needs a detective chief inspector to visit me. If you do need my help, please at least be honest with me.'

Tom smiled, as he quickly realised that he would not be able to play any word games with Mr Sax. 'Mr Sax, I apologise. Let me be frank with you. The main reason why we wanted to speak with you was so that you could tell us what you remember about the wedding and, in particular, about the time when Jacob became upset. We are not sure if it has any relevance to Mr Green's death. We are simply trying to identify anything unusual which might have happened with him or his family prior to his death, and this may or may not be one of those occasions.'

'Thank you, Detective Chief Inspector Stone. I accept your apology. Isn't there an English saying about honesty always being the best policy? I would expect that to be especially the case with policemen.'

Tom laughed. 'You are, of course, correct. I promise that from now on I will be totally open with you.'

'We will see,' replied Mr Sax, with a slight laugh. 'So, what is it you want to know?'

'Perhaps you could start by telling us how you and Jacob came to know each other and become friends.'

'I have to tell you it's a long story,' he replied.

'Please take as long as you want. We have plenty of time,' said Tom.

Mr Sax then recounted one of the most extraordinary stories that Tom and Milner had ever heard.

He told them about how it had really begun, for them, in the spring of 1944, when the Nazis decided to instigate a major purge of all Hungarian Jews. The course of the war was, by then, turning in favour of the Allies. This, though, seemed to become the trigger to undertake one of the most frenzied periods of killing in the entire period of the war. Over 400,000 Jews from Hungary alone were rounded up and transported to Auschwitz II, or, as it later became known,

Auschwitz-Birkenau. The vast majority of these people would die in the camp.

'One night we found our home surrounded by German soldiers, together with some Hungarian police. They used loudspeakers to inform us that we had fifteen minutes to pack one suitcase per family. If we didn't then leave our home, they would come in and get us. Most of the families were then led to a holding yard where our belongings were pillaged by the Hungarian police.'

'Did they steal your belongings?' asked a puzzled Milner.

'Not all of our belongings, just anything valuable they could find,' answered Yitzhak. 'If they couldn't find anything they would take you into a building and beat you. "Where is your gold? Where is your money?" they would shout, either until you told them or until they lost interest and moved on to someone else.'

When Milner didn't respond, Yitzhak continued. 'We were told we were all being resettled and would be given work when we arrived at our final destinations. They even showed us postcards, supposedly from others who had already been resettled, saying how they had work and plenty of food. Of course, they were not genuine postcards, but, at the time, we wanted to believe they were. It showed just how gullible we were then that, even after we were loaded into the cattle trucks and the doors locked, we still believed their lie.

'There were so many of us packed into each truck, including many children, that we had to take turns to sit down. It was dark and icy cold. There were no blankets, just some dirty straw on the floor. If you needed the toilet you had to use a single bucket, which was emptied every day. At first the smell became almost overpowering but, after a while, we got used to it. The journey took six days and some in our truck died along the way, usually babies or very old people. So, after a few days of this, we realised this was no normal resettlement. What we didn't know was the hell which awaited us at Auschwitz.'

Yitzhak then described what happened when they arrived in Auschwitz. How a specially constructed railway line which took people directly into Auschwitz, with the terminus just a few hundred metres from the actual gas chambers, had conveniently been laid down so as to minimise the processing time.

He told them how, after they had all disembarked, they were arranged into two lines. The young, fit and able-bodied were directed towards the right, whilst the old, infirm and mothers with children all went to the left.

'When I got off the train there were lots of soldiers with dogs. However, I immediately noticed quite a lot of strange-looking people in striped blue and white uniforms. They seemed to be making sure the people kept moving by hurrying them along. To be honest, at first, I thought they were people who must have escaped from the local lunatic asylum. When I was got off the train, one of them came up to me and told me to say that I had a trade. So, when one of the SS guards asked me if I had a trade, I lied and told him I was a carpenter. Although I was a strong nineteen-year-old at the time, it was probably that which saved my life, because I was immediately sent to join all of the other similar men on the right.'

'And what about the others?' asked Milner, already knowing the answer but not able to prevent himself from asking.

'Do you really want to know, young man?' asked Yitzhak.

Milner just nodded, and so Yitzhak told him.

'My mother, father and brothers and sisters were all sent to the left. I can, even today, remember Mother turning around to look for me. I waved back but she didn't notice me. Even then I fully expected to see them all again shortly. That was the last time I saw them.'

He once again went quiet and Tom could just detect how he seemed to swallow hard before he continued. When he did, though, he did so with a thin smile on his face. 'In order to prevent any panic they had been told they were heading for the showers where they would be washed and deloused, after which they would be reunited with their families and assigned to one of the many barrack blocks on the site. In order to preserve this lie, once they had arrived at the "showers" they were even told to remember the number of the peg on which they had hung their clothes. But what they could not possibly realise was that they were being marched to the end of the narrow track and towards their ultimate destination: not showers but a gas chamber and, after that, the crematorium. Less than an hour after arriving at Auschwitz they would all be dead. Of course, to begin with, I didn't fully understand what was happening to everyone, including my own family.' He hesitated briefly before adding, 'It is a small relief for me, actually, that I didn't know what was about to happen to them, although it wasn't too long afterwards before I was fully aware of the horrors of what happened in this place.'

Once again, he was briefly silent, almost as though he was vividly remembering that particular time. He then went on. 'We were taken to what was known as "the sauna", where we all had our heads shaved, showered and then were tattooed with our personal identification number. I still have mine.' He rolled up his left sleeve, revealing a faded but still visible set of numbers.

'What were you then expected to do?' asked Milner, now fully engrossed in Yitzhak's story.

'Most were destined to become slaves, working for the Nazi war effort until they died from disease, hunger or sheer exhaustion,' answered Yitzhak. 'I, though, was destined for something entirely different.'

As Yitzhak described this, Tom found it very difficult not to avert his eyes from him. He had an almost mesmeric presence and, although he had shown brief glimpses of emotion as he recounted his experience, it was almost as if he were describing something which had happened to someone else.

He continued with his account, describing how he had been accommodated in one of the rectangular wooden huts which were systematically arranged in long lines throughout the site. Inside, along the entire length were three levels of bunks and he was allocated a space on the lowest level, which he shared with two other prisoners. Opposite the bunks was a long, narrow, concrete latrine channel, whilst in the centre were a stove and brick-built chimney. The hut where he was located, along with a couple of other similar ones, was set apart from the vast majority of other huts.

It was here Yitzhak had first met Benjamin Green's father, Jacob, and Rabbi Aphron's father, Josef, both of whom had also seen their own parents and siblings marched towards the gas chambers and their final fate.

Once again, it was Milner who interrupted him with a question. 'You mentioned that you didn't have the same tasks as the other prisoners. So what was it you actually did?'

For a second time Yitzhak appeared to show some reluctance to continue his story. 'Young man, are you sure you want to hear this?'

This time it was Milner who hesitated and, with some trepidation, said, 'Well, yes.'

'We were all selected to be part of the *Sonderkommando* section. Have you ever heard of that?' he asked, looking straight at Milner.

'No, I'm afraid I haven't,' Milner answered.

'Have you, Detective Chief Inspector Stone?'

Tom simply nodded his head.

Yitzhak then continued, although now in a tone of voice which was devoid of any emotion. 'We were allocated to gas chamber number 2. In total there were about a hundred of us who worked there at any one time. Our job was to dispose of the victims who had been murdered in the gas chambers. After the people had been gassed we went into the room, removed all of the bodies and threw them into the ovens. By the autumn of 1944, every day, almost 5,000 people were killed like this.'

Once more he hesitated. 'Do you want me to go on?'

Milner simply nodded this time.

'Sometimes, as we were removing them, we came across a few who were not dead. They were usually the ones who had fought their way to the top of the pile as they tried to breathe.'

'What happened to those people?' asked Milner quietly, concerned, once again, that he might already know the answer.

'After we carried them out, the SS guards shot them,' replied Yitzhak, again without any obvious emotion.

He immediately continued. 'We placed the bodies in the ovens, which, with typical German efficiency, had been built next to the gas chambers. Near the end, when there were too many bodies for the ovens, we just dug incineration pits and threw the bodies into them. When they had burnt we shovelled up the ashes and dumped them into the nearby Vistula river.'

Yitzhak suddenly stopped speaking and, looking directly at Milner, said, 'Does that shock you, young man?'

'I'm not sure I could have done that,' answered Milner quietly.

'That's what I also thought when I realised what I had

joined. But it wasn't long before, like everyone else, I just saw it as a job and a way to stay alive. Even though we were given no choice – if anyone refused they were taken to the gas chamber themselves – I'm ashamed to say I soon lost all feeling and emotion. By then it was just a job. Whatever humanity I had possessed when I arrived had long been drained from me. A few times some of the group would even discover members of their own family amongst the pile of bodies. Can you imagine that? Can you imagine anything worse than seeing your mother or father's naked dead body amongst a pile of other corpses? But they still did their job.'

'Didn't you warn the people who were being sent to the gas chambers?' asked Milner, now fully absorbed by Yitzhak's account. 'At least they would have had a chance.'

Suddenly Yitzhak became quite angry. 'Why? What good would that have done? They would have all been murdered anyway. Probably machine-gunned. Much better for it to happen quickly, without them suspecting, rather than enduring the agony of knowing. None of us could possibly know what it would be like if a mother actually knew she was taking her own children to their death.'

Milner looked as though he remained unconvinced, but before he could say anything, Yitzhak continued, 'Sometimes, though, when some of the newcomers asked where they were going, the guards would just point to the sky.'

Milner was relieved to suddenly hear a knock on the door, which then immediately opened, and Mr Sax's daughter appeared with another pot of tea. 'I thought you might need a refill. I know what my father is like when he starts speaking. He can go on a bit.'

'That's very kind of you,' replied Tom. He hesitated for a moment. 'You must be so proud of your father.'

'Yes, we are. As I'm sure you have heard, his life has been a very interesting one.'

Tom was tempted to reply that this was probably the under-statement of all time, but did not feel confident enough to actually say it. Instead, he made do with, 'It's a real honour to meet your father.'

Chapter 34

After his daughter had left, Yitzhak said, 'Are you sure you want me to carry on?'

'Please do, Mr Sax,' answered Tom, genuinely now fixated on Mr Sax's account of his time in Auschwitz-Birkenau.

'In return for carrying out our tasks we did receive certain privileges from the SS guards. As they wanted us to carry out our jobs efficiently we were given better food, cigarettes and even, sometimes, when we were sick, medicines. I soon realised, though, that even most of these had been brought into the camp by those who had been sent to the gas chambers. But, by then, we didn't care as long as we received an extra potato or piece of bread.' He continued, although this time much more quietly, 'Strange, isn't it, how so-called civilised people can so quickly be reduced to valuing human life in terms of a small potato?'

'What happened, though, to anyone who became too ill to work?' asked Milner. 'Were they then murdered?'

'Yes. They were immediately taken to the gas chamber. Later, the SS introduced a policy where they systematically began to kill members of the *Sonderkommando*. They did this so we couldn't tell anyone what was happening. The ones who were killed were then replaced by other newly arrived prisoners. The average life expectancy of a *Sonderkommando* was about three months. The Nazis were nothing if not efficient.'

'Why, then, do you think that you and the others managed to survive so long?' asked Tom.

'Self-preservation is a very powerful motive. But we also learned to live by our wits, and, of course, luck also played a key part. You quickly came to realise it was much safer if you were not noticed and did not give any excuse for the SS guards to select you. We soon learnt the art of becoming invisible, at least as far as the guards were concerned. Also, perhaps we had skills which some of the others didn't have and these were valued by the Nazis.'

Tom was interested to know what these skills were, but it soon became obvious Yitzhak was not about to elaborate and so he quickly decided not to pursue the point. Instead, he took up a different question. 'It sounds as though you could have been murdered any day. That must have been unbearable to live with, not knowing if you would be the one chosen.'

'It was for some people,' replied Yitzhak. 'There were many suicides in the camp. For those it was much easier to choose death rather than continue the life they were living.'

'Didn't I read how there was an uprising at one point, when some of the prisoners tried to escape?' asked Tom.

'Yes, you are correct. Information had reached the camp that prisoners in Sobibór and Treblinka, some of the other camps in Poland, had tried to escape. Of course, we didn't know the full story or outcome, but I suppose what we didn't know we simply made up, as we wanted to believe it. So in October 1944 it was our turn to try. For some time the rumours had grown about an even bigger purge, by the Nazi guards, on members of the *Sonderkommando*. As I said, every few months, they eliminated most of the existing prisoners and replaced them with new ones. By this time there was a well-established camp resistance in place, and they warned those that worked at one of the other crematoria that they were due to be murdered. So, the next morning, those in the *Sonderkommando* attacked the SS guards and *Kapos*, killing a few of them. They had planned to blow up the gas chambers and crematoria and then escape, taking their chances in the surrounding woods.'

'Surely they needed some explosives?' asked Milner. 'So how did they manage to get hold of them?'

'Some of the women prisoners worked in a munitions factory which was part of the camp complex. Over a period of a few months they smuggled out small amounts of gunpowder, wrapped in bits of cloth and hidden on their bodies. They then passed these to members of the camp resistance, who converted them into explosives.'

'Did anyone manage to escape?' asked Milner.

'One of the crematoria was partly destroyed and a few did get out of the camp, but they were all soon recaptured. They were all then forced to strip and lie face-down, before being shot in the back of the head. In total, over 400 of the *Sonderkommando* were killed on that day. So, you can see, Detective Chief Inspector Stone, there were some people in the camp who didn't just accept their fate. They tried to do something about it. Even though they died, every single one of them was a hero.' Suddenly, Yitzhak's previous equanimity disappeared as he showed real emotion; a solitary tear started to roll down his cheek. 'But I was not one of them, Detective Chief Inspector Stone, and not a single day goes by without me regretting that fact.'

Everyone remained silent for what seemed like an extended period of time. Eventually, Yitzhak, having now regained control of his emotions, spoke.

'The strange thing is that many people, including other Jewish prisoners, considered us to be collaborators for helping the Nazis to carry out their mass murder. Even today, some of those survivors still feel this way. Over the years it was often better not to mention how I had been part of a *Sonderkommando*.'

'But surely you had no choice,' suggested Milner.

'There's always a choice, young man,' he answered. 'I chose to live rather than die, whilst others dealt with the situation in their own way.'

'The Allies must have known what was happening,' said Milner. 'Why didn't they try and do something?'

'Like what?' asked Yitzhak.

As Milner, clearly not expecting his question, didn't immediately answer, it was left to Tom to provide a suggestion. 'Couldn't they have tried, at least, to bomb the railway lines leading into the camp? That might have held up the arrivals of new prisoners.'

'We wanted them to. If they had done that, then it might have also given us a chance to escape,' Yitzhak said, before adding, with surprising anger in his voice, 'But they didn't. A few times during the summer of 1944 we could see the American planes flying over on their way to bomb the synthetic rubber factory at Monowitz. It was only a few miles further east from where we were, so they could easily have done it. But, for some reason, they chose not to. I heard after the war they had taken a decision that bombing the factories would shorten the war and so save many more lives. Maybe it was the right decision, but to us, in the camps, it didn't seem so at the time. It just reinforced our view that we had simply been forgotten.'

Tom, sensing how Yitzhak's emotions were once again beginning to rise, decided to move on to a different subject. 'I understand it was whilst at Auschwitz that Josef met his wife. How did that happen?'

Even Yitzhak now appeared to be relieved by Tom's new line of questioning. 'Yes, Ethel also arrived in early 1944 along with her mother, father, older brother and younger sister. Her brother, who was about twenty years old, had broken his leg and, as he needed a crutch, was of no use to the Nazis. Everyone, apart from Ethel, went straight to the gas chambers. She was about eighteen at the time but was quite tall. I think that was what saved her.'

'Why was that?' asked Milner.

'As I say, she was tall and looked physically fit and so they could set her to work.'

'What did *she* do?' asked a now intrigued Milner.

Yitzhak started to laugh. 'What did she do? She was sent to work in Canada. That's what she did.'

Although Tom had read about this, and so knew what he meant, it was clear Milner didn't.

'Canada? What was that?' Milner asked.

'It was a special part of the camp. Its official name was Sector B11G, but everybody called it *Canada* because it was full of riches. Just how we imagined the real Canada to be. A land of riches. Although people were only allowed to bring a single suitcase with them, they usually tried to hide their more valuable belongings by, for example, sewing them into the lining of their clothes, or in secret compartments in their suitcase. It was the job of the women who worked in Canada to search and then sort all of the prisoners' belongings. It was incredible what they found. Cash, in all types of different currencies, diamonds, rings, necklaces, gold coins and even bond certificates. Despite the ingenuity of the prisoners, the vast majority of it was discovered. There was so much cash that a separate section was set up by the Nazis to sort it into different currencies, count it, record it and then send it back to Germany.'

'Were you involved in this as well?' asked Milner.

Yitzhak looked directly at him, before a thin smile appeared on his face. 'Do you really think the Nazis would let a bunch of Jewish prisoners anywhere near things that valuable? The women prisoners' job was simply to find the valuables. The sorting and recording roles were staffed entirely by SS people and overseen by officers. Even they, though, were not trusted with all of these riches. Every now and again, there were crackdowns by a different SS section. They would turn up, unannounced, and check all of the records, open up all of the lockers and even carry out body searches on their colleagues.'

He then continued. 'After everything had been searched, and any hidden items found, everything remaining was then sorted into clothes, suitcases, spectacles, hair and tooth-brushes and even children's toys. Nothing was wasted.'

Milner, not deterred by the answer to his previous question, and now gaining more confidence, asked a more obvious question. 'What happened to it all, after it had been sorted?'

'It was all recorded, packed up and sent back to Germany to help the Nazi war effort. Some of it, especially the warm clothes, eventually found its way to their soldiers who were fighting on the eastern front.' He paused before adding, in a more subdued tone, 'Do you know when the Russians arrived at Auschwitz in January 1945, they also found almost seven tons of human hair, bagged and ready to be sent back to Germany?'

'What could they possibly use that for?' asked a clearly shocked Milner.

'They used it to make padded jackets, again for their soldiers on the eastern front. Ingenious, really. As I said, nothing was wasted.'

Before anyone could ask any follow-up questions, Yitzhak continued. 'Towards the end, though, when the Russians were getting closer, there was mass panic amongst the Germans, and all order and discipline was breaking down daily. We knew the camp had always been rife with corruption, theft and looting, but by then it had become a free-for-all amongst the Nazi officials and SS guards. There were rumours that they were all helping themselves to the cash, gold and jewels. In fact, anything that was valuable, especially if it could be easily carried.'

'So, how did Ethel and Josef meet if they worked in different parts of the camp?' asked Tom.

'For a while one of Josef's jobs was to fill up a wheelbarrow with the clothes of those who had died in the gas chambers and take them to Canada for sorting. He waited, out of sight, until everyone was locked in the gas chamber, and then collected all of their clothes. The route through the camp took him past the block where all the women working in Canada were housed. It was while he was doing this that he first met Ethel. He told me how, one day, they just started talking, and so each day afterwards he would bring her a slice of bread or a small potato. I suppose it was then they became much closer.'

'I understand it was during their time in Auschwitz that Ethel became pregnant. Weren't the male and female prisoners kept apart from one another?' asked Tom.

Once again Yitzhak gave out a short laugh. 'Detective Chief Inspector Stone, you have obviously never been locked up in a camp where you think each day is your last, and there are women as eager as you are not too far away. What is your English expression? Where there is a will, there is a way. And there were always ways to do this, if you had the right things, especially something which you could bribe the *Kapos* with.'

'You mentioned *Kapos* before. Was that the name of the Nazi guards?' asked Milner.

'No, they were other prisoners, usually criminals or thugs, who the Nazis appointed to apply discipline within the camp. They were considered to be the most privileged prisoners and so took their duties very seriously. But,' he added, after a short pause, 'they were still happy to take bribes in return for turning a blind eye and allowing us to spend a few minutes with the women.'

'You say *us*. Does that mean you also took part?' asked Milner.

Yitzhak looked directly at him before answering. 'Of course I did. I've already mentioned that to Detective Chief Inspector Stone. You must not judge me based on today's morals. As I have told you, by then none of us had much humanity left inside us, including, incidentally, the women prisoners. They were in a far more vulnerable situation even than us. Lots of them were raped by the SS guards and *Kapos*, and some of them decided it was better to submit than to fight them. A few even became the regular lovers of some of the SS guards and officers. Like all of us who were there, they would do anything to stay alive.'

Once again, an uncomfortable period of silence followed before Tom spoke. 'So it was then Ethel conceived Josef's baby, later Rabbi Aphron?'

Yitzhak smiled. 'She certainly became pregnant then, and it's likely that Josef was the father.'

'Likely?' asked Tom, surprised by Yitzhak's reply. 'You mean that it's possible he wasn't the father?'

'It's certainly possible,' answered Yitzhak. 'There were rumours some of the others in the camp had also ... how shall I say? ... been intimate with her, and, even if that was true, she certainly wasn't the only one who was more than happy to share their favours in return for a small piece of bread or cigarette.'

Tom looked directly at Yitzhak. 'Would you mind if I asked you a very personal question? I would totally respect your decision if you chose not to answer it.'

Now it was Yitzhak's turn to look at Tom, the hint of a smile once again appearing on his face. 'Detective Chief Inspector Stone, when you have lived as long as I have and done some of the things which I've done in my life, personal questions do not really affect you as they might affect someone else. I'm afraid that's another consequence of my time in the camp.'

'Were you and Jacob some of those other men who slept with Ethel?' asked Tom. He noticed Milner shifting uncomfortably in his chair.

Yitzhak, as he had earlier suggested, was totally unmoved by Tom's direct question, other than letting out a loud laugh. 'I think describing it as "sleeping with Ethel" suggests something totally different to what actually happened. It was raw, emotionless sex, Detective Chief Inspector. We did it whenever and wherever we could. But to answer your question, yes, we both had sex with Ethel. As time went by, Ethel became more choosy, and it was then that Josef seemed to become her regular partner. He fell in love with her and so we had to be careful not to mention our time with her. Anyway, let's just say there were other fish in the sea.'

Chapter 35

Tom took a quick look at his watch and was amazed to see how much time had gone by since they had arrived at Mr Sax's home, and yet they still hadn't come to the part about the wedding. Nonetheless, this had become one of the most incredible and moving stories he had ever heard. It wasn't every day, he thought, that you had the chance to listen to someone who not only had first-hand experience of Auschwitz, but could also describe it in such an evocative way.

'What happened after the camp was liberated?' asked Tom, now interested to hear about this part of Yitzhak's life story.

'The Russians arrived at Auschwitz in January 1945. For the few weeks before that the Germans were in total panic. They knew the Russians were getting closer by the day, so they started burning all records and files. They also set up a separate section whose job was to blow up the gas chambers and crematoria in order to try and remove all evidence of what had happened there.' Once again Yitzhak paused briefly before saying, almost to himself, 'What they couldn't remove, though, were our memories.'

He then continued. 'By then, though, there were only about 2,000 prisoners left in the camp, mainly women, children or those who were infirm. A week or so earlier, a few of the prisoners who were still reasonably fit and healthy, including us, had been marched to a nearby railway station and packed into open-top railway trucks which then headed west into Germany. The vast majority, however, weren't quite so lucky. They were not selected for the trains and so were forced to walk to their next destination. It was the middle of winter, freezing cold, and snow was falling. Not surprisingly, many of the weaker prisoners died during that journey. Those who had become ill or too weak to keep up were shot by the SS guards. Later, when the guards started to become more jittery, they just shot whole groups of prisoners so that they could get away from the Russians. But, as I said, we were the lucky ones. Eventually, we reached our destination – Dachau – and, for the next few months, we were put to work as slave labourers in their remaining factories.'

'Were you still with Jacob, Josef and Ethel then?' asked Tom.

'Jacob, Josef and I were on the same train, although not in the same truck. Ethel, though, had left a week or so earlier, with most of the other women. It was only after the Americans liberated Dachau that we saw Ethel again.'

'It's incredible, with everything going on, you were able to meet Ethel again,' said Milner.

'A lot of incredible things happened at that time, young man,' Yitzhak replied. 'But just to be able to have a shower, wear clean clothes and eat proper food seemed incredible to us. After Auschwitz, when the Americans arrived, it was like paradise.'

'What were your jobs in Dachau, before you were liberated?' asked Tom, fully aware of the place's infamous reputation.

'By the time we arrived the camp was already overcrowded. As I said, all able-bodied prisoners were being moved from the camps in the east as the Russians continued to advance. In a way we were lucky to end up in Dachau,' said Yitzhak.

'Lucky?' repeated Tom. 'But I thought Dachau was one of the worst camps for atrocities.'

'I meant lucky in terms of it being in an area of Germany which the Americans got to before the Russians. It was located close to Munich in Bavaria and the Americans liberated it on the 29th of April, 1945.' He then added, almost wistfully, 'It's a day I will remember until my final breath.'

He went on. 'We quickly realised, if we were going to die, it was likely to be from disease or starvation. In fact, after the war, it was estimated about half of all of the prisoners died this way in the final few months. Typhus was becoming the main killer. Not surprising, really, with all of the overcrowding and poor sanitary conditions.'

'So, did you have the same job there as in Auschwitz?' asked Milner.

'No, thank God,' he answered quickly. 'By this time, the Nazis were starting to realise that the war was lost and so they all seemed to be making preparations for its end. To begin with, though, we lived and worked in one of the Dachau sub-camps. By then the area was being regularly bombed by the Americans and so the Nazis decided to build underground factories so war production could continue. We didn't know it at the time, but that's where their first jet fighter was going to be built. Anyway, some time in April – I can't remember the exact date – we were all moved to the main camp. When we got there it was chaos. Some of the regular guards told us the Americans would be arriving soon and so to try and do everything to stay alive until then. Of course, they too, by then, wanted to be captured by the Americans. The SS guards, though, were different. They knew, with all of the atrocities they had committed, how they were likely to be severely punished – even shot – so they went on a sort of final, crazed killing spree, and thousands of prisoners were murdered as the Americans got closer. We were just lucky we weren't amongst them.'

'What happened when the Americans arrived?' asked Tom, once again totally absorbed by Yitzhak's account.

'Of course, to begin with we were all ecstatic. Somehow we had managed to survive. But we quickly saw how the dying had not stopped. By then many prisoners were just too weak and ill to survive, and so lots more died in the weeks after liberation. After the first few days our joy turned to anger, and so we directed that anger at the captured SS guards.'

'What, you attacked them?' asked Milner.

'*Attacked* is one word to describe it, young man,' answered Yitzhak. 'I suppose *taking revenge* would better describe what happened.'

'Were many of the guards killed?' asked Milner.

'Yes, we killed them,' Yitzhak explained, in a matter-of-fact tone. 'And we enjoyed doing it,' he added, almost for effect.

Tom and Milner remained silent, as they took in what Yitzhak had just said. Eventually Tom, deciding that asking for any further details relating to this would probably be fruitless, instead asked, 'Were you still there when the Americans forced the local Germans to visit the camp to see for themselves what had been going on there?'

'Yes, I was,' he replied. 'They acted as though they had no idea what had happened. But they only lived a few miles away and quite a few German civilians even worked there, so they must have known. Most were walking around with masks over their faces to try and keep out the terrible stench of death. But some of the American soldiers made them remove the masks. They were mostly old men and women, but I still couldn't keep myself from hating them.'

Chapter 36

'So, how did you finish up in this country?' asked Tom, gently moving Yitzhak on to more recent times.

'We couldn't go back home to Hungary because the Russians were there and, from what we knew about them, they were almost as bad as the Nazis. We later heard a lot of the women who had remained in Auschwitz had been raped by the Russian soldiers. A few weeks after our camp was liberated, a few British officers and civilians suddenly appeared and began asking if anyone wanted to come to this country to work in the factories, in coal mines or on farms. We all decided, as there was nothing left for us anywhere else, we didn't have anything to lose. All of our families were dead and the Russians now controlled Hungary. So, why not?'

'But it must have been obvious that Ethel was having a baby. Was that not a problem?' asked Tom.

'Many women had had babies in the camps, so why should it be a problem? And, anyway, Josef was in love with her. He was just so happy to be back with her again. He told the British she was his wife.'

'So, when did you all arrive here in England?' asked Milner.

'Once we had all been accepted, things moved very quickly. We were each given a travel pass, which got us to a Belgian port, and then a ship over to Dover. We arrived on September 14th, 1945.'

'Had Ethel's baby been born by then?'

'No. Her son was born later that month in England.' Yitzhak took a sip of his tea and then resumed his story. 'To begin with we all worked on a farm near Maidstone, but after a few months there we moved to London.'

'What? Were you given different jobs?' asked Tom.

A smile appeared on Yitzhak's face. 'Let's just say we made the decision ourselves. It was a chaotic time here. Many foreigners were arriving all of the time, and so it wasn't too difficult to just disappear. No one was going to waste time trying to track down a few Hungarian Jews.'

'But why this part of London?'

'When we set off we didn't really know where we were going. But, on the way, we met another Jewish man from Hungary, who had an uncle who lived in Ealing, and so we just came along with him. For a while we all lived in two rooms at his house, but a few months later me and Jacob managed to find a bigger room in another house close by.'

'How did you earn money?' asked Tom. 'Did you get jobs?'

A thin smile appeared on Yitzhak's face. 'Times were different then. We had learnt many skills in the camps, not all of them strictly legal, and so we were both able to get money.'

'You mean by criminal activities?' asked a clearly shocked Milner.

'Let's just say we did what we had to do. But no one ever got hurt. We had seen too much of that already. Even though your country had rationing, to us it was still a land of plenty. The black market was everywhere and over the next few years we became very good at buying and selling things which people wanted. It was a good time,' he said, wistfully. 'I am so lucky to have found this country to live in. I will be grateful until my dying day.'

'I'm sure you have nothing to be grateful for, Mr Sax,' said Tom. 'Did you all stay in contact?'

'To begin with, yes, but, as the years went by and we had our own families, we drifted apart a bit, although I stayed closer to Jacob than to Josef and Ethel.'

'Didn't you ever consider writing about your experiences?' asked Milner. 'Yours is such an incredible story.'

Yitzhak looked directly at him, before answering, in a voice laced with rare emotion, 'Young man. Why would we want to remember our experiences? Remember seeing our families marched off to their death? Remember all of the other things which we saw, and sometimes did ourselves, in the camp? I've spent most of my life trying to forget about them.'

Milner suddenly looked as though he wanted the ground to swallow him up, and an uneasy silence followed until Tom spoke. 'But, Mr Sax, you seemed able to recount your experiences to us just now.'

Yitzhak didn't immediately respond. Finally, though, with

contrition having now replaced his earlier anger, he said, 'I apologise to you, young man, for my sharpness. You didn't deserve that.'

'You have absolutely no need to apologise, Mr Sax. I wasn't thinking,' answered Milner.

'No. It actually was a very reasonable question. I think some of the others – Jacob definitely – at some stage kept a journal. I heard that Ethel did as well. Josef, I know, just wanted to forget.'

Tom, realising that now might be a good time, decided to ask him about the wedding. 'Speaking of Jacob, could you please tell us what happened at the wedding?'

'It is not a mystery. I'm not too sure why you think it is so important. It was after the main wedding ceremony, and I was seated at a table next to Jacob and the rest of his family. Hannah, the bride, and her husband, Aaron, came over to all of the tables to meet their guests and thank them for attending. When she was directly in front of Jacob he suddenly began to shout. To begin with it seemed to be in excitement. After a short while, though, it became obvious he was becoming more and more upset. Benjamin and his wife tried to calm him, but it only seemed to make him even more upset. It was then that I went to him.'

'I understand you were able to calm him down,' said Tom. 'What did you do?'

'Nothing really,' he answered. 'All I did was say a few consoling words in Hungarian. In fact, I can't even remember exactly what they were. He did, though, stop crying.'

'Was he still calling out Hannah's name?'

'Hannah's name?' replied Yitzhak with a degree of surprise. 'He wasn't saying *Hannah*. He was using the Hungarian word for "mother". *Mama*.'

'*Mama*?' repeated Milner. 'But the other people we've spoken to are sure he was calling out Hannah's name.'

'Young man,' answered Yitzhak, 'I might be an old man, and have lived in your country for a long time, but I can still remember a few words of my native language, and know the difference between *Hannah* and *Mama*.'

'I'm sorry, Mr Sax,' said Milner. 'I didn't mean to ...'

But before he could finish, Yitzhak said, 'It's me who should apologise to you. Sometimes, I'm not as polite as I should be for a ninety-year-old man.' He smiled. 'I like you. You are a very nice young man, and when you become this country's top policeman I hope you'll remember your time today with old Yitzhak.'

*

Tom and Milner were on their way back to the station. For the first few minutes of their journey, they had travelled in complete silence, both still trying to fully comprehend the story which Yitzhak had just recounted. Eventually, though, it was Milner, unable to restrain himself any further, who spoke first.

'I think that was the most moving thing I have ever heard in my life. I just can't begin to imagine what effect it has had on Mr Sax's life. It's also really sad to know he is now the only one of the four who is still alive.'

For once, Tom was not inclined to be deliberately provocative or facetious with Milner. 'I agree. That must be very difficult for him to bear. We should be grateful for the fact you and I were able to hear it first-hand from a person who had lived through those times. It was just so ... humbling.'

Milner could sense that Tom was finding it difficult to speak, something he had never seen before.

Another extended period of silence followed before Milner, once again, spoke. 'Do you think he was correct when he said Jacob was calling out *Mama*?'

'I've got no doubts about that,' replied Tom. 'Why, do you doubt Mr Sax?'

'Not at all,' replied Milner, 'especially now that I've met him.'

'Exactly,' answered Tom.

'So, do you think there is any significance in that?' asked Milner.

'I really don't know, although he must have said it for a reason,' replied Tom. 'Perhaps Hannah reminded him of his own mother.'

'Yes, that certainly possible,' said Milner. 'But, if that's the case, what was it which caused him to say it, and in such an emotional way?'

'Well, given that he'd seen his parents literally walk to their death in Auschwitz, that would be as good a reason as any,' said Tom. 'I think we should go and see Mrs Green again. Perhaps she can provide the answer.'

135

DC Bennett was waiting for them when they returned to Tom's office.

'Sir, I've been to see Mr Stephenson again, just to see if he'd been able to recall anything else.'

'He was the one who found Mr Green's body, wasn't he?' asked Tom. 'And?'

'Afraid not, sir. There was something, though, which might be of significance. He said that he'd seen a car driving in the opposite direction to him, as he was walking towards the spot where Mr Green's body was found.'

'Why would that be significant?' asked Milner.

'He remembered that the car appeared to be going far too fast for such a road.'

'What? As though it was trying to get away from the area quickly?' asked Tom.

'Well, that would be one possibility,' answered DC Bennett.

'Could he say anything else about the car? Registration number? Make of car?'

'It was dark and so he didn't see too much. He did mention, though, that it was quite a large car and was probably a dark colour.'

'But it wasn't the same car which he already mentioned. The one with the two people in it. Is that correct?' asked Tom.

'That's right, sir. It was a different car.'

'And what time was this? Could he remember?' asked Tom.

'I did ask that, of course. He estimated it was about ten minutes before he saw the other car. So around 10.10pm, give or take,' he answered.

Tom didn't immediately reply as he considered what DC Bennett had just told him. Finally, he said, 'Well, that's something, I suppose. I'm not too sure it has got us any closer to finding out who killed Mr Green, though, except we've now got two cars to check out.' He then added, almost as an afterthought, 'The timings don't quite stack up.'

'In what way?' asked Milner.

Tom picked up a black marker pen and walked towards the whiteboard that was sited in one of the corners. He began to write times on it, vertically and in chronological order.

'Mr Green left his house at 9.45pm. It's a fifteen-to-twenty-minute walk to the synagogue, but we know he never arrived there. So, let's assume it took him fifteen minutes to get to the lay-by where his body was found. That means he was there at about 10pm.'

Tom then started a new vertical line. 'Mr Stephenson saw the car, driving fast, at about 10.10pm, and then the other car, with the two people in it, driving into the lay-by at about 10.20pm. Finally he found Mr Green's body at 10.30pm.'

'So what's your point, sir?' asked DC Bennett.

Tom continued to stare at the time chart. 'I'm just wondering what Mr Green was doing between, say, 10pm and 10.20pm, when the car drove into the lay-by.'

'Perhaps he had not walked all the way there but had been picked up, and it wasn't until 10.20ish that the car in which he was travelling drove into the lay-by. Whoever the driver was then murdered him,' suggested Milner.

'That's certainly possible,' agreed Tom. 'But it would suggest Mr Green probably knew the person who was driving the car. Otherwise, why get into it? Don't you remember his daughter mentioning how it was a nice evening and he'd said he wanted to walk to give himself some thinking time? Also, it would mean they had stopped, probably to talk, before arriving at the lay-by at 10.20pm. Anyway, if that is the case then it would at least eliminate the possibility that it was a random attack. It must have been someone who he knew, otherwise why would he get in the car?'

As Tom and Milner both continued to take in this new information, DC Bennett suddenly spoke. 'There is one other possibility, of course.'

'Go on,' said Tom.

'What if Mr Green was already dead?' He carried on. 'Suppose the two people who Mr Stephenson saw driving into the lay-by had gone there for other reasons. Mr Stephenson did say how it was occasionally used by fly tippers. So, what if they'd found Mr Green's body, panicked and then left quickly? According to what one of the forensics people told me, the imprint of the tyre marks close to Mr Green's body suggested a speedy exit. I don't know exactly how they could interpret it that way, but he was very confident. Anyway, if you remember, there was another set of fresh tyre marks found in the lay-by, albeit further away from Mr Green's body. Perhaps the other car, seen speeding away at about

10.10pm, is the one we should be concentrating on. At least that would fit more logically into your timeline, sir.'

Now it was the turn of all three of them to remain silent. Finally Tom, turning to face Milner, said, 'Give Mrs Green a call to arrange a time when we can go and see her again. And check with forensics to see if they have anything yet on the two sets of tyre tracks found in the lay-by.'

He now looked at DC Bennett. 'If what you are saying is correct, then we need to find our fly tippers as soon as possible. So that's your next priority. Find out who they are. In the meantime, why don't you tell me what the plan is for Saturday night?'

Chapter 37

It was just before midnight and Tom, together with DC Bennett and DC Jones, was in the front room of Jim King's bungalow in Hayes. Although Milner had not been asked to attend he had, nonetheless, persuaded Tom to have one of the more heavily built officers also there inside, in addition to the four other uniformed officers who were in place outside the bungalow.

Earlier in the day Jim King, the owner of the bungalow and himself a former police sergeant, had pleaded with Tom to be allowed to stay with them, there in his bungalow. Not surprisingly, Tom could not allow that but, after further discussion, a compromise had been agreed whereby Jim could stay outside along with the others.

They had arrived there, as unobtrusively as possible, earlier that evening. The house was now in complete darkness, ensuring there was little likelihood they would be seen by anyone.

They didn't have to wait much longer before DC Bennett's mobile phone began to vibrate.

'Looks like we've got some activity outside,' said one of the officers quietly, over the phone. 'Two people. Both males and both wearing dark hoodies. They've parked their car at the top of the road and have already walked past the front of the bungalow a couple of times. So they are definitely interested in it.'

He then excitedly added, 'Hang on. Looks as though they've decided this is the right place after all. They are just approaching the front door. Yes, he's just inserting the key. You should start to hear it now.'

DC Bennett gave the thumbs-up sign and everyone silently went to their allotted place in the bungalow. Almost immediately they heard the key being turned and then the door opening.

The door was quickly closed and a voice immediately said, 'Sweet as a nut. It's like shelling peas. You take the bedrooms and I'll search the front room. Just look for cash and jewellery. These old farts always have their valuables stashed somewhere. And remember to keep your gloves on.'

Tom and DC Bennett were positioned in the front room and suddenly the door to the room was opened, followed immediately by a beam of light.

'Are you looking for something?' asked Tom, as calmly as possible.

The man, not expecting this, was momentarily almost transfixed, and it was only when DC Bennett switched on the light that he started to recover his senses. By then, though, it was too late and DC Bennett threw himself at the intruder, followed by two of the uniformed officers who had suddenly entered the room.

Tom, under strict instructions from Milner to stay away from any possible rough stuff, could see that, fortunately, his involvement was not required. The man was already lying face-down on the floor, with a pair of handcuffs just about to be placed on his hands.

Tom squeezed past them and made his way to one of the bedrooms, where he could hear a lot of noise. When he got there he could see there was a bit of a stand-off. Jim, despite the efforts to keep him out of the fray, had evidently come into the house. The second intruder had a small bedside table lamp in his hand and was threatening to use it if anyone approached him. All this did, though, was provide further motivation for Jim to decide this wasn't a situation he was going to tolerate any longer. Tom's appearance in the room provided just the distraction that Jim needed and he suddenly rushed the man, hitting him before he could react. Although Jim was in his sixties he was still powerfully built and the force of his blow was enough to cause the man to drop the lamp, as he attempted to protect himself.

'You might want to think again before you break into my home,' Jim said.

'Has anyone gone to their car?' asked Tom. 'They might have an accomplice.'

'All in hand, sir,' replied DC Bennett.

'Good,' Tom said, as much to himself as in response to DC

Bennett. 'And don't forget to get the search warrant. We need to take a look in the place where they work before anything can be moved.'

A thin smile appeared on DC Bennett's face. 'That's in hand as well, sir,' he said.

'Right, read them their rights and then get them down to the station for charging, before we wake up the entire street,' said Tom.

He then turned towards Jim. 'Thanks, Jim, for agreeing to let us use your house, and sorry about the damage. Just let me know what's been broken and I'll make sure you are reimbursed.'

Jim looked around the room. 'Don't worry about that. There doesn't seem much broken anyway. It'll just be more paperwork for you to fill in. And, to be honest, I quite enjoyed it. It was just like the old days.'

Chapter 38

As Tom didn't arrive home until the early hours of Sunday morning he decided, so as not to disturb Mary, to sleep in the spare bedroom. He always found it difficult to get to sleep after the type of operation he and his colleagues had just been involved in, and today was no exception. Although it wasn't exactly the Great Train Robbery, nonetheless it was still very satisfying when an operation went exactly to plan, especially as he knew through painful experience how events could, and often did, go wrong. It was also satisfying to see just how much DC Bennett's confidence had increased since he had become a permanent part of the team. It wasn't too long ago, due to circumstances not of his own making, that DC Bennett's personal and professional life had fallen into a spiral of depression and self-doubt. In fact, he had been within days of resigning from the force before Tom had offered him this particular role. Although DC Bennett was quite a bit older and more experienced than Milner, he had quickly accepted, to his great credit, the fact that Milner, as DS, was his superior. It was gratifying, for Tom, to see just how well they worked together as a team.

As he lay there in bed, suddenly all of these thoughts were interrupted when the bedroom door opened.

'I thought I heard you return,' said Mary. 'Didn't you want to sleep with me?'

Tom sat up. 'Of course I did, but I didn't want to wake you. Also, I knew I wouldn't be able to get to sleep straight away.'

'How did it go?' she asked.

'Very well,' he answered. 'We caught the men who had been carrying out the burglaries just as they were trying to burgle a different house.'

'That's good,' she said, slipping into bed alongside him. She leant over and kissed him. 'I think I might be able to help you sleep.'

Later that morning they were seated in the offices of an estate agent, not far from Tom's house in Staines.

'So, when were you thinking of putting your house up for sale?' asked the well-dressed young man on the other side of the table.

'Well, straight away,' answered Tom. 'We'd like to sell as quickly as possible.'

'Okay,' the man replied. 'If I could take down your details, I'll then be able to give you an idea of how long the process is likely to take.'

For the next ten minutes or so, Tom answered the young man's questions. For someone who had spent all of his adult life asking the questions himself, this was a very odd experience.

Eventually, the man seemed to have all of the information he needed.

'The next stage is I will come and visit your property, take some photographs, and then write up the details for our website. I know the area where you live quite well. In fact, we have just closed on a property there within the past couple of weeks. After I've made my visit I will be able to provide you with a valuation within a day or so and, provided you are happy with it, it should be on the market a few days later.'

After they had arrived back at Mary's house, she said, 'Are you sure you want to sell your house? Wouldn't it be more sensible to rent it, at least for the next year or so?'

'No,' answered Tom. 'If I kept the house it would almost be like I'm not sure about us and am keeping my options open. I want to make a complete break.'

'Are you happy for us to keep living here?' she asked.

'Of course I am. There's just the two of us, so we don't need a bigger house, and, anyway, it's your home.'

'I just don't want you to think you have to give up everything, that's all.'

Tom took her hands in his. 'Look, I'm gaining far more than I'm giving up. The most important thing, as far as I'm concerned, is that I'm with you. And anyway,' he added, with a laugh, 'I don't want to be reminded, every time I open the front door, of the time I was shot.'

'You are doing it again. Why do you always make jokes about it?' she asked.

'Probably because it's my way of dealing with it,' he answered.

'That's the first time I've ever heard you admit that,' said Mary, surprised by Tom's sudden bout of uncharacteristic openness.

'Well, I suppose there's a first time for everything. You know by now that I've never been a touchy-feely type of person.' He paused before adding, almost reflectively. 'Perhaps that's the reason why I seem to have spent most of my life alone. Anyway, I know, with you, I have to be more open and honest. I can't always guarantee I will succeed, but at least I will be trying.'

'The reason why I love you is because of the person who you are, not because of the person I want you to be. All I'm asking is that we are both honest with one another,' she said. 'Is that too much to ask?'

Tom pulled her towards him and kissed her, before saying, 'I think I need you to help me sleep again.'

Chapter 39

'I spoke with Mrs Green first thing and she agreed we could meet with her any time later this morning,' said Milner.

'Good. So why don't we leave immediately?'

Milner hesitated briefly, as though he were reluctant to leave.

'Is there anything else?' asked Tom, sensing Milner had something else to say.

'Well, yes, there was something which I'd like to discuss.' Before Tom had the chance to ask what this was, Milner provided the answer. 'I still have the file which you gave to me. I was wondering if you still want me to hang on to it.'

'I do, if that's okay with you. Well, at least for a little while longer. I know it must be frustrating for you, but please trust me on this one.'

Milner realised it was very rare, if it had ever happened at all, that DCI Stone had asked for his trust, and so instantly realised just how important it was to him. 'Of course I trust you, sir,' he answered, before once again hesitating.

'I sense a "but" coming,' said Tom.

'It's just that you did promise to let me know what's in it.'

'I'm not sure I ever did,' Tom replied, 'and, anyway, why is it so important for you to know its contents? I will tell you, but only when I think the time is right to do so. Can we at least agree on that?'

'It's just that it is clearly very important to you and I feel I might be able to help with whatever it is.'

A thin smile appeared on Tom's face. 'I know you do,' he said. 'And I appreciate it, and that's why I will tell you at some stage.'

This seemed to satisfy Milner, and it was reflected in his tone when he next spoke. 'Thank you, sir.'

*

A short while later and Tom and Milner were, once again, seated in Mrs Green's front room. As before, she was joined by her two daughters. This time, though, a man was also present.

'This is my son, Daniel,' explained Mrs Green. 'He lives in America but came back for his father's funeral.'

Ruth, Mrs Green's older daughter, was seated alongside her and, as she said this, immediately took hold of her hand.

Tom spoke quietly. 'I'm very sorry to have to trouble you again, especially so soon after your husband's funeral, but we think there may be one or two things which you can help us with in our investigation.'

'So you haven't caught anyone yet. Is that what you are saying?' asked Ruth, her voice already rising in anger.

'Ruth, please,' said Mrs Green. 'I'm sure the police are doing everything possible.' She looked back at Tom. 'What is it you think we can help you with?'

'Thank you,' answered Tom. 'When we last met you mentioned how your father-in-law had become upset at the wedding and kept shouting the name *Hannah*.'

Daniel, who, up until now, had remained silent, suddenly said, 'What the hell has this to do with Papa's death? Ruth is right. You should be spending your time looking for the killer, not wasting time on what Grandpapa said at a wedding months ago.'

'I understand your frustration,' answered Tom, as patiently as possible. 'But please bear with me.'

This seemed to have the desired effect because, when Ruth next spoke, it was in a much more reasonable tone. 'Yes, Grandpapa did get upset. As we told you last time it was when my daughter came over to speak to us, later at the reception. He suddenly became overcome with emotion and it was then he started to call out her name.'

Milner now spoke for the first time. 'What if we told you your grandfather was not saying *Hannah*? In fact he was saying *Mama*.'

'*Mama*?' repeated Mrs Green. 'Why would he say that?'

'Well, that's what we were hoping you could tell us,' said Tom. 'Perhaps Hannah reminded him of his mother.'

'But his mother died about seventy years ago in Auschwitz,' said Mrs Green.

'Sometimes people, especially older people, find it easier to remember things from long ago than remember events which happened far more recently,' suggested Tom.

'But Hannah was his great-granddaughter and so he'd seen her lots of times. I can't ever remember him confusing her with his own mother,' said Ruth.

'Anyway, how do you know that's what he was saying?' asked Daniel, evidently not impressed by Tom's possible explanation. 'You weren't there, but we were.'

Tom then told them about how they had viewed the wedding video and seen for themselves just how upset Jacob had become. More importantly, he also told them about what Yitzhak had said with regard to his friend's use of the Hungarian word for 'mother'.

'With respect to Yitzhak,' said Daniel, 'he is a very old man, and sometimes older people want to believe things.'

'That's possible,' agreed Tom. After his meeting with Yitzhak, he didn't for one second doubt Yitzhak had heard correctly, but nonetheless he judged it was probably best not to say this right now.

'But I thought you told us that Papa had also mentioned Hannah's name to the paramedics,' said Rebecca, Mrs Green's younger daughter.

'He did. We double-checked with the paramedics,' explained Milner. 'Given the circumstances it wasn't easy for them to fully make out what your father was saying, but, nonetheless, they are almost certain that's what he was trying to say.'

'Okay, perhaps Grandpapa did say *Mama*. But if Papa said *Hannah* then there is no coincidence. I really don't understand why all of this is of so much interest to you,' said Daniel.

A brief, uncomfortable silence followed before Tom, deciding not to respond to Daniel's comment, spoke. 'Did your grandfather leave any documents? A journal or diary, letters, photographs? That type of thing.'

'He did leave a few items,' answered Mrs Green. 'I know he kept all of the letters he received from Magda, his wife, before they were married, but Benjamin dealt with all of that after his father died.'

'Do you know if they are still available?' asked Tom.

'I'm sure they are here somewhere, most probably with all

of Benjamin's other possessions,' Mrs Green said. She then began to cry. 'I just can't bring myself to go through them,' she added, between sobs. 'It would bring back so many memories.'

'I totally understand,' said Tom, sympathetically. 'Perhaps, when you feel you are able to, you could allow us to take a look at them. I understand it's quite unusual but, as I've said previously, it might help us with our investigation.'

Daniel was clearly not going to let this go unchallenged. 'First, you ask about whether Grandpapa said *Hannah* or *Mama*. Now you would like to go through all of his personal belongings. I can't possibly see how any of this is going to help with the investigation into Papa's death. In fact, all it will do is distract you from what you should be doing: finding whoever murdered Papa.'

This time Tom had little choice but to respond. 'I can assure you, Mr Green, my officers and I will not become distracted. We are doing everything possible, and that includes exploring every connection, however indirect, to find whoever did this. I have been a police officer for over thirty years, and during that time I have seen many situations where crimes have been solved due to seemingly unimportant connections. I share your frustration, but all I can ask is that you give me your total support during this investigation. It's more than likely there will be nothing within your grandfather's possessions which will help, but, if that does turn out to be the case, at least we can then positively discount it.'

Tom's little speech seemed to have the necessary effect on Daniel. 'Okay,' he said, albeit grudgingly. 'If you think it's important, I guess we have no choice but to agree to it.'

Before Tom could respond, Ruth spoke. 'You said there were a couple of things which we might be able to help you with. Or was it just about what Grandpapa said at my daughter's wedding?'

'There was one other thing,' said Tom, looking at Mrs Green. 'Did your father-in-law keep in touch with any of the others who were at Auschwitz with him, apart from Mr Sax?'

'It depends whether or not you mean recently. Josef, of course, died about twenty years ago and his wife, Ethel, died two or three years ago. Before she died, though, she and Jacob did start spending more and more time together. It was really nice to see them renewing their old friendship. After all, they shared a lot of experiences in their lives.'

'They certainly did,' replied Tom. 'When we met with Mr Sax, he described some of those experiences.' He hesitated. 'It was very humbling.'

For a while, no one spoke, and the silence was only broken when Tom stood up. 'I do appreciate your time, particularly so soon after Mr Green's funeral. I would imagine there were a lot of people there.'

'Yes, he was well liked,' replied Ruth.

'I assume Rabbi Aphron officiated at it,' said Tom.

'Of course. He is our rabbi. We have known him and his family for a very long time. His son is married to Ruth. They were all there to pay their respects,' said Mrs Green. 'As I have mentioned previously, Rabbi Aphron and his family have been at the centre of our local Jewish community for many years. Samuel, in particular, has been a great source of strength to our family – well, not just ours, but many others as well – over the years.'

'Thank you once again,' said Tom. 'And, if you do find any of your father-in-law's belongings, I would appreciate it if you could give me a call.'

Daniel looked as though he was just about to make a comment, but resisted the temptation and instead put a comforting arm around his mother, who by now had started to weep quietly.

As they walked towards their car, Milner said, 'Daniel had a good point when he highlighted the lack of any coincidence, or any connection at all, between what his grandfather and father had said.'

'On the other hand, there might be a connection, but we just haven't found it yet,' replied Tom, a little mysteriously.

Chapter 40

'Good news, sir,' said an excited DC Bennett, once they were back at the station. Before either Tom or Milner could ask the obvious question, DC Bennett provided the answer. 'We carried out a search of the car repair garage and managed to find some of the items stolen during the first few burglaries.' He opened his notebook and started to read from it. 'There was a pair of gold earrings, and matching necklace, which belonged to Mrs Rogers, as well as a watch belonging to her husband. All the items match perfectly with their descriptions provided by Mr and Mrs Rogers. In fact, on the back of the watch there is even an inscription relating to Mr Rogers.'

'Anything else?' asked Tom.

'That's it, I'm afraid, sir. No cash, of course. It's probable they also managed to get rid of the other stuff some time earlier.'

'So, what did the owner of the garage have to say? Did he admit his involvement?' asked Tom, hopefully.

'No. He denied knowing anything about what his two employees were up to. He's hanging them out to dry, in my opinion. Unfortunately, unless they decide to implicate him, we have absolutely nothing to hold him on. I haven't given up on that, though. I intend to interview them again and lay it on thick how anyone else who might have been involved will still be able to benefit from their little enterprise whilst they are banged up somewhere. As you know, it's amazing how any misplaced loyalty often suddenly disappears when they know what's ahead of them.'

Before Tom could respond, DC Bennett carried on. 'There was some other good news, though. The receptionist did admit her involvement. Apparently she's the girlfriend of the matey who Jim managed to land one on. She was the one who got chatty with the customers and managed to find out when they would be away. She claimed her boyfriend forced her to do it. I can't see it myself but, anyway, she's now admitted her involvement.'

Tom didn't immediately answer. Finally, though, he said, 'Just make sure the paperwork is done properly. We don't want to give their defence team any opportunity to get them off on a technicality. And you are right about the owner. Keep the pressure on the others. I'd like to nick the lot of them if possible.' He paused. 'Could you let me have the items belonging to Mr and Mrs Rogers? I just need to borrow them for a short while.'

Although DC Bennett looked slightly puzzled by Tom's request, he nonetheless knew it was probably unwise to ask why he needed them. So he simply said, 'I'll let you have them straight away.'

Later that same day Tom received a call from Rebecca Green. She described how, after Tom and Milner had left their house, they had all agreed that she and her brother Daniel should go through their father's belongings. They realised, notwithstanding Tom's request, it was a job which would have to be done sooner or later. All of Jacob's personal belongings, she told him, had been contained in a rectangular metal box. Tom thanked her for letting him know and agreed he would call round to collect them the following morning.

*

As Tom drove home his thoughts kept returning to the incredible story which Yitzhak had told him and Milner about his time in Auschwitz. He hadn't realised just how much it had affected him until he had found himself lying awake at night, remembering vividly what he had been told. Of course, he had seen, on television, documentaries about the Holocaust and, in particular, about Auschwitz, the most infamous of all of the Nazi death camps. But it was one thing to see those events in black and white; it was another thing entirely to hear about them from someone who had actually been there and survived the experience.

In truth he wasn't any closer to finding out who had killed Benjamin Green. As ever, though, he knew that, if he could at least find a potential motive, it would go a long way to help provide him with the answer.

But, before he finally arrived home, he had to do something

else, and that was why he later found himself seated in Mr and Mrs Rogers' front room in Hillingdon.

'I understand DC Bennett has already informed you we have been able to recover your items. I just wanted to bring them along to show you.' Tom produced a pair of earrings and matching necklace, together with Mr Rogers' watch, and placed them on the small table immediately in front of him. 'I will need to take them back until we have finalised all of our evidence, but, as I said, I thought you might want to see them.'

Mr Rogers picked up the watch and inspected the inscription on the back. 'Thank you,' he said, after a brief silence. 'Although we said we just wanted whoever did this to be caught, this watch means a lot to me. My mother and father bought it for me on my twenty-first birthday.' It was clear Mr Rogers was suddenly overcome with emotion.

'I also wanted to let you know we have arrested the people who did this and I'm sure they will all get a custodial sentence.'

'Thank you so much. You don't know how much this means to us,' said Mrs Rogers. 'At least I will be able to sleep again now that I know they won't be doing it again.'

Chapter 41

The following morning Tom had collected the metal box from Rebecca Green. It was now on the table in front of him, in his office.

It was much bigger than he had imagined and, as he looked at it, he could immediately see that there were a number of features which clearly distinguished it as something quite unusual. Most obviously there were the four short, finely decorated metal legs on which the main body of the box stood. A narrow silver rim had been soldered to both the top and bottom of the box, and the sides were intricately decorated. It was also clearly old. The extensive tarnishing over the surface, together with a few dents, was testament to that. He put on a pair of thin latex gloves, as he was determined not to contaminate any potential evidence which the box might reveal.

The box had a large keyhole on the top, which provided some security, although the reality was that a little force, judiciously applied, would probably have been as effective as any key. Nonetheless Tom used the large key, also provided by Rebecca, to open the box and was immediately surprised to see that the box was not even half full. He carefully removed the contents and placed them on the table before examining the box in more detail.

He turned the box over so he could see its underside. He spotted a small, circular indentation, presumably where the manufacturer's stamp had been pressed, but couldn't immediately make out any name. He then carefully flipped it back over, placed it on the table, and turned his attention to the contents. After a very cursory examination he decided to sort them into four separate categories. The first one, and the one which contained the most numerous items, was for all of the letters. They were all bundled together, held in place by pieces of very fragile-looking string. The second one had just a single item: something which resembled a journal or small writing book. The third category was for the dozen or so photographs which were in the box. The final one also had the one solitary item, which Tom picked up and examined in more detail. Although quite faded and with some of the wording smudged, it was clearly an identity card. In the centre was a grainy head-and-shoulders photograph of Jacob, under which had been typed his full name, *Jacob Greenbaum*, his date of birth, *20th August 1927*, and a brief description of his distinguishing features. Stamped at the top of the card was *Auschwitz II*.

He was wearing the standard Auschwitz prison uniform. His blue and white striped cap looked far too large, as did the striped 'pyjama' coat which hung from his shoulders. Based upon his date of birth, Tom estimated Jacob's age, at the time the photograph was taken, to be about seventeen. The now-faded photograph, together with the standard prisoner uniform, somehow gave the impression of someone much older. Jacob's expressionless face and vacant eyes suggested a person almost devoid of any human feeling. Tom continued to examine the card for a while longer, completely transfixed. If ever there was a photograph which evoked the hopelessness of the situation, he thought, then surely this was the one.

Almost reluctantly he put the identity card down and picked up the small writing book to open it at the first page. Although he couldn't understand what Jacob had written, as, he guessed, it was all in Hungarian, he could make out the date of the first entry. It was the 26th September 1945. He quickly flicked through the rest of the pages and could see that the entries continued fairly regularly for a few years until they eventually became much more infrequent and finally stopped entirely in the middle of the 1950s.

Next, he turned his attention towards the photographs. Most were quite small in size, with the smallest only about two inches square and the largest about four inches by six in size. A couple of the photographs had that old, sepia-style quality about them and showed a young man and woman, both dressed quite elegantly. The woman was seated whilst the man stood stiffly behind her with his right hand placed on her shoulder. Neither, though, was smiling. Instead, both had a very serious look on their face, almost as if the occasion was far too formal for frivolities. There was a selection of photographs featuring a baby and a small toddler. Others showed a young boy and then, finally, a teenage boy – all presumably photographs of Jacob as he grew older and taller.

Tom picked up the largest photograph and, for some time, examined it in more detail before finally placing it back with the others.

Finally he picked up the bundle of letters and very carefully untied the string and quickly flicked through them. He estimated that there were about twenty in total. He selected the one at the bottom of the pile and looked closely at the front of the envelope, which had a British stamp stuck on it. It was addressed to Jacob Greenbaum and was dated 15th March 1947.

Tom very carefully took out the letter, which comprised two pages, unfolded it and laid it down on the table. Like the journal, it was written in a foreign language. He turned to the second page and cast his eye down to the bottom. He could make out the signature as belonging to Magda Berger. He then opened a few more letters at random, which confirmed they too had been written by the same person who, later, would become Jacob's wife.

Just as he was about to replace the journal and letters in the metal box, he suddenly noticed a small envelope which had become hidden amongst the larger ones. He took it out and could immediately see that the address had been written in a totally different handwriting style. He examined it in more detail and, like all of the others, it was addressed to Jacob. What was surprising, though, was that the postmark was dated 18th August 2013.

He carefully opened the envelope and took out the letter. It consisted of just two sheets of special A5 writing paper and all four sides were covered in neat handwriting, all in English. At the very end he noticed Ethel Aphron's signature.

He quickly read the letter and then put it back into its envelope and placed it on the table, before putting all of the other letters, together with the journal, back in the metal box. The photographs, identification card and Ethel's letter he then put into separate protective plastic bags.

Tom leant back in his chair and considered what, if anything, he had actually learnt from now being able to see all of these items. He was hoping there might be something of importance contained within the letters or journal. Something which might give a clue as to why Mr Green was murdered. For that to happen, however, he knew he would first have to know what the letters actually said and so would need them, together with the journal, to be translated.

He had mixed feelings about this, aware that he was intruding into someone's personal life. Perhaps he had now become far too fixated on the real-life experiences of Yitzhak, Jacob, Josef and Ethel during their time together in Auschwitz. There was, of course, no evidence, so far, which linked Mr Green's murder with the events of over seventy years ago. But, despite this lack of evidence and the absence of any obvious motive, somewhere deep inside him he felt his inbuilt antennae, which had often, in the past, proved to be so prescient, were beginning to spring into life. He just hoped, as he continued down this particular path, he wasn't missing something much more obvious, due to this growing obsession with events which had happened before he had even been born.

Chapter 42

More out of curiosity than for any logical investigative reason, Tom decided to take Jacob's metal box along to an antiques dealer, hoping the dealer might be able to tell him a bit more about the origins of the box. Joshua Porter owned an antiques shop in Windsor and Tom had been part of the team which had recovered some of the items stolen from Joshua's premises about ten years previously.

'Good to see you again, Joshua. Thanks for seeing me so soon,' said Tom.

'It's a pleasure to see you again, Detective Chief Inspector Stone.' He paused for a moment. 'Well, perhaps not always a pleasure, but at least this time, I assume, it's more of a social visit.'

'Actually, I was hoping you could help me this time.'

'Really?' replied Joshua. 'Well, I'll try my best.'

Tom, having earlier removed the contents, took the box out of the bag in which he had carried it, and placed it on the cloth conveniently located on the small desk in front of Joshua.

'What have we here?' asked Joshua, clearly intrigued.

'I was hoping you could tell me,' replied Tom, who then briefly told Joshua about its known history.

Joshua very carefully picked the box up and began to examine it, starting with the lid and then the sides before turning it over to view the underside. He then took out a magnifying glass, from the top drawer of the desk, and used it to examine the pressed indentation.

'Very interesting,' he said, still peering through the magnifying glass. 'It looks like it was made in Poland, or possibly Hungary, but certainly somewhere in central Europe, probably around the end of the nineteenth century. It also looks like the manufacturer's name is Weisser. But I will be able to confirm that later. Lots of this type of thing appeared on the market immediately after the end of the Second World

War. Not surprising, really, given what happened to most of their owners.'

'What do you mean?' asked Tom.

'Well, the people who originally owned them were murdered in the camps, and their property was stolen, hidden or simply left behind when they were being transported there. Those who survived may have needed to sell their personal items just to feed themselves and their families, and of course the stolen ones would probably have been put up for sale. Anyway, for whatever reason, as I said, lots of such items suddenly became available.'

Tom didn't respond to what Joshua had just said. Instead, he was deep in thought, wondering how the box had originally come into Jacob's possession.

Joshua put the box back onto the desk, 'It's a nice piece of work but, unfortunately, because it is quite plain, not something which would attract a lot of interest if it were to go to auction. I may be wrong, of course, but I don't think you will be able to retire on any sale proceeds.'

'That's a shame,' replied Tom, with a laugh, grateful for Joshua's little joke. 'I was hoping it would fund my retirement.'

Joshua picked up the key, unlocked the box and lifted the lid. 'Again, not good news, I'm afraid. The hinges are fairly bog-standard and there's nothing of interest, that I can see, on the inside walls.' He placed his right hand inside the box and started to feel around, before once again picking up his magnifying glass to look in more detail inside it. After a while he put the magnifying glass back down on the desk, put both hands into the box and, with thumb and index finger, squeezed each side of the box.

Suddenly a look of satisfaction appeared on his face. 'Hello. What's this?' he asked, rhetorically, as he took out a thin metal plate. 'You might want to take a look inside.'

Tom peered into the box and could immediately see that it was no longer empty. He reached into his pocket, pulled out a pair of latex gloves, put them on and very delicately took out the box's contents: an old photograph. He placed it on the desk alongside the box and then closed the lid.

Tom picked up the photograph and straight away recognised the same young woman who had featured in many of the other photographs. This time, though, she was the only person in the photograph, which looked as though it had been taken on her wedding day. 'Could I please borrow your magnifying glass?' he asked.

Joshua passed it to Tom, who examined the photograph with much more deliberation. He could feel his heart rate increasing. After a while he handed the magnifying glass back to Joshua.

'Is that what you were expecting?' asked Joshua, looking at the photograph in front of him.

'I'm not sure what I was expecting,' Tom answered truthfully.

'It's not uncommon,' explained Joshua, 'for these sorts of items to have a secret compartment. If you know what you are looking for, sometimes they are quite obvious. What is clever with this one, however, is that whilst the box itself is so unremarkable, the release mechanism inside was extremely well hidden.'

'Well, it was certainly that,' said Tom. 'I must have looked inside the box half a dozen times and not spotted anything.'

'As I said, you have to know what you are looking for,' said Joshua.

Tom couldn't resist picking up the photograph one more time and taking another look before placing it into one of his protective plastic bags.

He suddenly found himself smiling. 'At least the old antennae are still working,' he said quietly.

'What did you say?' asked Joshua.

'Nothing very interesting. Just talking to myself,' he replied.

Chapter 43

After dinner Tom suggested to Mary that he had a DVD which they could watch together. This came as a real surprise to Mary as she knew Tom didn't especially like watching films. By his own admission, he didn't have the patience to sit down and spend over two hours staring at a screen. This was way above his normal boredom threshold. When he told her it was a wedding DVD, she was even more puzzled, and it was only after a few questions that the real reason emerged. He gave her some of the background to Mr Green's murder and, finally, explained how the photograph had been found in the metal box by Joshua.

Tom switched on the television and placed the DVD in the player. He pressed 'play' and it sprang into life. When it got to the part where Jacob became upset he paused the DVD.

'You are more likely to know about this type of thing than I am,' he said generously, 'so how would you describe the necklace which Hannah, the bride, is wearing?' He had paused the DVD at a point where Hannah, wearing the necklace, was clearly visible.

'Why?' asked Mary, a puzzled expression appearing on her face.

'Just bear with me,' replied Tom. 'I'll tell you shortly. So, what would you say?'

'It's difficult to see it clearly,' she said, leaning forward to get a better view.

Tom pressed the 'zoom' button on the television remote and the image suddenly increased four times in size.

Mary turned to look at Tom. 'When did you learn to do that?' she asked with genuine admiration, knowing how he could never be described as tech-savvy.

'I've been practising,' he answered, clearly pleased with himself. 'And, anyway, Milner told me what to do.'

'Perhaps you could ask Milner to also explain to you how to work the washing machine,' she said.

'Ha, ha. Very funny,' he said in reply. 'I know my limitations. I think that might be one step too far.'

'Very convenient,' she said, with a short laugh, before concentrating on the image of Hannah. She instinctively moved closer to the television. 'Well, it's still a bit difficult to see, but it looks like an oval garnet stone, set in beaded gold and surrounded by... one, two, three, four, five, six, seven, eight, nine, ten, eleven teardrop garnet stones, all of which hang from a gold chain.' She paused before adding, 'It's lovely and beautifully complements Hannah's slender neck.'

This time it was Tom's turn to look at Mary with genuine admiration. 'That's why I asked you to describe it. It's unlikely any man – particularly me – could ever have described it the way you just did. You made it sound like a living thing. I've mentioned before how you would make a great policewoman.'

'Thank you, but I suspect there's more to being a police officer than being able to describe a necklace.'

Tom put on his latex gloves and carefully removed the photograph from the plastic bag. 'I'd rather you didn't touch this, but could you now take a look at it and see if you think it's the same necklace that Hannah was wearing, or just something similar?'

Tom held the photograph in front of her whilst she looked closely at it. After a while she sat back. 'I can't be absolutely sure when the photograph is black and white. It's more difficult to differentiate all of the features.'

'But?' said Tom, a bit impatiently.

'But I would say it is the same or, if not, something which is very, very similar.'

Tom placed the photograph back into the plastic bag. 'Yes, that's what I thought as well.'

'Can you now please tell me what all this is about?' she asked.

So Tom told her. He told her about Mr Green's murder and the moving conversation with Yitzhak, when he had recounted the time he had spent captive in Auschwitz. He told her about his own meetings with the Green family and about the metal box, containing Jacob's personal items, which they had entrusted to him. He told her about Jacob's emotional outburst at Hannah's wedding and his own meeting with Rabbi Aphron. And finally, he told her about how Joshua had found the secret compartment, within the box, containing the photograph which she had just studied.

Mary looked at Tom and then said, 'I can see all of this has really affected you.'

Tom didn't immediately respond. Eventually, though, he said, 'I would challenge anyone not to be moved by the story which Mr Sax told me and Milner. Despite hearing it directly from someone who was actually there at the time in Auschwitz, it is still almost impossible to fully comprehend the horrors which took place there. It's as if it's from a different time entirely and not from just seventy years ago.'

'Do you think it's all connected with the murder?' she asked directly.

'The only connection we are aware of, so far, relates to their time at Auschwitz. Once we have a better idea as to why Mr Green was murdered, I might be able to answer your question with a bit more confidence.'

As he said this he couldn't help thinking how all of this might just be a wild goose chase.

Chapter 44

The next morning Tom arrived at the station earlier than normal, although still not early enough to beat Milner, who, along with DC Bennett, was waiting for him to arrive.

'Don't you ever go home?' Tom asked jokingly. 'Remember what they said about work and Jack.'

Milner stared at him with a look of genuine puzzlement. 'Who is Jack, sir?' he asked.

'Never mind,' answered Tom with uncharacteristic patience.

Milner had, over the past year or so, become a bit of an expert at reading his boss's body language, and today his instincts were telling him that his boss appeared to be in a particularly buoyant mood. And his instincts were confirmed when DCI Stone began to update them on his meeting with Joshua and the subsequent discovery of the photograph.

'That's amazing, sir,' said Milner. 'So, your theory about the connection between Jacob's outburst and Mr Green's murder was correct.'

First thing that morning Tom had phoned Mrs Green, who had confirmed that the young woman featured in the photo was indeed Jacob's mother on her wedding day.

'I'm not sure I actually said that, Milner,' answered Tom. 'At the moment it's just a coincidence.'

'And you don't believe in coincidences, do you, sir?' added Milner.

Tom looked Milner suspiciously, before a thin smile appeared on his face. 'Am I really that predictable?' he asked.

'Not really, sir,' Milner replied, a little cautiously. 'But, anyway, even if you are, you're right more times than not.'

'Good answer, Milner. I think, with diplomacy skills like that, you are perfectly qualified to go right to the very top of the force. Isn't that right, DC Bennett?'

'I couldn't possibly comment, sir, not having any diplomacy skills myself,' DC Bennett answered.

'You and me both,' said Tom. 'Anyway, what would you propose we do next?'

It was DC Bennett who spoke first. 'I think we should go and speak with Hannah, the bride, and find out where she got her necklace from.'

'I agree,' said Milner. 'If we know that, then it might lead us closer to finding out why Mr Green was killed.'

'I agree,' answered Tom. 'Although, first, I think we should show it to Rabbi Aphron. It's possible he might know more about it than his granddaughter, but let's tread carefully. It *might*, after all, just be a coincidence and, if that is the case, we don't want to make the situation any worse than it already is.'

'You also mentioned a letter to Jacob from Rabbi Aphron's mother,' said Milner. 'Did it include anything interesting?'

'Interesting? I suppose it depends who is reading it,' Tom replied, a little too sharply. He quickly carried on. 'She and Jacob had clearly met for coffee just a few days earlier. The first part of the letter was mainly about family members, what they were doing with their lives and how proud she was of all her grandchildren and great-grandchildren. There was also an entire paragraph complaining about the cost of the coffee and cake which they had bought in the café. The most intriguing bit, however, was a reference to a man named Oskar and how he was "different from all of the others". I'll read that part to you.'

He then picked up the letter and began to read.

'It helped that I was finally able to speak with you about Oskar. It's a great comfort to me to know that I have you there as a true friend. It's a long time ago now, but I find myself thinking about him more and more as time goes by and I get nearer to the end. He was different from all of the others and, without his help, I'm certain I wouldn't be here enjoying cake and coffee with you, my special friend.'

It was DC Bennett who asked the question that they were all thinking. 'So, who is Oskar?'

When there was no answer, Tom said, 'Right. In the meantime could you take the wedding DVD and get a few enlarged, close-up stills of Hannah wearing the necklace? Also take the photograph and letter and get them checked for any fingerprints and DNA. You never know. Then take the photo to the tech boys and see if it's possible to add colour to it.' He handed Milner the plastic bag containing the black-and-white photo.

'Is that it?' asked Milner.

'No. I'd also like you to start the process of translating all of the letters and the journal into English. Then take a few copies of them. The same with Jacob's identity card and the other photos. When you've started all of that, we will go and visit Rabbi Aphron.'

'Is that all?' asked Milner, with a hint of sarcasm. 'Just as well I have lots of spare time.'

Tom looked at Milner, smiled and said, 'My mum used to say to me that if you want something done quickly, always give it to the person who is the most busy.' He then added, almost as an afterthought, 'And, as you know, your mum always knows best.'

Chapter 45

Not long after Milner and DC Bennett had left, Tom received a call from Jenny, now Superintendent Birch's PA.

'Good morning, sir,' she said, in her usual cheery and polite tone. 'Superintendent Birch has asked me to find out if you are available any time today to see him.'

Tom looked at his watch. 'Actually, now would be a good time, as it's possible I will be tied up this afternoon.'

'I'll just check to see if that's okay,' she said. 'I'll call you straight back.'

Almost immediately she called again. 'Yes, now is also fine for Superintendent Birch. I'll have a coffee waiting for you.'

'That would be very nice,' he replied. 'It will be worth seeing Superintendent Birch just to drink your coffee again.'

A short while later and he was seated in his old, temporary office on the fifth floor, a pot of coffee on the table in front of him.

'Thanks, Tom, for making time to see me and, by the way, congratulations on the burglary investigation,' said Superintendent Birch. 'I've read the report. Looks like you got a good result there.'

'Well, it was mainly DC Bennett who led the operation, although, I have to say, the burglars weren't the brightest criminals I've ever come across.'

'Dim or bright, it doesn't really matter. The main thing is they won't be carrying out any more burglaries on elderly people's homes. How's the murder investigation coming along? Have you made any progress with it?'

'Yes. Coincidentally, I think we've just had our first break.'

Tom then updated him on the recent development regarding the secret photograph as well as what they were next proposing.

'As you say, sounds like a bit of a breakthrough,' Superintendent Birch said, sitting back. 'Anyway, I'd appreciate it if you could keep me informed. When you first mentioned it to me, I feared it might have been racially motivated. I'm sure you've heard that, in some parts of the country, there has been an increase in so-called hate crimes recently, many involving Jewish people, and that's not counting the increase in vitriol which is on social media nowadays.'

'Well, actually, sir, we might have to think again on that one.'

'Really?' asked Superintendent Birch, clearly betraying his increased concern.

So Tom told him about the letter which Rabbi Aphron had received just days before Mr Green, a prominent man within the Jewish community, had been murdered.

'Hmmm. That's worrying. Let's hope it is just a coincidence. Anyway, if there are any other resources you think you might need, just ask.'

'Thank you, sir,' replied Tom. 'I'll let you know if there are.'

Tom could sense that this wasn't the main reason why he had been asked to see Superintendent Birch, and this was quickly confirmed.

'The main reason why I wanted to see you relates to some very good news. I have just been informed by DCS Small that his recommendation you receive a gallantry medal, in recognition of your work relating to the Grace case, has been accepted.' A big smile appeared on his face. 'Very many congratulations. It is thoroughly deserved.' He held out his right hand and Tom automatically responded by holding out his own.

Although the possibility of this had been raised by DCS Small previously, Tom thought he had made it perfectly clear that he was unable to accept it.

'I'm sure everyone in the station will be delighted for you. It's a great honour,' said an effusive Superintendent Birch. Tom could see that he was genuinely pleased for him, and this suddenly added to Tom's already increasing sense of anxiety, especially bearing in mind what he was just about to say.

'I'm sorry, sir, but I thought I'd made it clear to DCS Small that I could not accept a medal.'

'Why on earth not?' asked a now bemused Superintendent Birch. 'From what I know about the case, not only did you put yourself in danger, but your immediate family was also threatened by Grace. Notwithstanding this you continued to pursue Grace, and the other family members. To my mind, and, more importantly, clearly to other more senior officers, your actions went above and beyond what would normally be expected of any police officer in those circumstances.'

Tom remained silent whilst he collected his thoughts.

'Would you mind telling me why you can't accept it?' Superintendent Birch asked, in a much more subdued tone.

'I'll repeat what I said to DCS Small. I do not believe I did anything different to what thousands of other officers would have done. I suspect one of the main reasons is that I was shot. But, if anything, that was due to my own carelessness. After all, I was shot on my own doorstep, not on a stakeout, or leading a near-suicidal assault on well-armed criminals.'

What he didn't mention was how he also thought that this award might, perhaps, be some sort of *quid pro quo* for his continuing silence with regard to the case he had brought against Commander Jenkins and Charles Cope. He couldn't be certain, of course, but the timing did seem to be far too coincidental for his liking.

'Tom,' replied Superintendent Birch, 'of course I respect your views, but I feel, if I may say so, you are being unduly hard on yourself, as well as far too modest. Awards such as these aren't handed out like sweets. There is a very clear vetting process, which involves quite a number of senior officers. The relative rarity of any being awarded is testimony to that.'

'I understand all of that, sir,' Tom answered patiently, 'but I'm afraid I haven't heard anything, since my conversation with DCS Small, which has made me change my mind. I do respect your position on this, but I really cannot accept it.'

'Of course, it's your right to decline, and I have to respect it. I will inform DCS Small of your decision.' He paused. 'But I still think you are making a mistake.'

Chapter 46

'It certainly looks very similar, but, of course, it's difficult to be one hundred percent certain. Even if they're identical, it might just be because they were two of a number of similar necklaces which were made,' said Rabbi Aphron.

Tom and Milner were, once again, seated in the same small office located towards the rear of the synagogue. They had just shown Rabbi Aphron the old photograph of Jacob's mother, wearing the necklace on her wedding day, together with a still of Hannah taken from the DVD. The first picture, originally shown in black and white, had been edited by the station's techies, so that now it was resplendent in full colour.

'That's perfectly true,' said Tom, in response to Rabbi Aphron's possible explanation. 'But would you accept that it would be a remarkable coincidence?'

When he heard DCI Stone's use of the word 'coincidence', a thin smile appeared on Milner's face.

'Well, yes, I suppose it would be, although coincidences do sometimes occur,' Rabbi Aphron said, not very convincingly. He then went on in a far more assertive tone, with renewed confidence. 'Even so, I fail to see how this could possibly be connected to Benjamin's death.'

'That's exactly what we are trying to determine. It would at least help if we could discount any possible connection,' said Tom. 'Could you please tell us how your granddaughter came to be wearing the necklace?'

Rabbi Aphron looked suspiciously at Tom. 'Now you seem to be involving Hannah in this. I don't think you are being completely honest with me, Detective Chief Inspector Stone.'

Tom's expression remained unchanged as he said, 'I'm sorry if you think that, but I can assure you I am being totally honest with you. I'm simply following up on one possible connection, that's all. As I just said, if we could discount this then that would also help.'

This appeared to satisfy Rabbi Aphron, at least for the moment, as he then provided the answer to Tom's earlier question. 'It originally belonged to Mother. We found it after she died. It was one of a number of similar pieces of jewellery we came across when we were clearing her personal items. I had no need for them and so, as is often the tradition in Jewish families, I gave them to my children, Sarah, David and Emmanuel. As you know, Hannah is Emmanuel's daughter and so, again as is our custom, it was perfectly natural for her to wear it at her wedding.' He paused briefly and then said, 'A wedding is an extremely important occasion within the Jewish faith. It not only celebrates the union of two people but also provides the perfect opportunity to reinforce the sanctity of the family unit. Something to which our faith attaches great importance.'

'You mentioned how the necklace was one of a number of items found when you went through your mother's possessions,' Milner said. 'What other items did you find?'

Rabbi Aphron's earlier suspicion suddenly resurfaced. 'Why is it now you seem to have developed an interest in Mother's other items of jewellery? I could just about accept that the necklace might be of interest to you, but I really do fail to see why anything else would be.'

'It's a question of context,' answered Milner. 'For example, there might have been a matching ring or pair of earrings.'

Rabbi Aphron's expression suggested he remained far from convinced. Nonetheless, he answered Milner's question.

'In actual fact, if I remember correctly, there were two rings, although both of them were in a totally different style, together with a bracelet. None of them were a match to the necklace,' he replied, before hesitating slightly, as if he were about to say something else. When he didn't, it was Tom, picking up on his hesitation, who next spoke.

'Was that everything?' he asked.

'Yes, it was,' Rabbi Aphron answered firmly.

There was a brief silence before Tom said, 'Thank you very much. We do appreciate that.' He paused. 'Do you know how your mother came to own them?'

'Detective Chief Inspector,' Rabbi Aphron replied, his voice rising in obvious anger, 'I resent your implication that, somehow, these were not Mother's. As I told you and your colleague earlier, it is traditional for such items to be handed down from generation to generation. Do you not own anything which belonged to your mother or father?'

'I'm sure I do,' Tom answered.

'Yes, well, it's the same within our families,' said Rabbi Aphron.

Tom waited until he felt Rabbi Aphron's anger had abated, and then said, in as reasonable a tone as he could manage, 'Would it be possible to take a look at the necklace? At least then we would be able to see for ourselves if it is likely to be the same necklace worn by Jacob's mother, or a totally different one.'

Rabbi Aphron had, by now, regained his usual equanimity. 'I'm sure that would be possible. I will speak with my son, Emmanuel, first. I wouldn't want to cause undue alarm to Hannah, especially as it was her wedding day.'

'Thank you,' answered Tom. 'And I agree with what you said about not upsetting Hannah. That is the last thing we would want to do. Perhaps your son could bring it here for us to see?'

'Yes, that's a very good idea. I'll speak to him and contact you as soon as I have it.'

Tom took out a copy of the letter which Ethel had sent to Jacob the year before she died. 'There is one other thing which I was hoping you might be able to help us with.'

'As I've told you previously, Detective Chief Inspector Stone, if I can, I certainly will,' he replied.

Tom passed the copy of the letter to Rabbi Aphron, who began to read it. As he did so, Tom said, 'It's a letter which your mother wrote to Mr Green's father. In it she makes reference to someone named Oskar. Would you have any idea who he might be?'

Rabbi Aphron was still reading the letter and so didn't immediately answer. Eventually he said, in a slightly more aggressive tone, 'Where did you get this from and why are you reading Mother's private correspondence?'

'It was given to us by Mr Green's family and was part of a collection of items belonging to Mrs Green's father-in-law,' Tom replied calmly.

Once again, Rabbi Aphron quickly regained his composure. 'I apologise for my reaction. It was just such a shock to see a letter written in Mother's handwriting.'

Tom didn't reply and instead, as he so often did, let the silence do the work for him.

'I'm afraid I really can't help you. I have never heard of anyone named Oskar, and certainly I never heard Mother mention that name.'

Tom stood up and offered his hand to Rabbi Aphron. 'Thank you once again for your time, and I apologise if any of my questions caused you any offence.'

'I'm sure you were only doing your job,' replied Rabbi Aphron, not very convincingly.

*

'What do you think, sir?' asked Milner, once they were in the car and heading back to the station.

'What do I think about what?' answered Tom, who had been deep in thought as Milner drove.

'The necklace, sir. Rabbi Aphron did seem genuinely surprised when we showed him the two photos.'

'He did, yes. But I still have this feeling there's something else,' Tom replied.

'Yes, I agree, sir. I thought he was going to say something else when you asked him if they found any more of his mother's items, apart from the necklace, rings and earrings.'

'I'm glad you thought that, because so did I. I think we should ask the question again when we go back to look at the necklace,' said Tom.

'He also seemed to get quite angry when you showed him the letter.'

'Well, I don't blame him for that. Wouldn't you get angry if someone showed you a private letter which your mother had written?'

'I suppose so,' said an unconvinced Milner.

'Anyway, I'd like you to find out if there was someone – a guard or officer – whose Christian name was Oskar, who was at Auschwitz between March 1944 and January 1945. I suggest that you start by taking a look at those who worked in or around Canada, as that was where Ethel worked.'

'How am I supposed to do that, sir?' asked Milner. 'After all, it was a long time ago.'

'I've got no idea,' Tom answered. 'That's for you to find out. Anyway, aren't the Germans renowned for keeping meticulous records?' Then, suddenly thinking of a related question, he asked, 'Did you make a note of the names of Rabbi Aphron's children?'

'I did, sir,' replied Milner. 'Their names are in my notebook, but I think, if I remember correctly, they were Sarah, David and Emmanuel. It's Emmanuel who is Hannah's father and Ruth's husband.'

'That's right,' remembered Tom. 'Whilst you're looking for Oskar, why don't you also run a check on all of the Aphron family members?'

Milner looked slightly puzzled. 'Even Rabbi Aphron?'

'Why not?' answered Tom. 'Anyway, there's not a lot more we can do with this part of the investigation, until Rabbi Aphron gets back to us. So, whilst we are waiting, I suggest you and DC Bennett go back and review all of the information we have so far: the items found near the murder scene, the DNA and PM reports, the update on the two sets of tyre marks, the statement of the man who found the body, as well as the statements of the other people who were at the meeting that night.'

'Are you still thinking about your mum's advice to give jobs to those who are the busiest?' Milner asked, with a light laugh.

Tom laughed in return. 'Exactly. And, after you've done that, you can take the rest of the day off.'

Chapter 47

When Tom arrived back in his office, he immediately spotted the yellow Post-it note which had been stuck onto his computer screen. On it someone had written *call Superintendent Birch's PA urgently!!!* He suspected he already knew what it was about, but, when Jenny answered his return call, he said, in a slightly faux-puzzled voice, 'Was Superintendent Birch trying to get hold of me?'

'DCI Stone? Good, glad you got the message. Yes. Superintendent Birch would like to meet with you, as soon as possible.'

'Any idea what it's about?' asked Tom.

He noticed just the briefest hesitation in Jenny's voice before she replied. 'I'm not too sure, but it must be urgent because he's been trying to get hold of you for most of the day.'

'As you say, sounds important. I'm free now, so why don't I come up immediately?'

'I'll let Superintendent Birch know that you are on your way,' she answered, with clear relief.

Just a few minutes later and Tom was in Superintendent Birch's office.

'Tom. Thanks for coming up. I know you've probably got lots of things to do, but I needed to speak with you urgently.'

When Tom did not ask the obvious question, Superintendent Birch continued. 'It's about the award. I passed on your concerns about accepting it to DCS Small, but he was ... well, how can I put it?'

Tom helped him out. 'Not very happy?'

'To be frank, it was a little stronger than that.' He paused for a while. 'Tom. I'd really like you to review your decision. I know I have no right to ask you to do this, as we've only just started working together, but I genuinely feel you are making the wrong call with this. No doubt you think I've been put under pressure by the top brass to help you change your mind, and, to be perfectly honest, there is something in that. But, and I'm asking you to trust me on this, if I felt you were doing the right thing, I would, one hundred percent, support your decision. I genuinely don't think you are making the right choice.'

This time it was Tom's turn to acknowledge Superintendent Birch's strength of feeling. 'I do respect your view, sir,' he answered, before adding, 'Could I ask if I now actually have a choice?'

Superintendent Birch let out a short laugh. 'Well, I suppose we all have choices, but there are usually different consequences which come with those choices.' Once again he paused briefly. 'Look, Tom, why don't you just accept it in the spirit in which it is intended? If nothing else, it will be a real boost to the station. The one thing I've learned in my short period here is how well respected you are.'

Tom smiled to himself, recalling the time, not that long ago, when he considered himself to be almost *persona non grata* as far as his colleagues were concerned.

Superintendent Birch, having noticed Tom's smile, asked, 'Why are you smiling?'

'I just wish all of those annual reviews I've had to endure over the years had mentioned that.'

Now it was Superintendent Birch's turn to smile. 'Yes, I know what you mean. I often thought they were just a box-ticking exercise, which was quickly completed and then filed away until the time of your next review.'

Superintendent Birch's admission seemed to have the desired effect because, when Tom next spoke, he said, 'What if I think about it?'

'That's all I can ask,' answered a now more hopeful Superintendent Birch. 'Although I would add that we don't have much time on this. The formal letters are due to go out in the next few days. Why don't you speak to your partner about it? It might help.'

'Yes, thank you, sir, I will,' Tom answered, suspecting he already knew what Mary's reaction might be.

Chapter 48

'That's wonderful news,' said a clearly delighted Mary, before embracing him. 'I'm so proud of you. When will you receive it?'

Tom pulled away from her. 'I knew you weren't listening,' he said, with clear annoyance in his voice. 'As I said, I'm not sure I will accept it.'

'Why on earth not? Surely they must believe you deserve it, otherwise why offer it to you? I'm sure a lot of thought goes into their decision,' she said, echoing Superintendent Birch's reasoning.

'I'm sure it does,' he replied, 'but I honestly don't think that I do deserve it. It would be like taking something under a false pretence.'

'But you got shot.'

'Mary, unfortunately quite a few police officers get shot, and not all of those receive awards.'

Tom could sense that Mary was now beginning to become angry and frustrated with him, and this was immediately confirmed when she next spoke.

'Sometimes, I really don't understand you,' she said sharply. 'Well, maybe I do but just don't like it.'

'What do you mean?' he asked.

'It's almost as though you get some perverse pleasure out of playing the maverick.'

'Maverick?' repeated Tom.

'You know exactly what I mean,' she said, now quite angry. 'A non-conformist. Someone who always likes to take a counter-approach, just for the sake of it.'

Tom didn't immediately reply, hoping the silence would allow Mary's anger to dissipate. When he did reply, it was with a light laugh, as he tried to further defuse the tension. 'I see that as a compliment, actually.'

It was immediately clear, as she walked away from him,

that his attempt had backfired spectacularly and only further inflamed the situation, which was now in real danger of getting totally out of hand.

'Mary, where are you going?' he asked, abandoning his previous levity.

'I'm sorry, Tom,' she answered, without even turning around to face him. 'When you are acting like this I just don't want to be near you.'

He followed her. 'I think you are making a big thing about this. Let's not argue over it.'

Mary stopped and turned to face Tom at last. 'It's not just this, is it? It's always the same with you.'

'What do you mean?' he asked, shaken by her aggressive reaction.

'You know exactly what I mean,' she replied sharply.

'Well, actually, I don't,' he answered, equally sharply.

'We've had this same conversation many times. I've got to the point where I'm almost scared to say anything nice about you in case you belittle or make a joke about it. I'm proud of you, but it's as though I'm not allowed to say it. How can that be a good basis for a relationship, let alone a marriage?' She began to sob quietly and, when Tom moved towards her, she held up her right hand and said, 'Don't. Just leave me alone.'

An uneasy silence followed, before she continued, between sobs, 'You said you would try to change, but that's never going to happen, is it? How can I marry someone who won't even share their feelings with me?'

Tom was temporarily shellshocked as he wondered how things had deteriorated so quickly, unable to find any words which might be appropriate for the situation. Eventually, he simply settled on, 'I'm sorry.'

When Mary next spoke it was clear that she had regained some control of her emotions. 'Tom, it's not your fault. We can't help being who we are. We just have to face the fact we are very different.'

'I'm not sure what you are saying,' he said apprehensively.

'I think we have just been hiding from the truth. What I'm saying is that I think it would be wrong for us to get married,' she replied, in a matter-of-fact manner.

'Do you really mean that?' he asked.

'Yes, I do,' she answered, worryingly calmly.

Chapter 49

'Are you okay, sir?' asked a concerned DC Bennett the following morning, at the station. 'You don't look too well.'

Not surprisingly Tom had spent an almost sleepless night as he lay in bed, playing back, in his mind, all of the things which Mary had said. It was true that this hadn't been the first time they had had that type of conversation, and so her strength of feeling shouldn't have come as such a surprise to him. But it had, which suggested he simply had not taken those conversations into account.

The rest of the evening had been very tense, with neither of them engaging in any meaningful conversation. Mary had gone to bed early, leaving Tom alone to consider the full implications of what she had said. Eventually, he had also gone to bed, but not to the one he shared with Mary. The following morning had been, if anything, even more tense, with barely a word passing between them, and it was almost a relief when he left for work.

'I'm fine, thanks,' he replied, somewhat disingenuously.

'I ran another check on all of the CCTV cameras within a two-mile radius of the murder site,' explained DC Bennett. 'If you remember, initially we didn't think there were any nearby. Well, that's true, as there aren't any very close by. I eventually found one which had only recently been fitted by a small garage, though, about a mile from our site.'

'But what are you looking for?' asked Tom. 'There must been hundreds of cars to view. If you don't know what you're looking for, it sounds a bit of a forlorn hope.'

Tom could sense, from the expression on DC Bennett's face, he didn't necessarily agree. 'Well, at first, I thought that as well. So, to begin with, what I did was concentrate on a very limited time period, from 10pm to 10.30pm.'

DC Bennett had now got Tom's full attention. 'Go on,' he said.

'What I was looking for was the car containing the two people, which Mr Stephenson saw pull into the lay-by at 10.20pm. So, if I managed to see a car matching that description, say, twenty minutes either side, then it's a reasonable chance that car would be of interest to us.'

'And?' asked Tom, suddenly displaying his usual impatience.

DC Bennett began to smile broadly. 'There were quite a few which fitted that time frame, but at least it was at night and not earlier in the day, and so there wasn't as much traffic. Anyway, there were only four cars where there were just two occupants. One of those had two female occupants whilst another had a woman driver and young child. So, for the time being, at least, I've discounted those. So that leaves just two cars.'

'But, if these two only came from the single CCTV camera, then that would exclude any cars which might have gone to and from the lay-by from the other direction,' suggested Tom. 'Also, what about the other car that Mr Stephenson saw earlier, the one which he said was going fast? Did the CCTV footage capture any car which initially had two people in it, but later just the one?'

Tom could sense DC Bennett was now slightly deflated. Despite this, impressively, he quickly regained his earlier enthusiasm. 'Unfortunately, I didn't see anything like that, sir. As you said, there was no CCTV coverage of cars approaching from the other direction.'

'Hmmm,' said Tom, now not quite as optimistic, as he considered what DC Bennett had just told him.

Before he could further comment, though, DC Bennett continued. 'I know my theory has a few potential holes in it, but at least it gives us a 50:50 chance of finding the car. In fact, I would actually say the odds are better than 50:50.'

'Why's that?' asked Tom, slightly puzzled.

'Well, one of the cars with two people in it was clocked at 10.17pm, heading towards the lay-by, and again at 10.25pm heading back in the same direction as it had come from. So that narrows it down significantly to just an eight-minute window. I would say that makes it very interesting to us.'

He fell silent, giving Tom time to, once again, consider this latest information.

Eventually, Tom said, 'Could you get anything else from the footage? Make of car or, better still, the registration number?'

The broad smile returned to DC Bennett's face. 'It was dark, but we've got a good idea of the model. More importantly, though, we managed to get a clear print of the registration number. In fact, we got the registration numbers of both cars. I've already run a check on both of them and so we now also have two names.' He opened his notebook. 'One is a Peter Thornton, who lives in Park Royal. The other is a Robert Thomas, whose address is in Chiswick.'

Not for the first time, Tom was silent as he pursued his own line of thought, and so DC Bennett took his lead from Tom and remained quiet.

Finally, Tom broke the silence. 'Right, go and pay them both a visit and bring them in.' He then added, 'And make sure you have enough uniform in support. We don't want them to make a break for it.'

'Don't you want to come along, sir?' asked DC Bennett.

Tom was tempted to go with DC Bennett, if only because it would provide a brief distraction from last night's emotional outburst. But he knew, unless he and Mary resolved this, one way or another, he would constantly be thinking about its implications and unable to do the job he was paid to do.

'I'm sure you can handle it. And, anyway, I have something else which I need to do.'

Chapter 50

'What are you doing here?' asked Mary, a look of genuine surprise on her face. 'Is there a problem?' she added with growing concern.

After his meeting with DC Bennett, Tom had quickly decided he could not let the situation with Mary drag on any longer. He had tried to concentrate on work issues but just couldn't get it out of his mind. Finally, he had resolved to go and see her, and so that was why he was currently standing in the flower shop that Mary owned in Bagshot. Although the shop was empty of customers, one of Mary's part-time assistants was there, putting together a large bouquet of flowers.

On the way there Tom had thought about what he was going to say to Mary, but all he could now think of was to say, 'Is there anywhere we can go? I'd like to talk with you.'

'I suppose we could go to that small café just around the corner,' she replied, although, to Tom's ears, at least, not very enthusiastically.

A short while later they were both seated in the café.

'I just wanted to say sorry about yesterday,' Tom said. 'I spent the night worrying about it and just couldn't concentrate on anything when I was at work. I thought it best, rather than wait any longer, to come and see you.' He looked directly at her. 'I'm sorry.'

She didn't immediately respond and Tom was prompted, against his usual professional rule, to say something else. Just as he was about to do this, Mary said, 'You don't have to apologise. You … we ….are who we are, and that's not going to change now. If it's any consolation, I also didn't sleep very well. But,' she added, slightly disconcertingly, 'despite knowing how we are different, I still find it very difficult to cope with. It's almost as though you won't let me get close to you.'

'That's just not true,' answered Tom, as calmly as he could manage.

'Well, that's the way I feel,' she replied.

'Is it just because of this award?' he asked. 'Or is it something else?'

'It's not just that, although, in many ways, it's a perfect example of what I was just talking about. There have been other times, as well, when I've felt the same.'

This was not how he had hoped it would go. He'd made up his mind he would tell Mary the real reason why he felt he was unable to accept the award. But now it seemed that wouldn't be enough. Nonetheless, the stakes were clearly very high and so he decided to tell her nonetheless.

'I know you said yesterday was not just an isolated example,' he said, 'but at least let me tell you why I feel I couldn't accept the award.'

'But you told me all of this yesterday,' she said.

'What I told you yesterday was certainly true, but the main reason is that I feel it is only being offered to me in order to buy my silence.'

'Buy what silence?' she asked, a puzzled expression appearing on her face.

Tom took a deep breath before he answered. 'My silence relating to a murder.'

'Murder? What murder?' she asked, now totally confused.

So Tom told her. He told her about the murder of Susan Chambers and the subsequent death in prison of Jimmy Griffiths, the man who had been found guilty of murdering her. He told her about the involvement of a serving senior government minister, as well as Commander Jenkins, in her death, and how they had instigated the subsequent cover-up. He told her briefly how he himself had uncovered all this and what had happened when he had confronted them with the evidence. Finally he told her about his recent conversation with Sir Peter Westwood and DCS Small, when they had suggested the award. What he didn't tell her about, however, were the veiled threats he'd received, and the existence of the second file, currently with Milner, containing all of his accumulated evidence. Those, he decided, were two steps too far.

'That's incredible,' she said after he had finished. 'I can't believe this type of thing still goes on today. It's almost like a spy story.'

'Funnily enough, that's exactly what the Commissioner said,' he replied.

'So that's why you feel you can't accept the award, is it? You see it as some sort of bribe.'

'I do,' he said, 'although, to be perfectly honest, even without this, I think I would still have refused the award, for the reasons I gave yesterday.'

Suddenly Mary smiled. 'I knew you were quite stubborn but, I'm ashamed to say, I didn't realise just how principled you were.'

'I'll take that as a compliment, then.'

Mary didn't immediately respond, perhaps carefully considering what she would next say.

'What will happen to the minister and Commander Jenkins?' she eventually asked.

'I don't know for sure, but the Commissioner assured me that both would shortly be leaving their posts, although I suspect neither of them will be charged.'

'That's outrageous,' she said, her voice now rising appreciably with her increasing anger. 'How can they be allowed to get away with this just because of who they are and who they know?' Her anger suddenly disappeared. 'And you've been living with this all of this time. That must have been terrible for you. Have you not spoken with anyone else about it?'

'Only you, just now,' he answered quietly.

'What? Not even David?' she asked.

'There were a couple of times when I was tempted but then thought better of it.' Once again, he could have taken the opportunity to tell her about the file that he had given Milner for safe keeping, but decided not to.

'So what made you tell me?' she asked.

'The thought of losing you,' he simply replied.

Chapter 51

It was later the same day and Tom, after he'd left Mary, had returned to the station. They had decided that, perhaps, the café wasn't the right place to discuss something as important as their future relationship.

As Tom drove back to the station, his mind, as usual, was dissecting everything which Mary had said to him, and not just her words but also their tone, together with her associated body language. In truth he was looking for any sign which might suggest that she, too, was regretting the emotion and seriousness of yesterday's conversation. Whilst he couldn't highlight any one moment which might give him hope that this might be the case, he nonetheless came away thinking there were now some grounds for optimism. As the full reality of what she had heard had sunk in, she had become more and more angry. Not with him but with his superiors. If anything, as her anger had increased, her support and respect for him seemed to grow in direct proportion, and it was this which provided the grounds for his optimism.

He still had all of these thoughts in his mind when he arrived at the station, but it wasn't long before they had to take a back seat.

'Sir,' said Milner, 'some good news.'

Tom didn't need to hear these words to see that Milner had some positive news to impart. Just as Milner had learnt to recognise Tom's body language signals, so Tom could see, almost immediately, if Milner was about to tell him something good or bad.

'We could do with some good news,' answered Tom. 'What is it?'

'Forensics have come back with their preliminary analysis of the items which were in Jacob Green's metal box.'

'And?' said Tom, displaying his characteristic impatience when these situations arose.

'The letters, journal and Jacob's identity card, not surprisingly, had evidence of both Jacob's and Mr Green's fingerprints on them.'

'As you say, not surprising, really, given that Mr Green sorted through them after his father's death.' He paused briefly, looking directly at Milner. 'I hope there is a "but" to follow.'

Milner smiled and didn't disappoint. '*But* Mr Green's prints were also found on the photograph which you found in the secret compartment.'

'Actually, Milner, it wasn't me who found it, but I'm happy to take the credit nonetheless.' As often happened when Tom had been told something of importance, he didn't immediately respond to the revelation itself, choosing, instead, to consider all of the possible consequences.

'So that means Mr Green must have deliberately put the photo there,' said Milner with an almost childish excitement in his voice.

Finally, Tom said, 'Now, that is interesting. The key question, though, is why would he go to the trouble of hiding that particular photograph, out of all of the ones that were in the box, in such a secret place? It must have been very important to him.'

'Exactly what I was thinking, sir. I took a look at all of the other photographs, many of which also featured Jacob's mother. The only difference was that, in this one, his mother was wearing the necklace.'

'It seems as though, for once, Milner, we are both on the same wavelength. Despite everything, I do believe you are, at last, starting to think like me.'

Milner laughed and then said, in a more serious tone, 'This is all starting to point, yet again, towards the wedding. Do you think Mr Green was killed because of that photograph?'

'It's a possibility, especially as you know what I think about coincidences, but we should also try to keep an open mind. We don't want to fall into the trap of being too selective with the evidence and then trying to fit it into our theory.'

Tom then went on, 'What it does mean, however, is that we need to meet again with Rabbi Aphron. So get on to him and see if there's any news as to when we can take a look at the necklace his granddaughter was wearing at her wedding.'

Just as Milner was about to leave, DC Bennett appeared. 'Good news, sir,' he said.

Tom gave a light laugh. 'Have you and DS Milner been coordinating this?'

'Not sure I follow you, sir,' DC Bennett answered, clearly puzzled.

'Don't worry,' replied Tom. 'Ask DS Milner later. Anyway, what have you got?'

'Actually we've got Peter Thornton in one of the interview rooms, and he's telling quite an interesting story.'

'One of the car owners, wasn't he?' asked Tom. 'Okay, why don't you tell me?'

So DC Bennett told him. Earlier in the day, he, together with a few uniformed officers, had visited Mr Thornton's house in Park Royal. Fortunately he was at home at the time although, not surprisingly, he was clearly shaken when he opened his front door to be confronted by a number of police officers. DC Bennett had introduced himself and stated that they were there on account of an investigation relating to the murder of Mr Green. DC Bennett had then informed Mr Thornton that they had reason to believe he had been at the murder scene around the time that Mr Green was murdered and that, as a result, they would like him to accompany them back to the station for questioning.

'Did he resist?' asked Milner.

'Not at all,' DC Bennett answered. 'In fact, it was as if he couldn't wait to get out of the house.'

'Really?' asked Milner. 'Any obvious reason for that?'

'Yes, there is, sir. To begin with, when we got back, he denied ever being anywhere near Ealing on that particular night. But he quickly changed his story when we showed him the CCTV footage and the prints of the tyre marks found alongside Mr Green's body, which, incidentally, perfectly match the tyres on Mr Thornton's car.'

'Thank goodness for forensics,' said Tom. 'So, what was he doing there? Is he our man?' he asked without any great enthusiasm.

'I'm afraid not, sir. He was there for ... well, let's say more basic reasons. He is having an affair with a work colleague and that, apparently, is their place.'

'Very romantic,' said Milner. 'In a lay-by, where there's lots of fly-tipped rubbish.'

'Yes, well, despite DS Milner's disapproval, these things happen,' said Tom. 'Have you checked his story yet with the lady concerned?'

'Not yet, but it does sound genuine. That was the reason why he seemed keen to come down to the station. He didn't want his wife to know what he's been up to,' explained DS Bennett.

'Okay, so let's assume he's telling the truth,' said Tom. 'The more important questions then are what happened when he got there, and did he see anybody else around?'

'I think I can partly answer those, sir,' suggested DC Bennett. 'Just as Mr Stephenson said, they got there at about 10.20pm. As they pulled into the lay-by, Mr Thornton said they spotted something, or somebody, on the ground. He got out to investigate, realised it was a body and then immediately drove off.'

'Did he check to see if Mr Green was still alive?' asked Milner.

'No. He said all he could think about was that, if he were to get involved, it would probably come out why he was there. So he panicked and left.'

'And what about seeing anything else?' asked Tom.

'Nothing, I'm afraid, sir.' When there was no immediate follow-up question, DS Bennett said, 'I left him writing up his statement. I suspect he will have some explaining to do when he gets home.'

'It's not the result we were hoping for, but good work anyway,' replied Tom. 'Okay, the good news is we can now discount the 10.20 car. So far, Mr Stephenson seems to be the ideal witness, so we should now focus our efforts on finding the second car. The one which he saw earlier, driving away fast in the opposite direction.' He looked at DS Bennett. 'Any news there?'

'The only news is what we know already, from Mr Stephenson's description. It was a large, dark-coloured car.'

'Not much to go on,' suggested DS Milner.

'It's better than nothing,' replied Tom, surprisingly cheerfully, given how their most hopeful lead had just come to a dead end. 'I suggest you now extend your CCTV examination further afield. Say, within a three-mile distance of the lay-by. At least you only have to look in the one direction.'

'And what exactly am I looking for?' asked DS Bennett.

'A large, dark car, of course.'

Chapter 52

Just as Tom was thinking about leaving for home, his phone rang.

'DCI Stone here.'

'DCI Stone, this is Samuel Aphron. You asked me to call you so we could arrange a time when you could take a look at Hannah's necklace.'

'Yes. Thank you for calling back,' he answered. 'Do you have a time when this would be possible?'

'Actually, I do. I've now spoken with my son, Emmanuel, and we would both be available this evening, if that's convenient for you. Say, at 7pm?'

The main reason why Tom had been planning to leave was so he could continue the discussion with Mary he had started earlier. Although they had discussed quite a lot, there were still more things which had been left unsaid.

'That would be fine,' he replied. 'Where do you suggest?'

'I was thinking here, at the synagogue, might be best. Unless, of course, that's not convenient for you.'

'No, that's not a problem. I look forward to seeing you there at 7pm.'

Tom immediately called Milner, who, surprisingly, had already left the station.

'Yes, sir?' Milner said as he answered his phone, a hint of apprehension in his voice. It wasn't often DCI Stone called him, but when he did it nearly always resulted in a further increase in his workload. And this particular call was no exception.

'Where are you, Milner?' asked Tom.

'Actually, sir, I'm on my way home. I have something planned for tonight,' he replied, as vaguely as he could manage.

'Well, I'm afraid you'll have to rearrange it. If you would like, I'll speak with Jenny,' Tom said mischievously.

There was a period of silence before Milner answered. 'I'm sure I can manage that by myself, sir. Anyway, what's happened?'

So Tom told him about his recent phone call from Rabbi Aphron and their planned meeting later that evening.

'Okay, I'll be back at the station shortly,' Milner answered, the merest hint of brusqueness detectable in his voice.

True to his word, it wasn't long before he had returned. As he walked into the office, Tom said, 'Thanks for coming back. I just thought you'd want to be there.'

'Yes, well, thanks for giving me the opportunity,' Milner said.

Other than smiling, Tom didn't respond to Milner's undisguised sarcasm. Instead he said, 'Right, let's just run through what we know.'

*

It was just before 7pm and, once again, they had arrived at the synagogue. The small room, now including Rabbi Aphron's son Emmanuel, was even more crowded than usual.

Although there was a facial similarity between Emmanuel and his father, that was where the resemblance ended. Whilst his father was dressed, not surprisingly, being a rabbi, quite conservatively, Emmanuel, apart from the traditional skull cap, was dressed in a much more modern fashion. He looked to be in his mid-to-late forties and wore a button-down blue shirt, light brown casual trousers and a pair of tan brogues.

After the introductions had been made, it was Emmanuel who addressed the reason they were all there.

'I understand you'd like to take a look at this,' he said, carefully taking out the necklace from a protective bag and then placing it equally carefully on a small table.

'Not that I'm an expert on this type of thing, but it is a beautiful necklace,' Tom said with genuine admiration. 'Would you mind if we took a photograph of it?'

'Please go ahead, but I'm puzzled as to why you are so interested in my grandmother's necklace,' said Emmanuel.

As Milner took a few photographs of it, Tom answered Emmanuel's question. 'I'm sure your father has mentioned to you how we believe it to be the same necklace which was worn by Benjamin Green's grandmother on her wedding day, almost a hundred years ago.' Tom then showed Emmanuel the photograph that had been found concealed in the secret compartment.

'It certainly looks like Grandmother's necklace,' Emmanuel said, as he closely examined it. 'But why would that have any connection with Benjamin's death?'

'I've found, over the years,' explained Tom, 'that any connection, in cases such as this, is always worth investigating.'

When Emmanuel didn't respond, Tom asked the most obvious question. 'Your father said you found this amongst your grandmother's possessions. Do you know how she came to own it?'

'To be honest, I'm not now sure. I assumed she had inherited it but, if it *is* the same one as Benjamin's grandmother was wearing, then it would seem that's not the case. I can only think that Jacob must have given it to Grandmother just before she died. They shared many experiences in their early lives, and, as I think Father has already told you, they had renewed their friendship in their later years. Perhaps he wanted her to have it.'

'Yes, that is certainly one possibility,' agreed Tom. 'Although it would have been more logical if he had given it to his own son, or even granddaughter.' He looked towards Rabbi Aphron. 'After all, I think it was you yourself who mentioned how it's a Jewish tradition for items like this to be passed down to the next family generation.'

When there was no response, Tom continued, once again directing his question at Emmanuel. 'Your father also mentioned how there were other items of jewellery, apart from the necklace, which you found amongst her possessions. Did you bring those along with you?'

'Yes, I did,' Emmanuel replied, before opening a small jewellery bag and placing the contents on the table, alongside the necklace.

'Were you aware that your grandmother owned these items?' asked Tom, looking at the other pieces of jewellery.

'No. I can't ever remember her wearing them, and certainly she never mentioned them to me. Perhaps Jacob gave her these as well?'

'Would you mind if DS Milner also photographed these?'

'Not at all,' answered Emmanuel. He paused. 'Father says

you think Benjamin's murder was racially motivated. Do you have any suspects yet?'

'Actually, what I said was that it *may* have been racially motivated but, at this stage, we are keeping an open mind,' said Tom.

'Were you aware Father received a threatening letter, just a few days before Benjamin's death?' Emmanuel asked. 'I was a bit annoyed with him, as he has only just told me about it.'

'Yes, your father showed us the letter. In fact, we took it away so that forensics could take a look at it.'

'Good. Well, let's hope you are able to find something before anything else happens and it becomes open season on us.'

'I'm sure it won't come to that,' replied Tom reassuringly. 'What makes you think it might?'

'There has been quite a lot of coverage in the local media about our plans for the extension to the synagogue. Even our preliminary application for planning permission generated quite a lot of animosity, and all the signs are that it will only get worse as we seek final planning approval. We are seeing this more and more in other parts of the country, and so it wouldn't be a surprise if we were next.'

Tom looked at Emmanuel. 'As I said, I'm sure it won't come to that.'

He could see from Emmanuel's expression that he didn't share Tom's optimism.

Milner now spoke. 'Were there any other items of jewellery amongst your grandmother's possessions?'

'No. This was everything,' answered Emmanuel. 'Why? Were you expecting anything in particular?'

'Not at all,' replied Milner quickly. 'What about any letters or diaries? Did she leave any of those?'

Emmanuel looked towards his father. 'Not that I'm aware of. What about you, Father?'

'You've asked me this already,' Rabbi Aphron said, directing his attention towards Milner, 'and I said then, she hadn't. Are you saying you don't believe us?' His tone was unambiguously accusatory.

'Absolutely not,' Milner replied. 'It just seems a bit strange, given how your mother was such a prolific writer, that she didn't leave anything.'

'Yes, I thought that as well,' agreed Emmanuel. 'When we were going through all of her possessions I was really surprised not to find any letters.' He paused briefly. 'Father did mention a letter, though. One which, apparently, Grandmother wrote to Benjamin's father. Would it be possible to see it?'

'We don't have it with us right now, so I'm afraid you won't be able to see it. Plus, of course, I suppose it now belongs to the Green family. I'm sure, though, especially as you are related, they would let you read it.' Tom paused before continuing. 'What I can tell you is that, in the letter, your grandmother mentioned a man named Oskar. I wonder if, at some point in the past, she mentioned his name to you.'

'I can't say she did, but, anyway, why is a German man so important to you?' Emmanuel asked.

'I wouldn't quite describe it that way,' Tom said. 'It's just one of many different lines of enquiry we are currently pursuing.' He then went on, 'I'm sure your father has already mentioned to you how Mr Green had contacted him, earlier on the day he was murdered, so that he could speak with him about something important relating to your daughter's wedding. As you are Mr Green's son-in-law, I wonder if he ever mentioned this to you.'

'Yes, Father did tell me about his phone call, but Benjamin never mentioned anything like that to me.'

Rabbi Aphron, who had, so far, let his son do most of the talking, cut in. 'Why do I get the feeling, Detective Chief Inspector Stone, you are not telling us the full story here? Is it because of the potential racial motive and, if not, what could Benjamin's death possibly have to do with Mother's necklace and Hannah's wedding? I do hope you are spending as much time trying to actually find Benjamin's killer as you seem to be asking us about jewellery.'

'I can assure you that we are,' Tom replied, not fully answering his questions.

Not for the first time, Rabbi Aphron's expression suggested he was not entirely convinced.

'To be frank, Detective Chief Inspector,' interjected Emmanuel, 'I have to tell you this is a view also shared by my wife's family. As Father says, it does all seem very strange.' He then carried on, in a more conciliatory tone, 'But, as you have said, you are the police officer with many years of experience, and so I'm sure you have your reasons. Of course, we will continue to help in whatever capacity you think is required. We just want the person who murdered Benjamin to be caught as soon as possible, before anyone else gets hurt.'

Tom stood up and offered his hand, first to Rabbi Aphron and then to his son. 'Thank you very much for showing us your grandmother's necklace, together with the other pieces of jewellery. Please rest assured that we *are* doing everything possible to arrest this person. If there is anything else which you feel might help us, please don't hesitate to contact either myself or DS Milner directly.'

*

It was almost 9pm before Tom arrived home.

'I thought you'd try and get home a bit earlier, especially given what you told me this morning,' said Mary, her slight brusqueness taking him a little by surprise.

'Yes, I'm sorry. Milner and I had, unexpectedly, to go and see Rabbi Aphron – you remember, I told you about him and the necklace. Anyway, I'm sorry. I should have called you.'

'That's okay,' replied Mary. 'I shouldn't have been quite so sharp with you. It's just I've been worrying all day about what you told me when we were in the café.'

'You shouldn't worry,' said Tom, as reassuringly as possible.

'Really? Based upon what you told me, I think there's a lot to worry about.' She looked at him very intently. 'There's nothing else, is there? Something which you are not telling me?'

'If there were anything else, I would have told you,' answered Tom. Although he felt bad about not telling Mary absolutely everything, he didn't consider this to be lying to her. His judgement was that there was nothing to be gained, at this stage, by telling her about the threats or the existence of the file copy. In fact, he suspected, if he were to tell her, this would only unnecessarily add to her already increasing sense of anxiety and concern.

Tom's response appeared to reassure her and, when she next spoke, she said something which he hadn't expected.

'I've been thinking about what you told me and, for what it's worth, I agree with you about not accepting the award. I still believe you have earned one, but I can now see how,

194

especially with what happened to the woman who died, you would consider it to be tainted. So I think you should politely decline the offer but still make them aware of why you are doing that.' She paused for a moment before adding, 'Although I'm still annoyed with you for not telling me when we first discussed it last night.'

'I know,' answered a contrite Tom. 'It was something which I will always regret.'

Mary reached forward and took hold of Tom's hands. 'I don't want you to always regret it. That's not the point. All I want is for us to have the type of relationship where we can trust one another. Surely that's not too much to ask?'

'It's not, and, if it's any consolation, it's what I want as well. But sometimes I make the wrong choices. It's not because I don't love you; it's because I do love you.' Even he was surprised that those particular words had fallen from his mouth.

Mary stood back slightly and said, 'Do you really mean that?'

'Of course I do. As I've told you before, I don't want to lose you.'

'I still can't believe people such as Commander Jenkins and that government minister are able to get away with murder, simply because of who they now are. Is there nothing which can be done to make them pay for their crimes?'

Tom's thoughts, once again, returned to the file which Milner was keeping for him. 'I suspect the only way to achieve it would be if I myself pursued this.' He looked directly at her. 'Is that something which you would be happy for me to do?'

'What would happen to you, if you were to do that?' she asked, pointedly.

'I just don't know, is the honest truth,' he replied. 'The establishment have a tendency to close ranks in situations such as this. There's also the possibility – how big a possibility, I don't know – that there would be a campaign to undermine and discredit me. And, as we saw with the Grace case, it might also involve you. Are you willing to take that risk?'

Mary didn't immediately reply, as she considered what Tom had just told her. Eventually, though, she said, in a very deter-mined tone, 'I just want you to know, whatever you decide, I will be there to support you.'

Chapter 53

'How was your evening?' asked Tom, when he was back in his office the next morning. 'Did you and Jenny still manage to spend some time together?'

Milner looked at his boss with a hint of suspicion, having failed, so far, to assess his body language. 'I'm afraid not, sir,' he answered. 'When I received your call, I spoke with Jenny and we decided that it would be better if we postponed it. Hopefully, unless something else unexpectedly crops up, we'll be able to see each other tonight.'

'Well, let's hope so,' answered Tom, without, at least to Milner's ears, any great optimism. 'Would you like me to speak with her? At least then I can confirm that it was my fault.'

Very briefly a look of almost horror appeared on Milner's face. 'Thanks, but I don't think that is now necessary.'

Tom didn't pursue this point. 'Anyway, do you have anything for me?'

Milner appeared relieved that they were now in more familiar territory. 'Actually, I do, sir. It's with regard to Oskar. I managed to obtain a contact name within the Berlin police force, and, after a couple of back-and-forth emails, was then given the name of someone who might be able to help.' He went straight on, denying Tom the opportunity to interrupt. 'His name is Johan Straub and he heads up a government records department which houses details of all known serving German officers during the Second World War. So I contacted him last night and, amazingly, when I arrived this morning, there was an email from him waiting for me.'

'I told you,' said Tom, as though angling to take some credit for such a speedy response. 'That's German efficiency for you.'

Milner took out an A4 sheet of paper from the file he had

with him. 'I've printed off the email,' he said, before reading out the contents.

'Oskar Lang, born 21st April 1922 in Stuttgart, died 12th July 1989, was an SS Obersturmführer ...'

He looked up and said, 'The equivalent rank in the British army would be Lieutenant.' He carried on reading from the email.

'He arrived in Auschwitz in January 1944 and was assigned to the section which recorded and administered prisoners' possessions. He was stationed there until January 1945 when he was transferred to Dachau main camp. In April 1945 he was arrested by the US army when they liberated the camp and in January 1946 was sentenced to five years' detention by the US military authorities.'

As Tom remained silent, Milner continued.

'He was released in December 1950 and then settled back in Stuttgart, where he later married Andrea Weber in 1951. They then had three children, Heidi, born in 1952, Jurgen, born in 1953, and Hans, born in 1955.'

Once again Milner looked up from the email. 'So it looks as though this could very well be the Oskar who Mrs Aphron referred to in her letter to Jacob.'

Tom continued to remain silent as he followed his own line of thought.

'What do you suggest now, sir?' asked Milner, after an extended period of silence.

'Is that everything Mr Straub sent?' Tom asked.

'It is, sir.'

'Could you get back to him and ask if he is able to provide any information relating to Oskar's children? It would be interesting to know if they are still alive and, if so, where they currently live.'

'Why would that be of relevance to Mr Green's murder?' Milner asked.

'I'm not sure if it actually is,' replied Tom, 'but you never know. This case has already thrown up so many puzzles it would be inadvisable to stop looking, unless and until we come to a dead end. I just don't think we are at that point yet, though.'

Just as Milner was leaving, Tom suddenly said, 'Oh, and there's one other thing. Could you get hold of all of the items which were found close to Mr Green's body? I'd like to take a look at them myself.'

'Any particular reason, sir?' asked Milner.

'None really,' he answered, 'other than that they were all found close to where Mr Green was murdered. Anyway, maybe they will give me some inspiration. I think we need all the help we can get at the moment.'

Chapter 54

Tom received the phone call from Milner later that same night, informing him about another attack.

'How is Mr Weiss?' asked Tom, as soon as he arrived back at the station. It was now almost midnight and Tom had returned to the station immediately after the phone call.

'The last time I checked he was in quite a bad way, although it's not considered to be life-threatening,' answered Milner.

'Why don't you tell me again what you know about the attack?' asked Tom.

So Milner told him what he knew, although, at this stage, the details were still fairly sketchy. 'It looks as though Mr Weiss was attacked as he left the synagogue, when he was just about to get into his car. He was there to discuss the planning application for the extension. The meeting finished at about 10.15 pm, but Rabbi Aphron and Mr Weiss remained there for about another fifteen minutes.'

'Do we know why?' asked Tom.

'I've had a brief telephone conversation already with Rabbi Aphron but, as you can imagine, he is very distressed about this. Anyway, he'd asked Mr Weiss to stay behind for a few minutes, as he wanted his input into one of the specific issues relating to the planning application. Apparently Mr Weiss, before he retired, was a lawyer who specialised in commercial planning applications, and Rabbi Aphron wanted his advice on one specific aspect relating to the timing of their final application submission. Rabbi Aphron confirmed they finished just after 10.30 pm, and Mr Weiss left straight away.'

'I'm assuming this happened in the car park. Is that correct?'

'It did, sir, but by then the car park was empty, apart from the cars belonging to Rabbi Aphron and Mr Weiss.' He paused briefly and then said, 'And, as you know, there are no CCTV cameras there.'

'Okay, so what about the area? Can we get forensics there quickly?'

'Already on it, sir. They should be there now.'

They both fell silent until Tom finally said, 'I want someone at the hospital with Mr Weiss. Let's hope he is soon able to tell us something about his attacker. Also, go and visit all of the others who were at the meeting, to see if they spotted anything unusual after they came out of it. And, whilst you are at it, check their movements from the time the meeting ended until the time they arrived back home. I don't think we can rule anything out now.'

'Uniform are already at the hospital and I've asked DC Bennett to arrange for all of those at the meeting to be visited immediately.'

Tom smiled at Milner and said, with a laugh, 'So why did you call me? It seems as though you have everything in hand already.' He didn't allow Milner time to respond. 'First thing tomorrow ... well, later this morning,' he said, looking at his watch, 'you and I need to go and visit Rabbi Aphron again.' He paused briefly. 'That is likely to be another interesting meeting.'

*

'This is terrible,' said a clearly upset Rabbi Aphron. 'Simon is a very old friend of mine. Who would want to do this to him?'

It was 8.30am and Tom and Milner, not for the first time, were seated in the small room which doubled as Rabbi Aphron's office.

'Well, that's the question we are trying to answer. Do you have any idea?' Tom asked, as gently as possible.

'I can only think it has something to do with the extension of the synagogue. I knew there was some opposition but didn't realise just how strong that opposition was.' He hesitated briefly. 'I should have taken the threatening letter far more seriously. First poor Benjamin and now Simon.' He then looked directly at Tom and, now with anger in his voice, said, 'I asked you if Benjamin's murder could be racially motivated and you assured me it wasn't. But now this. Maybe you'll now start to take these attacks seriously.'

Tom waited a short while before answering. 'I'm not sure I ever ruled out it being racially motivated, but, irrespective of that, I can assure you that I and all of my officers are taking this very seriously indeed. Could I ask if you've received any other letters, similar in tone to the one you received just before Mr Green's death?'

'No, I haven't,' Rabbi Aphron replied, somewhat tersely. 'Well, not yet, anyway. Why? Are you expecting me to get another one?'

'I don't know,' answered Tom truthfully, 'but we shouldn't rule it out.' He went on. 'I understand Mr Weiss stayed behind at your request. Were the other people at the meeting aware of that?'

Rabbi Aphron suddenly stared intently at Tom. 'I can't believe what I'm hearing. Are you seriously suggesting one of my friends ... Simon's friends ... did this?' His anger now boiled over, as he almost shouted, 'This is outrageous. First you upset my friends, the Green family.' He looked at Tom with deep hostility. 'Yes, Ruth has told me all about your obsession with Jacob and what he did or didn't say at my granddaughter's wedding. Not content with that, you then make them hand over his possessions, including, incidentally, a private letter to him from Mother, even before they them-selves have had the opportunity to go through them. You then show me the letter, a letter which even I, her son, had not been given the chance to read first, and ask ludicrous questions about someone named Oskar. Not content with this, you then, disgracefully, accuse Mother of stealing a necklace once owned by Jacob's mother. And now you seem to be accusing my friends, here at our synagogue, of somehow being involved in the brutal murder of their friend Benjamin and now the attack on Simon. What next? Will you be arresting my grand-daughter for wearing stolen property?'

Tom and Milner both remained silent, hoping Rabbi Aphron's anger would soon blow itself out. Indeed, when he did next speak, it was without his previous hostility, but in a much more measured, ominously threatening tone.

'Detective Chief Inspector, a man in my position is not without some influence. I find your questions both deeply offensive and, frankly, borderline racist. I also have serious doubts about your competence and ability to actually find whoever is doing this. I intend to pass on these concerns to some of my friends, who, incidentally, hold senior positions within the Metropolitan Police Force. I also intend to make it abundantly clear that I have lost all confidence in your ability to protect our local Jewish community.'

He stood up. 'I would now like you to leave. I suggest you and your colleague' – at this point he turned to face Milner – 'direct your efforts to finding whoever is doing this, because, if you can't, then I will insist you be replaced by someone who can.'

Chapter 55

When they arrived back at the station, DC Bennett was waiting for them. 'How did it go? Was he able to shed any light on who might be doing this?'

It was Milner who answered. 'Not the best meeting I've ever been involved in, if I'm being totally honest.'

'What DS Milner is trying to say is that ... how can I put this? ... it was a bit of a disaster,' explained Tom, who then gave him a brief account of what had happened.

'Do you think he will carry out his threat to try and get you removed from the investigation?' DC Bennett asked.

'Given his level of anger and, no doubt, his contacts within the Met, I'm sure he will.' Tom let out a short laugh. 'I think it's only a question of time before I receive an invitation to visit the top brass at Met HQ.'

It was Milner who then asked the obvious question. 'Sir? Rabbi Aphron did make a good point about our focus on the necklace and wedding. Do you think all of this actually just might be a coincidence or, at least, a distraction? Maybe the attacks are, in fact, unconnected to the wedding and the necklace.'

It was something which Tom himself had thought a lot about recently, and so it was not a surprise Milner should now ask the very same question.

When Tom replied it was almost as much for his own benefit as it was a reply to Milner's question. 'In situations such as this, we should always be led by the evidence. So, let's review what we know.'

He then, without reference to any notes, began to summarise what they did know. 'Let's take the racial motive first. To begin with, both victims are prominent local Jewish people. Second, it would appear their plans to extend the synagogue have generated some local ill feeling. Next, and, I suppose, related, Rabbi Aphron received a clearly anti-Semitic letter, just days prior to the attack on Mr Green.' He paused momentarily. 'As far as actual evidence is concerned, we have very little. There were a few random items found close to Mr Green's body and two people were spotted, by Mr Stephenson, driving into the lay-by around the time of his murder. These, though, turned out to be a married man and a woman hoping for a bit of illicit sex. I think we can safely discount them from our potential list of murderers – although I suspect things might be very difficult at home, for the man, at least, for quite a while.'

When it became clear Tom had finished that part of his summary, DC Bennett spoke. 'Plus, of course, there is the other car which Mr Stephenson saw. The one driving fast, about ten minutes before he spotted the other car driving into the lay-by.'

'You are keen to pursue that line of enquiry, aren't you?' asked Tom.

'I just think we can't rule it out just yet. It might be nothing but, then again, you never know,' he answered.

'There was also the other set of fresh tyre marks which forensics found at the scene,' added Milner, in support.

'That's all true,' replied Tom. 'But it's still not a lot to go on. What was it Mr Stephenson said? He thought it was a large, dark-coloured car.' He paused. 'Is that it, or have I missed something?'

When there was no response, he carried on. 'Okay, let's look at the other side of the list.' Tom then began to count on his fingers as he went through the list. 'Firstly, we have the issue of the necklace worn by Rabbi Aphron's granddaughter at her wedding. I don't think there's any doubt now that it's the very same one owned by Jacob's mother. Secondly, it's clear – in fact it's on video – that Jacob became very upset when he saw Hannah wearing it. We've been told he was saying *Mama*, so it presumably brought back memories of his mother. Third, and related, probably the last thing which Mr Green said was the word *Hannah*. Fourth, there is a very strong connection between Jacob, Josef, Ethel and Yitzhak, based upon the time they spent together in Auschwitz. Fifth, and perhaps most importantly, Mr Green made it clear to Rabbi Aphron that he wanted to meet with him urgently to discuss something related to the wedding. Finally' said Tom, now holding up both hands, 'Mr Green's fingerprints were found on the photograph of Jacob's mother where she was wearing the necklace on her wedding day. The key question here is, why would he go to the trouble of hiding that particular photograph in a secret compartment within the box where his father kept all of his possessions?'

'To be honest, sir,' said DC Bennett, 'I'm not sure where all of that takes us. Some of it is obviously factual, but quite a lot is still circumstantial. Aren't we in danger of trying to join what little real evidence we do have with lots of circumstantial evidence? The reality is, with respect, sir, whichever theory we look at, there is very little hard evidence.'

For a moment, all three remained silent as they followed their own individual trains of thought.

It was DC Bennett who broke the silence. 'By the way,' he said, pointing towards a brown cardboard box in the corner of the room, 'in there are all of the items which we found in the lay-by. I understand you wanted to see them, sir.'

'Yes, thanks. Just leave them there and I'll take a look later,' said Tom.

'I've got something as well,' said Milner, as if he had just remembered something. 'It's an update from our German colleague.' He began to read from an email he had printed.

'Herr Lang's son Jurgen is, unfortunately, his only remaining offspring. His address, telephone and email details are given below. Please do contact me if you need any more assistance.'

Milner handed the email to Tom, who read it and then simply said, 'Stuttgart?' This appeared to energise Tom, who then said, in a far more upbeat tone, 'Do we have any news on Mr Weiss's condition?'

'Yes, and it's good news,' answered DC Bennett. 'He's awake, although very sore, and so has been given strong painkillers. The doctors won't let us see him just yet. We have to wait until he's had more rest and they are happy with his condition.'

'Okay, keep in touch with the hospital. I'd like to be there when he's able to speak. And what about speaking with the others who were at the meeting?'

'Meetings arranged for later this afternoon and evening. Do you want to come to those as well?' asked DC Bennett.

'No. I'm sure you and DS Milner can handle them. Just let me know immediately if anything significant comes out of them.' Tom turned to face Milner. 'Have you been able to run the checks on all of the people who attended the meetings?'

'I have, but nothing of significance, I'm afraid. None of them has any criminal record. Not even a parking fine, as far as I can see. Archetypal pillars of the Jewish community, and all have been successful in their business lives. Rabbi Aphron spent some time in Israel, back in the eighties. Apparently he attended a religious college, presumably related to his training to become a rabbi. As you asked, I also ran a few checks on his two sons and his daughter. All three also spent time in Israel, mainly working on kibbutzes.' Milner paused. 'Do you really think Mr Green was murdered by one of his friends?' he asked, in a tone of voice which suggested a certain degree of scepticism.

'Well, if he was,' replied Tom, 'I think we can safely assume whoever did it wasn't a friend in any true sense of the word.'

Chapter 56

It was sooner than even Tom had expected when he received the call. DCS Small's PA had called him first thing the following morning, and that was the reason Tom was now seated in DCS Small's large office.

'You've probably guessed why I've asked to see you,' said DCS Small.

'The way it's going at the moment, it could be for one of many things,' he answered, with a light laugh.

To Tom's surprise, DCS Small laughed in return. 'Well, that's true. You do seem to be ruffling a few feathers at the moment.'

'This time, though, I assume it's regarding the investigation into the murder of Mr Green.'

'That's correct,' said DCS Small. 'Yesterday, Commander Stern took a call from a Rabbi Aphron. Apparently he was extremely irate, and critical, concerning the way you are running the investigation into the murder of Mr Green.' He hesitated briefly. 'Basically, in addition to incompetence, he is also accusing you of being anti-Semitic.'

'So, presumably, he would like me to be taken off the investigation. Is that it, sir?'

'Well, yes, it is.' Once again there was a momentary pause, before he carried on. 'You don't appear to be that surprised.'

'Well, he did threaten to do that when DS Milner and I met him yesterday. My only surprise is that he has done it so quickly. He must have some good friends, high up in the force.'

'Apparently so,' agreed DCS Small. 'Anyway, the message has been passed down to me to get it sorted out, one way or another.'

'That sounds a bit ominous,' said Tom, his earlier levity returning.

'Well, I'm afraid I can't ignore it. Why don't you first tell me where you are with the investigation?'

So Tom told him, after which DCS Small said, 'His main criticism of you, apparently, is that you don't appear to be taking the racial motive very seriously and are fixated on what happened at his granddaughter's wedding. He feels you are waging some sort of vendetta against his family.'

'That's ridiculous, sir,' replied Tom. 'I'm just going where the evidence is taking me. I hope you don't believe what he's saying.'

'Of course I don't,' answered DCS Small reassuringly. 'But sometimes, unless you are aware of all of the facts, it's easy to see things very differently. I understand you can't divulge everything, but is there not something more specific you could share with him? At least then he would have a better idea of your thinking.'

'I'm not sure there is actually anything specific to share with him. You know how these things often work. In the absence of any real, hard evidence you tend to trust your instincts until something specific does emerge,' said Tom.

DCS Small seemed to consider what Tom had just said carefully before he finally responded. 'I do understand that it's clearly a very sensitive path you have to tread here. But let me ask you this. How close do you think you are to solving it?'

'At the moment, not very close at all,' Tom answered honestly. 'But it's entirely possible we will suddenly get a breakthrough and be able to wrap up the case. Unfortunately, of course, it's not something you can rely on. So, I'm afraid, it's as the saying goes ... it will take as long as it takes.'

'Although I totally understand what you are saying, I'm not sure that's exactly what Commander Stern wants to hear,' said DCS Small. 'What is it you propose to do next?'

'Actually, I was thinking of going to Stuttgart.'

'Stuttgart?' DCS Small repeated. 'Why on earth Stuttgart?'

So Tom told him about the reference, in the letter written by Ethel, to the man named Oskar, and how one of Oskar's sons, Jurgen, currently lived in Stuttgart. 'I just think it could be relevant to the investigation and, if not, then at least it would remove one potential line of enquiry, once and for all.'

DCS Small remained silent as he appeared to consider what to do next. Eventually he said, 'Okay. But this can't go on indefinitely. You have a week to demonstrate you are making progress. We'll meet again then to review the situation. After that, I'm afraid I can't guarantee anything. I'm actually already going out on a limb with the extra week. Commander Stern wanted to replace you straight away.'

'Nice to know who your friends are,' said Tom, once again with a light laugh.

'I'm sorry, Tom. It was the best I could do.'

Tom, realising it would be pointless to argue his case any further, said, 'Didn't someone once say that a week was a long time in politics? Well, let's hope it's equally long when it comes to solving murder investigations.'

Just as Tom was about to leave, DCS Small said, 'I understand Superintendent Birch has spoken with you about your gallantry award. Have you had any more thoughts on that, or are you still determined not to accept it?'

Tom suddenly smiled. 'Well, it might be a bit difficult to, on one day, accept such a prestigious award and then, on the next, be taken off a case because I'm considered to be a racist. I'll leave that one with Commander Stern to try and reconcile.'

Chapter 57

'Thank you very much for agreeing to see us. How are you feeling now?' asked Tom.

He and DC Bennett were seated at the side of Mr Weiss's bed, in the same hospital where, only a few weeks earlier, Tom himself had been. Tom and DC Bennett had gone to the hospital as soon as they had heard that Mr Weiss was now well enough to see them.

'Much better, thank you,' answered Mr Weiss, in a surprisingly clear voice, 'although my side still hurts. According to the doctor, I've broken a couple of ribs.'

Tom left it a while before, gently, saying, 'Are you able to tell us what happened?'

'I am, but I'm afraid there isn't a lot to tell,' he answered.

'Why don't you just tell us what you can remember, then?'

'I do remember our meeting ending and then walking towards my car. After that, everything is a bit hazy.'

'Were there any other cars in the car park?' asked DC Bennett, notebook in hand, in an attempt to prompt him.

'Only Samuel's – that's Rabbi Aphron – if I remember correctly, but I'm not totally sure about even that.'

'And you don't remember anything about the attack at all. Is that correct?'

'All I do remember is suddenly feeling the presence of someone behind me, followed by a blow to my face and then a shooting pain in my side. After that ... well, nothing.'

Before either of them could ask any follow-up question, Mr Weiss said, 'I suppose I'm lucky, really, considering what happened to poor Benjamin. Why do you think some people hate us so much, Detective Chief Inspector?'

'I can't answer that, I'm afraid, although I would say it's still not totally proven that the attacks were racially motivated.'

Mr Weiss looked at Tom, giving the impression he wasn't

totally convinced, but he made do with, 'I hope you are right.'

'Did your attacker say anything?' asked Tom.

'Nothing at all. As I said, I did sense the presence of someone behind me, but before I could turn around ... well, it was then I was attacked.'

'So you think there was just the one person,' suggested Tom.

'Yes; as far as I could tell, there was no one else there. But, again, I could be wrong.'

'I understand you stayed behind after the main meeting. Is that correct?' asked DC Bennett.

'Yes, Samuel had asked me prior to the meeting if I could remain behind. He wanted my input into the timing of the planning application. I have had experience in dealing with the local council many times in the past, and so he thought my input might be useful.'

'And was it?' asked Tom. 'Useful, that is.'

'Time will tell. One of the main determinants of whether or not a planning application is successful is local support or, of course, opposition. Councillors are human beings, after all. They would much rather make a decision which has popular support than one which would generate lots of animosity. But I'm not too sure what impact everything that has happened recently will have on our application. That is, of course, if we decide to still go ahead with it.'

'Why, is there some doubt about that?' asked Tom.

'I would imagine so, wouldn't you?' he answered. 'If Benjamin's death and, now, the attack on me are found to be connected to the application, then, yes, I'm sure that would cause some doubt.'

'Couldn't it also generate some sympathy, though?' asked DC Bennett.

'That's possible, I suppose,' replied a reflective Mr Weiss.

'You mentioned that Rabbi Aphron had given you prior notice of wanting you to remain behind,' said Tom. 'At what point did he actually ask you? Was it just before the meeting started or earlier than that?'

'It was earlier,' replied Mr Weiss. 'He called me the day before our meeting. Around 6pm, if I remember correctly.'

'Thank you very much for seeing us, Mr Weiss,' said Tom,

standing up. 'If there is anything else, however seemingly trivial, which you remember, please contact me or DC Bennett.'

Just as they were about to leave his room, Mr Weiss said, 'I do hope you soon find the person who is doing this, Detective Chief Inspector. My dread is that this sudden increase in violence against Jewish people will simply be the catalyst for even more, by giving encouragement to those people who would like to do us harm. It's not a pleasant feeling knowing that some people hate you.'

'We are doing everything possible to find the culprit, Mr Weiss,' answered Tom. What he didn't say was that he now only had another week to do it.

Chapter 58

'How may I help you, Mr Stone?' asked Jurgen Lang, in near-perfect English. Before Tom could answer, Herr Lang continued, 'I must admit I was very surprised when I received your phone call. It's not often I receive a call from a British police officer.'

'Yes, I'm sure it must have come as a bit of a shock,' said Tom.

After his visit to see Mr Weiss, Tom had returned to the station and, as soon as he was back in his office, had called the contact number that Herr Straub had provided. It was almost immediately answered by Herr Lang himself. After Tom had introduced himself he had briefly outlined the purpose of the call and why he would like to come and meet Herr Lang. Herr Lang had, not surprisingly, been puzzled by Tom's call, but had readily agreed to meet. He had been even more surprised when Tom had suggested they meet the following day.

So, early the following morning, Tom had taken the first flight out of Heathrow for Stuttgart. The flight left on time and, by 11am local time, he had arrived at Herr Lang's home, conveniently located on the south side of the city centre. The house itself was quite a large detached one and had been built towards the top of one of the many hills which overlooked the city. Unless all areas were like this, Tom suspected it was one of the more prosperous parts of Stuttgart.

'I'm sorry, but we don't have any English tea,' said Herr Lang. 'I hope you don't mind coffee.'

'Coffee would be fine,' answered Tom.

They were in a large room which had an impressive panoramic view of the city and the hills beyond.

'This is a wonderful home you have, Herr Lang,' said Tom, enjoying the view. 'Have you lived here long?'

Herr Lang laughed lightly. 'Have you started your enquiries already?'

Tom, still focussing on the view, didn't immediately understand the meaning of his question. 'No, I was just ... ah, I see what you mean,' he said. 'I'm afraid I'm not quite that clever with my questioning.'

'But,' said Herr Lang, 'to answer your question, yes, we bought this house back in the early nineties. Stuttgart has always been our home, although my work meant I spent quite a lot of time away.'

'If you don't mind me asking, what was your job?'

'Please, Mr Stone, you do not have to always show your normal English politeness. I understand it must be very important for you to come all this way to see me, here in Stuttgart, and so I promise I will try and answer all of your questions. Let us start by using each of our Christian names.'

Tom smiled. 'That's a very good idea.'

Jurgen began to explain. 'After my father had been released from prison he came back here to Stuttgart, his home before the war, and eventually set up a small manufacturing business which made parts, mainly for the auto industry. Eventually – and by that I mean after quite a few years – he had built it up and he had become a supplier to one of the main auto companies here in Stuttgart. If you have ever owned a Porsche motor car, then some of the parts would probably have been made by my father's company.'

'The British police force does not pay enough for me to have owned a Porsche, I'm afraid,' said Tom.

'Perhaps one day,' suggested Jurgen, before continuing. 'When I was old enough I also began to work in the business. Eventually, my father put me in charge of international sales and so I started to travel the world, selling our products. We Germans like to sell things to other countries. After my father died in 1989 I became managing director and stayed until a few years ago, when my own son, Dieter, took over the running of the company.' He poured more coffee into Tom's cup. 'Do you have children, Tom?'

'Yes, I have a son ... Paul. He lives in Australia,' Tom replied, never comfortable when this issue was raised.

'Australia? That is a very long way away. So you don't see him very often,' said Jurgen.

'Unfortunately not,' answered Tom, now desperate to move on to another subject. 'Did your father ever mention his role in the war?'

'I assume, by that, you mean his time as an SS officer in Auschwitz?' Jurgen suggested.

'Yes, as you know, that is the period I am especially interested in.'

Suddenly, Jurgen's calm and controlled persona appeared to waver slightly, before he replied. 'The older he became, the more guilt he seemed to carry. Of course, he never went into any detail about all of the horrors he had witnessed and, no doubt, the horrors he personally had been involved in. But, nonetheless, he did occasionally, when the mood took him, open up to us – that is to myself, my sister and my brother. I am in no way defending him, or other people like him, but he was only about twenty-one years old when he was assigned to Auschwitz. At first he was happy because it meant he wasn't going to fight the Russians in the east. By then, most sane people could tell Germany was not going to win the war and it was only a matter of time before the Allies were victorious. It wasn't long, though, before he realised that fighting and, perhaps, dying on the eastern front would have been preferable to what he saw and experienced in Auschwitz.' He fell briefly silent before saying, 'Have you ever been to Auschwitz, Tom?'

'I haven't, I'm embarrassed to say,' Tom answered truthfully. 'I have, though, recently spent quite a lot of time with someone who was a prisoner there at the same time as your father. In fact, it is highly likely that he saw your father whilst he was there. Yitzhak is now ninety years old and the only one of a group of four friends who is still alive.'

'I would like to meet him. Do you think that might be possible?' he asked.

Tom hesitated. 'I'm not too sure about that. He still has a very clear memory of events there. But you never know.' He then went on, 'Do you know what your father's role was in Auschwitz? I understand he had some sort of administrative role. Is that correct?'

Jurgen looked closely at Tom. 'Thank you for your choice of words,' he said, before, once again, falling silent for a while.

'This is always very difficult for us Germans,' he finally said. 'Anyone who worked there, whatever their role, must, of course, bear some responsibility for what happened, because it would have been impossible for them not to know what was occurring. It is a truly shameful period for my country. And it's a shame which, in many ways, we are still living with. As I said earlier, this was something which seemed to affect my father more the older he got. But,' he said in a more assertive tone, 'to answer your question, Father did have an administrative role. In fact, his job was to count, value and then record all of the possessions which had previously belonged to the prisoners. He then helped to arrange their transfer back into Germany.'

As Tom heard this he remembered Yitzhak's account of the role which German officers, such as Jurgen's father, had carried out in Canada. Their descriptions were almost identical.

Jurgen stood up and walked towards one of the cabinets located at the far end of the room, and opened its door. He took out a photograph and handed it to Tom. 'This is Father, and it was taken in 1943, just after he became an officer.'

Staring back at him was a handsome, fresh-faced young man in a formal pose. On his cap was the unmistakable, and sinister, death's-head badge of the SS. Tom continued to look intently at the photograph, unable to prevent himself from comparing it, in his mind, with the photograph of Jacob taken when he was in Auschwitz.

'Would you mind if I was to borrow it for a short while?' asked Tom. 'I will return it to you as soon as possible.'

Jurgen looked slightly puzzled by Tom's request but simply said, 'If you think it might help then, please, take it.'

'Thank you,' said Tom. 'What happened to your father after the war ended?'

'He left Auschwitz when the camp was evacuated in January 1945, and was then transferred to Dachau. Not long afterwards the Americans arrived and Father, along with hundreds of other SS personnel, was arrested. After the war had ended he was put on trial by the Americans, and then spent the next five years in prison, until his release in 1950.'

'What was he actually charged with?' asked Tom. 'I understand many other SS personnel were set free.'

'Some of the prisoners there had also been at Auschwitz at the same time as Father and they recognised him and ... well, I suppose I might have done the same if I had experienced everything they had.'

Tom now judged it was the right time to mention Ethel's letter.

'The main purpose of my visit, I suppose, is regarding this.' Tom took out, from his pocket, the letter. 'I'm sure you will be interested to hear the contents. It was written just a few years ago by a Hungarian Jewish lady who had been sent to Auschwitz in the spring of 1944, when she was about eighteen years old. She was assigned to work, within the camp, in a place which became known as Canada. Are you familiar with that term?'

Jurgen nodded.

Tom continued, 'Her name then was Ethel Engel, although, after her release, she married Josef Aphron, one of the other inmates. She sent this letter to a friend of hers, named Jacob – incidentally, yet another Auschwitz survivor – when she was in her late eighties. May I read it to you?'

With a hint of trepidation in his voice, Jurgen simply answered, 'Yes.'

Tom began to read.

'It helped that I was finally able to speak with you about Oskar. It's a great comfort to me to know that I have you there as a true friend. It's a long time ago now, but I find myself thinking about him more and more as time goes by and I get nearer to the end. He was different from all of the others and, without his help, I'm certain I wouldn't be here enjoying cake and coffee with you, my special friend.'

It soon became clear that Jurgen had been deeply moved by what he had just heard and it wasn't long before tears started to appear on both of his cheeks. 'Excuse me, Tom,' he said, taking a handkerchief from his pocket and wiping away the tears. 'It is very moving for me to hear such warm words about Father – especially from someone who was imprisoned there.'

Tom handed the letter to Jurgen, who silently read the

relevant paragraph. 'Are you sure that the Oskar who Ethel mentions is Father?' he then asked.

'Almost certainly,' Tom answered. 'According to your country's war records, your father was the only Oskar who worked in that part of the camp at the same time as Ethel was there. I think there is no doubt it is your father who Ethel is referring to in her letter.'

Once more tears appeared on Jurgen's cheeks. 'You can't imagine what this means to me, Tom,' he said. 'What Father and many other of my countrymen did, and were involved in, at that time, was horrific, but it is good he was still able to show just a small amount of humanity during those dreadful times.' He looked at the letter again, almost as though he needed to see the actual words again. 'Do you know what the help was, which Ethel mentions in her letter?' he asked.

'I don't, I'm afraid, but it must have been important for her to mention it seventy years later. I assume it involved helping her survive the camps, but that would only be a guess.'

'It would have been good to meet Ethel and speak with her about Father,' said Jurgen, undisguised sadness now in his voice. 'You mentioned that she married after the end of the war. Does she have any remaining family?'

Tom then told him about how, together with Josef, Jacob and Yitzhak, Ethel had found herself in England and then, upon arrival, she had given birth to Samuel – later Rabbi – Aphron. Finally, he told him about Rabbi Aphron's own children and grandchildren.

'That is quite incredible. All those people because Ethel lived,' he replied, reflectively. He then continued, 'But I'm sure you haven't come all this way just to show me the letter,' before quickly adding, 'although, of course, I'm very glad that you did.'

'Let me be very frank with you, Jurgen,' said Tom. 'My main reason for visiting you is because I believe you might be able to help in a police investigation I am leading, into the murder of someone who, in an indirect way, was also connected to your father.'

This immediately grabbed Jurgen's attention. 'Really? But how can that possibly be?' he asked doubtfully. 'I can't see how *I* can be of any assistance to you.'

So Tom told him.

Chapter 59

'Sir, I think you should see this,' said Milner.

It was the morning after his visit to Jurgen, in Stuttgart, and Tom had just arrived at the station. Milner passed him a newspaper and he immediately took in the headline:

LOCAL JEWISH COMMUNITY IN FEAR FOR THEIR SAFETY.

'Is this what I think it is?' asked Tom.

'I'm afraid so, sir,' answered Milner. He cleared his throat, a little apprehensively. 'I think you should read the rest of it.'

Tom began to read out loud.

'Following the murder of a prominent Jewish resident and the subsequent brutal attack on another, members of the local Jewish community are now fearful to venture out at night. One resident, who, understandably, did not want to be named, said, "Everyone is asking who will be next. I can't remember anything happening like this around here before. This has always been a very tolerant community where all different types of people have got along well with each other."

'It seems that these racist attacks could be linked to the impending planning application to build an extension to the local synagogue. We contacted West London police for a comment but, as yet, we have not had a response. Sources confirm, however, that the investigation is being led by Detective Chief Inspector Tom Stone.'

Milner allowed some time to elapse before he asked, 'Do you think we should talk to the press, sir?'

'I don't think we have any choice now, do you?' Tom

replied with resignation. 'I think the decision has already been made for us. If we don't then the press will simply fill in the gaps themselves, no doubt, helped by "unnamed sources". At the moment this is just a local story, but I suspect it won't be long before the national press pick up on it, and then it really will become a bit of a media fest. And anyway, if I know anything, it's that there will soon be pressure applied from the top to say something.'

'Do you want me to set it up?' asked Milner.

'You might as well before this spirals out of control,' he answered.

'Should we also ask one of the Green family members to take part? It might help to prompt the memory of other potential witnesses.'

Tom didn't immediately respond, as he weighed up the pros and cons of what Milner had suggested. After a short while, he said, albeit without any great conviction, 'I suppose so. It can't do any harm. Why don't you contact them to see if they would be willing to take part?'

After Milner had left, Tom spotted the brown cardboard box that DC Bennett had left in his office. He placed it on the table and then, carefully, removed all of the contents. Each item was in a separate protective, transparent plastic bag, and so he picked up each in turn, examined it carefully and then placed it back on the table. After a short while he selected one of the bags and re-examined it, before, once again, placing it back on the table.

He turned his attention to the contact chart that he and Milner had previously drawn up. He walked over to it, marker in hand, and started a new line with the names of Oskar and Jurgen Lang. As he looked at the updated chart his concentration was abruptly interrupted when his phone rang. It was Superintendent Birch.

'Tom,' Superintendent Birch immediately said. 'Glad you are in.'

Tom could instantly tell by the tone of his voice, together with the fact he had called himself, rather than asking Jenny to do it, that this was not a social call. This was quickly confirmed when Superintendent Birch, without any more preamble, said, 'Have you seen this morning's local newspaper?'

'Yes, sir,' he answered. 'Literally just a few minutes ago.'

'I thought you said this wasn't racially motivated.'

'I think what I actually said was that I was keeping an open mind.'

'And are you still keeping an open mind, as I understand there has now been another attack on a Jewish man? This, together with the threatening letter, would suggest something more targeted.'

'I do accept, sir, how all of the evidence points that way, but' – he hesitated briefly – 'for the time being, at least, I still think it best to do so.'

At first, Superintendent Birch was silent. After a while, though, he said, 'Well, I suppose you have your reasons. You'll remember how I offered you the option of more resources for the investigation. The offer still stands.'

'Thank you, sir. I'll certainly bear that in mind,' Tom replied, before telling him about the plan to hold a media conference.

'Look, Tom,' said Superintendent Birch, although this time in a much more amenable tone. 'As I said, I'm sure you have your reasons, and I will continue to support you, whatever you decide. In the meantime, I'll try and keep the top brass off your back, but I can't guarantee I'll be successful.'

'I really appreciate that, sir. Thank you,' Tom answered, knowing the clock was ticking and he now had less than a week to solve this before DCS Small's deadline expired.

Chapter 60

It was later the same morning when Milner reappeared.

'It's all set for tomorrow morning, sir. Here at the station at 10am,' he said. 'I've also spoken with Mrs Green, who initially was not keen to do it but, after speaking with her daughters, is now willing to be part of the press conference. She would, however, also like her daughter Ruth to be there to give her support. I didn't see this as a problem and I agreed. I hope that's okay with you, sir?'

'I can understand that. I only hope she does not break down completely, especially after all she has recently gone through.' He immediately went on, 'We do need to be clear, though, what we want to achieve by holding this press conference. What are your thoughts?'

'I think the main objective, as I said this morning, is to generate more publicity for the murder, in the hope it will trigger the memory of anyone who might have seen, or even heard, something. We know how the presence of the victim's family can often prompt this,' Milner suggested.

'I agree,' said Tom, 'but we do need to make Mrs Green and her daughter aware of this. What might help is if one of them was willing to read out a prepared statement along those lines. Will you speak with them about this?'

'I'll get on to it straight away, sir,' answered Milner. 'I'm already working closely with Jane, the station's new media liaison officer, regarding the logistics and organisation of the conference. She did say, though, that she would like to speak with you this afternoon about it, especially concerning the protocol of these events. I know you have been involved in quite a few of these in the past, but it's always advisable to remind yourself.'

'Thank you, Milner,' replied Tom. 'I look forward to meeting Jane.'

Not for the first time, Milner wasn't one hundred percent

certain of DCI Stone's true meaning, but, also not for the first time, he chose not to pursue it.

Milner then noticed the updated chart, now showing the two new names. 'Sir,' he said, 'with everything which has happened this morning, I forgot to ask how your trip to Stuttgart went.'

'It was very interesting,' Tom answered with obvious enthusiasm. 'As you know, I met with Jurgen Lang, and I'm now almost certain he is, in fact, the son of the "Oskar" who Ethel mentions in her letter. Actually, I have a photograph here of him.'

He took out the photograph, from a small folder, and handed it to Milner. As Milner looked at it, Tom said, 'Impressive-looking, isn't he?'

Milner didn't respond to Tom's question, treating it as rhetorical. Instead, he asked a question of his own. 'I see you've added their names to the chart. Does this mean you think they are connected to Mr Green's death?'

'I'm sure they are not *directly* connected but there is, undoubtedly, a common thread running through all of this,' Tom said, pointing at the chart.

'And that's Auschwitz, is it?' asked Milner.

Tom simply said, 'It is.'

'Were you able to find out anything new?'

Tom didn't reply immediately, as he considered his response carefully. 'Nothing startlingly new but a lot of good additional background information.'

'Like what, sir?' asked Milner, not content with such an ambiguous answer.

'Well, for a start, we now know what Oskar actually looks like and, as you know, it's always good to be able to put a face to a name.'

'Anything else?' asked a clearly underwhelmed Milner.

'Let's wait and see,' Tom answered, making it clear that he had now said, at least for the moment, all he intended to say.

Milner's disappointed expression clearly betrayed his feelings and this wasn't lost on Tom. 'Look, Milner, at this stage, there's nothing more I know to be fact than you know. If, and when, I learn anything else, you will be the first to know.'

As he heard this, Milner's thoughts immediately turned to the mysterious file which he was still holding for Tom. Nonetheless, he sounded reassured when he said, 'That's all I ever ask, sir.'

Chapter 61

It was the following morning and the press, together with other selected invitees, were gathered in one of the large rooms which doubled as the pre-conference reception area. Tea, coffee and various juices, together with a fairly restricted choice of biscuits, were all being served before the conference started. What was immediately obvious was how the number of press people who had turned up far exceeded the numbers expected. Tom's instinct that this local story might soon become of nationwide interest was proving to be prescient.

All the members of the Green family, with the exception of Mrs Green and Ruth Aphron, who were in a separate room, were there to provide their own physical and emotional support. Rabbi Aphron, together with his own children, Emmanuel, David and Sarah, were also in the room.

Tom had spent the previous couple of hours preparing his own statement and, with Jane, going through the running order of the conference. Mrs Green and Ruth had joined them later and it was agreed Ruth would read out an additional statement, on behalf of the Green family, appealing for further information.

As everyone took their seats in the conference room, Milner sneaked a look at the assembled people. 'The room is almost full. I can't believe so many people wanted to come to this. I thought it might be restricted to the local press and television. But it looks like a lot of the nationals are also here.'

'Thanks, Milner,' said Tom, with a hint of a nervous laugh. 'Just what I wanted to hear. Still, the more, the better. After all, we are trying to generate maximum publicity.'

Just then, Jane, the media relations officer, came into the small room where Tom and Milner were standing, immediately followed by Mrs Green and Ruth.

'Thank you for agreeing to do this,' said Tom. 'Hopefully, it will result in us receiving more information.'

It was Ruth who responded. 'I hope so, because this is becoming a real ordeal, especially for Mama.'

Before Tom could offer any further encouragement, Jane suddenly said, 'It's now ten o'clock. I think we should get started.' She then walked into the main conference room, followed by Mrs Green, Ruth and finally Tom. As they took their seats they were greeted by a sudden burst of clicks and flashes, as photographs were taken.

'Good morning and thank you very much for coming here today. My name is Jane Perkins and I'm media relations officer for West London Police. Also here this morning is Detective Chief Inspector Tom Stone, who is the lead officer on this investigation, and he will shortly begin by reading a statement. Mrs Green and her daughter, Ruth Aphron, are also here. After DCI Stone has finished his statement, Ruth will read one out on behalf of their family. Finally, after that, we will take some questions, but, as I'm sure you can imagine, this is a very stressful situation for all members and friends of the Green family, and so I would ask you to be respectful of that during your questions. DCI Stone,' Jane then said, looking towards him.

'Thank you, Jane, and thank you all for coming here today,' Tom said, looking at the mass of people in front of him. 'First of all I would like to pay tribute to Sylvia and Ruth for agreeing to take part in this conference. As you can appreciate, it has been a particularly emotional time for them, and it has taken remarkable courage on their part to agree to this.'

He then picked up an A4-sized sheet of paper. He could clearly see DCS Small and Superintendent Birch, who were seated next to each other on the front row, immediately in front of him. He began to read his statement. 'Benjamin Green was attacked between 10pm and 10.25pm on 23rd May, as he was making his way towards his local synagogue. We believe the attack took place where his body was later found, in a lay-by on Latimer Lane.'

As Tom read this out he could hear Mrs Green quietly sobbing.

'We would appeal to anyone who might have any information about this senseless attack, however seemingly trivial, to come forward. In particular we are interested to hear from the driver of a large, dark car, which was seen speeding away from the lay-by at approximately 10.10pm, to come forward so that we can eliminate that particular person from our enquiries.'

Tom then placed the sheet of paper on the table in front of him and continued. 'There has been speculation that Mr Green's murder, and the subsequent attack on another local Jewish man, Mr Simon Weiss, were racially motivated. At this stage there is no real hard evidence to substantiate this and so, until we do obtain such information, we will continue to keep an open mind.'

Even before Tom had finished speaking, a few of the assembled reporters started to shout out questions, prompting Jane to intervene. 'Could I please ask you to hold off any questions until after all of the statements have been read out?'

This seemed to have the desired effect. She continued. 'I'd now like to ask Mr Green's daughter, Ruth, to read out her statement.'

All eyes now transferred to Ruth, who, with a nervous tremor in her voice, began to read the prepared statement. Her hands were shaking slightly as she held the paper in front of her.

'Apart from being a father to me, Rebecca and Daniel, he was also a grandfather who had, earlier this year, seen his granddaughter, Hannah, marry. But he was also a loving husband who had been married to Mama for almost forty-two years, and, I know, was looking forward to spending many more years with all of his family.'

At this stage, Mrs Green's sobs became louder and it was with a supreme effort that Ruth continued to read her statement.

'Please, if there is anyone who knows anything about this, then I would beg you to contact the police. We do not want anyone else to have to go through what we are going through.'

She then immediately hugged her mother and both started to quietly cry. It was a display of raw emotion and, for a short while, the entire room was silent, with the silence only being broken by the low sobbing of Mrs Green and her daughter.

After a respectful period of time, Jane said, 'I'd now like to invite questions, but please bear in mind that, due to the ongoing investigations, it might not be possible to answer all questions.'

Immediately, there was an increase in noise as the reporters all began to shout questions at the same time. Jane, once again, had to intervene. 'I'm sorry, but it's impossible to hear your questions if everyone shouts at the same time. Sir,' she said, pointing towards one of the reporters who had been the most demonstrative. 'What is your question?'

'Detective Chief Inspector Stone,' he said. 'You said there is no hard evidence to suggest these attacks were racially motivated. But, by your own admission, both men attacked were members of the local Jewish community and attended the local Jewish synagogue. Surely this is more than just a coincidence. Also, I understand' – he then referred to a piece of paper he had in his hand – 'that Rabbi Aphron had, just before the first attack, received a letter warning him that these attacks would happen. Is that correct?'

'I'm sorry, but I'm not able to answer that,' replied Tom.

'But why not?' the same reporter shouted out.

'Because it is an operational issue,' he answered.

'Is it true you arrested someone but had to release them due to lack of evidence?' shouted someone else.

It took a while before Tom realised he was referring to Mr Thornton. 'No, that is not true. We did interview someone but released him, not due to lack of evidence but due to the fact he had nothing to do with the attack on Mr Green. I think that's quite an important reason. Don't you?'

'The local Jewish community are telling us that you are not taking these threats against them seriously,' shouted a different reporter. 'Why is that?'

'I take all threats seriously, irrespective of who they are aimed at,' he replied.

'So are you saying they have nothing to fear and it's perfectly safe to be out at night?' asked another reporter.

'I would recommend exactly the same as I would recommend to any other person who was out at night, especially when alone,' he answered.

'Do you have *any* idea, then, who might be carrying out these attacks?' asked someone else.

'We are currently pursuing a number of different lines of enquiry which the public can help us with. That's why I would appeal to anyone who has any information to come forward. As I mentioned in my statement, we are particularly interested in a large, dark car which was seen being driven quite fast, up Latimer Lane, at about ten past ten in the evening.'

But it was clear the reporters were only interested in the potentially racial aspect of this case.

'What happens if another Jewish person is attacked? Would you take it seriously then?' asked the same reporter.

'We take all attacks seriously,' answered Tom, calmly.

'We have been told,' said someone else, 'that you seem to be obsessed with something which happened at Mr Green's granddaughter's wedding. Is that right?'

This initially took Tom by surprise, and he immediately started to wonder how the reporter knew about this part of the investigation. 'No, I'm not obsessed with Mr Green's granddaughter's wedding. It's just one of many lines of enquiry which we are following.'

'Do you think there is institutional racism within the Met?' shouted someone else.

Tom looked closely at the man who had asked this and, despite being tempted to answer, chose not to respond to his question.

This line of questioning seemed to now set the tone and the entire conference was in serious danger of becoming a bit of a ping-pong game as the reporters continued to press the racial motive of the attacks, whilst Tom batted them back with his responses about lack of evidence and keeping an open mind.

One of the other reporters then shouted a question. 'Mrs Green, do you think that the police are doing everything possible to catch the person who murdered your husband?'

'I'm sure they are,' she replied quietly.

'And what about you, Ruth?' he asked.

Ruth looked directly at the reporter and simply said, 'No comment.'

*

Later, Tom was seated in Superintendent Birch's office. Also there was DCS Small.

'Well, that went well,' said DCS Small, with undisguised sarcasm. 'Couldn't you at least have been a bit more enthusiastic about the possibility of the attacks being racially motivated?'

'I didn't think I was being that *unenthusiastic*,' said Tom. 'I was simply being factual. Right now, there is no real evidence to suggest they were racially motivated.' He paused. 'Unless, that is, you know something which I don't.'

For a brief moment it looked as though a hint of anger appeared in DCS Small's eyes. But, if it did, it had just as quickly disappeared when he said, 'Look, Tom, all I'm asking you to do is to show a bit more understanding of the sensitivity of this situation when you deal with the press. And, incidentally, I don't think Mr Green's daughter exactly gave you a ringing endorsement.'

'Well, I do understand the family's frustration. Of course I do. It's in everyone's interests to get this solved as quickly as possible. But it would be not only irresponsible but also dangerous if we were to unnecessarily stoke this up as being racially motivated. If anything, until we have irrefutable evidence, we should be doing everything possible to avoid doing so.'

'I think, sir,' said Superintendent Birch, in support, 'we should just allow DCI Stone to conduct his investigation as he sees fit. I actually agree with him when he says there is no real evidence. Everything, including the threatening letter, could be deemed to be circumstantial. If we went to court on that basis, it would, quite rightly in my opinion, be thrown out immediately.'

Both Tom and Superintendent Birch waited for DCS Small to respond. When he did speak it was not in response to Superintendent Birch's point. 'Just make sure you keep me informed of any developments. I have a nasty feeling about this case. The sooner it's solved, the better for all concerned.'

Both Tom and Superintendent Birch noticed how DCS Small was looking directly at Tom when he said this.

Chapter 62

'Well,' said Tom, 'did you manage to get them?'

'I did, sir,' answered DC Bennett. 'I've sent them off already. I passed on your request for them to go to the top of their workload.'

'And?' asked Tom.

'Let's just say we now owe them a big favour.'

'Good,' answered Tom, with a light laugh. 'I suspect you've cleaned that up a bit. And what about the cars? Any luck there?'

'All done, sir, just as you asked.'

'Good,' repeated Tom, in a satisfied sort of way.

DC Bennett then continued, 'Forensics have come back with some more information regarding the other tyre marks. Based upon the pattern of the tyre tread, they have been able to work out what makes of car would need to have that type of tyre fitted.' He passed Tom a piece of paper, which listed the likely cars.

'Hmmm,' said Tom, as he read down the list. 'Could be very interesting.' He looked up from the paper. 'Any luck yet with CCTV? Weren't you going to widen the search area?'

'I have widened it, sir, but, as you can imagine, there is now a ton of footage to go through.'

'Well, keep looking. Do you need any help with it?'

'I already have quite a bit from the other teams, so I don't think any more would help right now. Anyway, let's hope we find something soon.'

As DC Bennett was about to leave, Tom said to him, 'And, with the other thing, don't forget to bring the results to me as soon as you get them back.'

DS Milner, who had been given the job of looking after Mrs Green and her family, now walked into the office.

'How are they?' asked Tom.

'They would like to see you,' Milner replied. 'They are waiting in the conference room.'

Milner suddenly looked uncomfortable and this was noticed by Tom, who said, 'You don't have to try and soft soap it for me. Just tell me what they said.'

'Let's put it this way,' said Milner, with a sudden surge of confidence. 'You are not their most popular policeman. In fact, I'd go so far as to say there is a real sense of ...' He hesitated.

'A real sense of what, exactly?' asked Tom.

'Well, animosity, really,' he replied. 'They have now gone beyond the point of thinking you are just incompetent.'

'I don't seem to have a lot of supporters in this investigation,' Tom said, as much to himself as in reply to Milner.

Milner looked slightly aggrieved by Tom's comment. 'I hope you aren't forgetting about me,' he said, before adding, 'even though you don't always share with me why you are doing certain things.'

As Tom looked at Milner he suddenly felt a pang of guilt. 'That's very good of you, Milner,' he replied, with genuine gratitude. 'It actually means a lot to me.' He then quickly added, as explanation, 'There are times when I don't tell you everything, that's true, but I always have my reasons. They may turn out to be the wrong reasons but, at the time, they are based upon my best judgement.'

'So,' said a suddenly emboldened Milner, 'is there anything you would like to tell me now?'

'No,' answered Tom, although the accompanying laugh eased the previous growing tension. 'Let's go and see my fan club.'

*

When Tom walked into the conference room, he was surprised to see just how many people were waiting for him. In addition to the Green family members, Rabbi Aphron and Emmanuel Aphron, as well as two other people who he didn't recognise, were also there.

It was Jane, the station's media relations manager, who spoke first. 'Ah, here's Detective Chief Inspector Stone. I was just telling Sylvia and Ruth how grateful we are to them both for agreeing to take part in the media conference.'

'Yes,' said Tom. 'Given the circumstances you both did very well.' He suddenly realised that this might come across as patronising and so quickly added, 'These things are never easy. I've been involved in quite a lot over the years but still find them daunting. Anyway, let's hope it will generate some new information for us.'

It was Rabbi Aphron who answered. 'Detective Chief Inspector. The last time we met I made it perfectly clear that I had lost all confidence in your ability to lead this investigation. I warned you then that I would be making my feelings known to those senior officers who I know within the Metropolitan Police Force. I'm afraid to say, after your performance today, I feel totally vindicated. More to the point, I now hope those same officers have come to the same conclusion as myself.'

'I'm sorry you feel that way, but I can assure you we *are* making progress and I'm hopeful we will soon be able to make an announcement to that effect,' Tom said calmly.

'Really?' asked Emmanuel. 'Then why didn't you say that when you had the opportunity earlier?'

'The main objective today,' Tom replied, 'was to try and obtain additional information. If I had said we were near to a breakthrough, then it's possible it would have put off those people who just might have that additional, important information.'

'So are you able to tell us what progress you have made?' asked one of the people who he hadn't recognised.

'I'm sorry,' said Tom. 'I'm not sure we've met before.'

'I'm David Aphron,' he replied, 'and this is my sister, Sarah.'

When there was no offer of a handshake, Tom replied, 'We have just received some important information regarding the make of car whose tyre marks we found in the lay-by. Also, we are hopeful that CCTV footage will soon provide even more information.'

'Is that all?' asked a clearly unimpressed Daniel, Mr Green's son.

'Sometimes that is all which is needed,' said Tom. 'There are a few other things which are of interest to us, but at this stage, I'm afraid, I can't provide any further details.'

'Why not?' demanded Ruth. 'It's our father who was murdered. How would you feel if it had been your father and the police wouldn't share with you what they knew?'

'As I have said previously,' replied Tom, as calmly as the

situation allowed, 'I will inform you as soon as I'm in a position to do so.'

Although Tom could sense the earlier outright hostility had abated a little, there was still a palpable sense of disappointment and frustration within the room by the time they all decided to leave.

As soon as they were back in Tom's office, Milner asked the question which Tom knew was coming.

'Sir? What exactly are the other things which are of interest to us? And also, I don't see any evidence of a major breakthrough.'

Tom was momentarily silent as he recalled his earlier discussion with Milner. Then he explained.

'But that's incredible. Are you sure?' asked a stunned Milner.

'Well, you can never be totally sure, of course, but certainly the evidence is growing daily.'

'What particular evidence *do* we have?' asked an intrigued Milner.

So, for a second time, Tom revealed his suspicions to him.

Chapter 63

The following morning, Tom, Milner and DC Bennett were all assembled in Tom's office. A selection of newspapers were spread across the table.

'Just when you thought it couldn't get any worse. Do you think they were actually there yesterday?' DC Bennett asked sarcastically. He picked up one of the dailies and read out the headline. '*Met Police failing to provide safety for local Jewish community.*'

He then went on to read the first paragraph.

'During a bad-tempered press conference yesterday, Detective Chief Inspector Tom Stone, the officer leading the investigation into the murder of one prominent local Jewish person and the more recent vicious attack on one of the deceased's friends, repeatedly refused to accept that the local Jewish community has been specifically targeted. This has led both family and friends of the deceased to question DCI Stone's competence, as well as his motives. Ruth Aphron, the daughter of the man murdered, said afterwards that their family, having lost all confidence in DCI Stone's abilities, are now calling for Stone to be removed from this investigation and replaced with someone who is more likely to be able to bring to justice the person who murdered her father.'

As DC Bennett placed the paper on the table and picked up a different one, Tom said, 'I wouldn't bother. They all pretty much say the same thing. What we need to keep focussing on is collecting evidence. That is even more important now we have this to contend with.' He gestured towards all of the papers on the table. 'More positively, you said earlier how the press conference generated quite a lot of calls. Anything interesting?' he asked, directing his question towards DC Bennett.

'Well, there was the usual stuff. Someone acting suspiciously nearby, although it was much earlier in the day. A car seen driving without any lights, although, again, not likely to be the car we are interested in. The next morning two men were seen following a local Jewish man. Someone also called in to say that if fly tippers were stopped from dumping their rubbish in the lay-by then this would not have happed.' He paused. 'But we took a call from a motorist who confirmed Mr Stephenson's observation about a car being driven fast. This particular man was with his wife and they were driving in the opposite direction to the speeding car. He remembered mentioning to his wife how the car was going too fast.'

'Did he remember anything else?' asked Milner.

'He did, yes,' answered DC Bennett quickly, 'and it could be very good news. He noticed it was a large BMW. He remembers this because, once again, he made a comment to his wife about BMW drivers always driving fast.'

'As you say, it could be good news,' said Tom. 'And what about the DNA results? When can we expect to get them back?'

'I checked with the lab this morning,' answered DC Bennett, 'and they are currently working on it. They did, though, make a comment, sir. Something along the lines of you not entirely understanding the meaning of the word *priority*. Apparently, you had already given them something else to work on, saying that was also a priority.'

'Was that another example of your mother's saying about giving work to those who are busy if you need something done quickly?' asked Milner.

'Exactly. Just wait and see if she was right,' Tom said, with a laugh. When he next spoke, however, his earlier joviality had disappeared. 'This, as is becoming increasingly obvious, could get quite nasty. I suspect it might even get worse before we can end this. So, in the meantime, we need to play this by the book. No shortcuts. Everything to be documented, and definitely no injudicious comments to *anyone*. There seem to be far too many leaks already for my liking. We keep the evidence we have close to our chests.' He paused. 'Whatever anyone says about our level of competence.'

'If what you say is correct, then surely we have enough evidence already to make an arrest,' suggested Milner.

'It's because I believe I am correct that we have to make sure we accumulate an irrefutable amount of evidence before we go for an arrest,' replied Tom. 'The key now is the DNA results. Those will give us something which is totally irrefutable.'

It was DC Bennett who articulated the main disadvantage of this let's-wait-until-we-have-more-evidence strategy. It was something which Tom had given a lot of thought to already. 'What happens if, in the meantime, there is another attack?'

'Well, then I have a real problem,' answered Tom. The use of the personal pronoun was not lost on Milner or DC Bennett.

Chapter 64

'But why would they say this when it's not true?' asked Mary.

It was later that evening and, if the morning papers hadn't been bad enough for Tom, the local evening paper's headline now took it to a completely different level.

Mary read out the headline.

'EXCLUSIVE: DETECTIVE LEADING THE INVESTIGATION INTO THE ATTACKS ON LOCAL JEWISH PEOPLE HAS ASKED FOR A BRAVERY AWARD.'

Even Tom had been stunned when Mary had first shown him the newspaper headline. As the investigation had progressed, it had taken so many unexpected twists and turns. It had really started with Yitzhak's moving description of his time in Auschwitz and then Dachau. It had affected Tom more than he had been willing to admit, and he had wondered if it was this which had brought him into direct conflict with both the Green and Aphron families. Then there were the accusations that he was not taking the attacks on Jewish people seriously enough, culminating in yesterday's hostile press conference. And now this.

'This is exactly the opposite of what you wanted to happen. Where did they get this story from?' she asked.

Tom had his own strong suspicions but decided, at least at this stage, not to share them with her. Instead, he replied, 'The press smell a good story here. As we've sometimes seen before, they are not beyond some creative journalistic sensationalism in order to sell more newspapers. The problem then is that it becomes a bit of a feeding frenzy, with each different newspaper or television station ratcheting up the sensationalism. It will eventually blow itself out, but by then the damage is often done.'

'You are going to respond to this, aren't you?' she said, holding up the paper.

'The most effective way to respond is to catch whoever has done this,' he replied.

'And are you close to doing that?' she asked, almost as if pleading for him to say that he was.

'I think we are very close,' he replied. 'We are just waiting for some DNA results to come back to us.'

But Mary wasn't about to let this drop. 'You *must* get your boss – it's Superintendent Birch, isn't it? – to speak to the press and tell them this is absolute rubbish.' She fell silent for a while before adding, 'Even if you were thinking of accepting the award, you can't accept it now, can you?' There was another brief silence, before she said, this time with a slight tremor in her voice, 'It's so unfair.'

Whilst Mary had been speaking, Tom's mind had been in overdrive as he considered where this story had come from. With this type of thing, he thought, to find the answer it was usually best to look for a potential motive, and who, particularly, would benefit from it.

It was only a short while later when his mobile rang and Tom could see it was Superintendent Birch. It wasn't difficult to predict the reason for the call. Mary's suggestion that he should speak with his boss was about to be followed even quicker than she had expected.

'Tom,' Superintendent Birch said without any pleasantries. 'I assume you've seen the headline in the local paper.' When Tom didn't immediately respond, he carried on. 'I'm so sorry. I just want to assure you I will do everything possible to find out where this story came from. And, of course, I will immediately issue a statement refuting the story. Do you have any idea where it came from?'

'Not really,' he answered, not totally truthfully. 'I suspect it's an attempt to discredit me. As to who is doing it ... well ... it could be a long list,' he added, with a surprising levity, given the seriousness of the situation.

'But you do believe it's connected with your current investigation,' suggested Superintendent Birch.

There was the briefest of pauses before Tom answered. 'I suppose so.'

The pause had not been lost on Superintendent Birch. 'Tom. Is there something else? Something which I should know about?'

'Not really,' Tom answered, trying not to openly lie to him. Superintendent Birch, being the perceptive copper he was, was obviously not totally convinced and this was reflected in the tone of his voice when he responded. '*Not really* is not exactly a ringing rebuttal.' He paused, hoping Tom might elaborate. When it became clear he wasn't about to, he continued. 'Well, if there is anything, I hope you feel you can discuss it with me.'

'Thank you, sir,' answered Tom. 'I appreciate that.'

Superintendent Birch clearly took the view that he had made the offer and it was now up to Tom to decide if, and when, to take it up. 'Anyway, I'll get a statement out as soon as possible.'

Unsurprisingly, Tom spent a restless night, finding it almost impossible to sleep. He had gone through, in his mind, all of the possible sources of the leak and, applying his principle of motive and beneficiary, kept returning to the same conclusion. But he also realised that now, even more than ever, the priority was to arrest whoever had been responsible for Mr Green's murder.

Unfortunately, that was just about to get more difficult.

Chapter 65

'What a load of cobblers,' said DC Bennett, after he had, once again, read the headline regarding the award.

He and Tom were together, waiting for Milner to join them. It was the following morning and, as he had found it difficult to sleep, Tom had left for the station much earlier than usual. So much earlier, in fact, he had arrived ahead of Milner. He knew he was more likely to be able to regain control of events if he was in the station, rather than worrying at home.

'You know that and I know that,' said Tom, 'but, unfortunately, again as we both know, some mud does stick in these situations.'

'Well, we'll just have to unstick it, then,' said a defiant DC Bennett.

'I appreciate your concern, but the most important thing is to focus all of our efforts on resolving the investigation. What we could do with are the DNA results. Can you chase them up again?'

'I already have, sir,' he replied, 'but I'll have another go. I'm already Mr Unpopular with the labs, so there's not much else to lose.'

Just then Milner arrived. The expression on his face suggested bad news and Tom immediately thought this was the result of the latest headline. It wasn't.

'I'm afraid there's been another attack, sir,' he simply said.

'Who was it?' asked Tom, trying to sound as calm as possible.

'Emmanuel Aphron,' answered Milner. 'Well, not him personally but his house and car. Last night, at around midnight, someone threw a brick through one of his windows. He was in bed at the time. When he went out to investigate, it was then he spotted how his car had also been vandalised. A Star of David had been sprayed onto the side of the car, with the words *No more Jews* underneath.'

'Are forensics there yet?' asked Tom.

'They should have been there first thing this morning,' Milner answered.

'Right,' said Tom. 'Let's get round there now.' He turned to face DC Bennett. 'Whilst we are there, you chase up the DNA results.'

Less than an hour later, and Tom and Milner were in the front room of Mr and Mrs Aphron's house. Outside, one of the forensics team was photographing the graffiti which had been sprayed on the side of Mr Aphron's car, whilst inside another team member was carefully bagging up various pieces of broken glass. Fortunately the curtains had been drawn and so most of the pieces had been confined to a fairly limited space just beyond the window. The brick that had been thrown through the window had ended up on the windowsill itself.

After they had seen the damage for themselves, Tom and Milner went to one of the other rooms at the back of the house, where Mr and Mrs Aphron were waiting. Also there was Rabbi Aphron.

'Now will you believe we are being targeted?' asked Rabbi Aphron, as soon as Tom and Milner had entered the room. 'Or are you waiting for someone else to be killed before you start doing something about it?'

Before Tom could answer, Ruth Aphron said, 'I can't believe you are allowing this to happen. What exactly have you been doing since Father was murdered? Apart, that is, from looking at wedding DVDs.' She suddenly began to cry and Emmanuel, her husband, immediately placed a comforting arm around her shoulder.

'Mr Aphron,' said Tom. 'It would be helpful if you could tell me what happened here last night.'

Tom's request seemed to reignite Ruth's anger. 'All you ever do is ask the same questions. My husband has already told the police what happened. Don't you ever speak to one another?'

'That's okay, Ruth,' said her husband. 'If it helps to find out who is doing this, then I don't mind how many times I tell them.' He looked at Tom. 'It was around midnight when I heard a loud crashing sound. At first I wasn't sure what it was, but I knew the noise had come from somewhere downstairs, at the front of the house. So I switched on the stairs light and went downstairs, went into the front room and could see a few pieces of glass on the floor. I pulled the curtains back and then saw the broken window and the brick on the windowsill. As I looked out of the window I thought I saw someone standing near my car, so I opened the front door and saw two people running away. It was then I also saw what they'd sprayed on the car.'

'So you didn't run after them,' said Milner.

Mr Aphron unexpectedly began to laugh. 'I didn't have anything on my feet and was wearing my pyjamas. So, no, I didn't run after them.'

'Could you describe them, then?' asked Milner, who had been making notes as Mr Aphron was speaking.

'Not really. By then they were quite a way from the house, and it was dark. But they were running quite fast, which, I suppose, suggests they were more likely to be young men.'

'And what about you, Mrs Aphron?' asked Milner. 'Can you remember anything about it?'

'I was in bed at the time and the crash woke me up. Manny shouted up to me to call the police just before he went outside to investigate,' she replied. 'I then came downstairs and saw what had been done. That's all I can remember.'

'Thank you,' said Milner. 'If you do remember anything else, however seemingly trivial, please let us know.'

Once again, Ruth's anger surfaced. 'What, however trivial? Like "did they call out *Hannah* or *Mama*?"'

'Ruth, please,' said Emmanuel.

An uneasy silence followed before Rabbi Aphron spoke, although this time without his earlier anger. 'Detective Chief Inspector. I'm sure you and your young sergeant are well-intentioned police officers, but, as I have said on many previous occasions, you are both clearly out of your depth with this particular investigation. I really don't know exactly what your motives are ...'

However, before he could finish what he was saying, Ruth interrupted. 'Well, I do. The great Detective Chief Inspector Stone wants to become a hero by getting his little medal. That's what it's all about. Isn't it?' she said, glaring directly at Tom.

Fortunately, Tom didn't have to answer Ruth's question, because her husband suddenly said, 'You mentioned, the last time, how you were close to making a major breakthrough. Could I ask exactly how close you are and whether that breakthrough is now based on these attacks being targeted at the Jewish community?'

'Certainly all of the available evidence points that way,' said Tom. 'But we should know for sure very shortly.'

'But how shortly?' asked Ruth.

'I'm hopeful we will have sufficient evidence within the next day or so,' he answered.

'*Hopeful?*' repeated Ruth. 'Is that the best you can do? That just about sums you up.' Contempt dripped from her every word.

*

'Did you speak to forensics?' asked Tom, as soon as they were in the car and on their way back to the station.

'I did, although they were a bit puzzled, to say the least,' Milner answered.

'They can join the club, then.' Tom paused for a moment, then said, more to himself than to Milner, 'I suspect I might be getting another call from DCS Small very soon.'

'Are you okay, sir?' asked Milner, his tone suggesting genuine concern for his boss.

'I'm fine, thank you, Milner,' Tom answered, a little too quickly for Milner's liking.

'You do know, don't you, sir, that, whatever happens, you will have my support?' Milner asked.

Tom, clearly touched, replied, 'Thank you, Milner. Although, with respect, I suspect it might be the support of some other people I need the most.'

*

They had been back in the station for a couple of hours when Tom's phone rang. He listened in silence to what the person on the other end was saying, before, himself, saying, 'Well, that didn't take long.'

The phone call itself was not unexpected. What was unexpected, however, was the reason for the call. It was DCS Small and he was informing Tom that he was being taken off the investigation.

'But I thought you said I had a week?' asked Tom.

'I'm afraid events have overtaken us. The attack last night was the final straw for HQ. They are very concerned by all of

244

the negative press coverage. The new team will be announced at 9am tomorrow.' A brief silence followed before DCS Small said, with what sounded like genuine sympathy, 'I'm truly sorry, Tom. I'm afraid this has now been taken out of my hands.'

'And what about the rubbish about me demanding an award? Apart from it being incorrect, as you well know, the story's timing proved to be very fortuitous, at least for those people who either wanted me off this case or simply want to discredit me. Where do you think that came from?' Tom asked, his voice now reflecting his increasing anger.

'Tom,' DCS Small answered in a calm voice, 'I know we've had our differences. It's true we are not the type of people who would naturally socialise together, but, for all of that, I do have great respect for you. I hope you can believe me when I say I would never leak anything against you.'

It wasn't lost on Tom how DCS Small had very cleverly avoided answering his specific question relating to the likely source of the leak. Despite this, however, his words had the desired effect and when Tom next spoke it was without the earlier anger. 'I actually believe you, sir.' This time it was Tom who paused before saying, 'But someone clearly would.'

After his conversation with DCS Small had ended, Tom took the opportunity to consider his options. He soon, though, came to the conclusion that none of them were especially career-enhancing. What was becoming obvious was that an attempt to discredit him had suddenly gathered momentum. The combination of his being taken off the investigation and the leaked 'award' press story suggested a coordinated strategy was now at play. It was a strategy which, if successful, could only end one way. His police career would be over and, more importantly, his reputation totally traduced.

As all of these thoughts went through his mind, he suddenly had a moment of clarity. He could either passively allow all of this to happen, or fight back and regain control of events. After all, he still had some time left. So he decided on the second option.

Chapter 66

'Tonight?' asked Milner. 'Are you sure?'

A short while earlier Milner and DC Bennett had returned to the office. As they had walked in, Tom had immediately noticed, from their body language, that they were probably bearing positive news.

Tom suddenly smiled, probably for the first time in many days. 'Why not?' he replied. 'As far as I can see, we now have all the evidence we need. The DNA results you've brought with you have just rubber-stamped that.'

'I agree,' said DC Bennett. 'We've been pussy-footing around this for some time now. Let's go for it.'

Milner was clearly not totally convinced by his colleagues' more gung-ho attitude. 'Like you, sir, I think we do now have enough evidence, but I'm worried that we are not giving ourselves enough time to properly plan the arrest. After all, sir, it wasn't that long ago you were making the point about how important it is to ensure we do everything by the book – especially given the sensitive nature of this investigation.'

'All of that is true, Milner. And, under normal circumstances, I would agree with you.' Tom then added, although this time with more deliberation, 'As we all know, given what has happened in the last few days, these are not normal circumstances. If we don't do it tonight, then we ... well, I, to be exact ... won't be doing it at all.'

Both Milner and DC Bennett looked at Tom with puzzlement. 'Why not?' asked Milner.

So Tom told them both about his earlier conversation with DCS Small and how a new team would be taking over the investigation tomorrow morning.

As usual, it was DC Bennett who succinctly expressed their reaction. 'Bastards. So we do all of the work, take all of the flak, are hung out to dry before being pulled off the investigation, leaving the way open for some other team to just walk in and make the arrest. Nice.'

'That's why I'd like to do it tonight,' said Tom. 'And, incidentally, Milner, you are quite right. We do need more time to plan for the arrest. Despite the evidence, we all know that there are all sorts of things which could go wrong. If they do, I had better start learning to play golf.'

After a short pause, whilst Milner and DC Bennett fully took on board the likely consequences of any foul-up, Tom continued. 'Look, I'm not asking you to do this. You both have many years of your careers still ahead of you. So, if you choose not to be involved, then I totally understand. In fact, I wouldn't blame you. I'd even be willing to put that in writing. At least then you'd both be covered. All I ask, though, is you let me know, one way or another, as soon as possible, especially given the little time which is left.'

'You are joking, aren't you, sir?' said DC Bennett. 'I'd pay good money to be able to see this through, whatever the consequences. You can count me in.'

All eyes were now on Milner. Suddenly a broad smile appeared on his face. 'Just try keeping me out of this,' he said.

*

For the second time that day they were all assembled in the front room of Mr and Mrs Aphron's house. It had already been restored to its former, pristine condition. The broken glass had all been removed and the broken window replaced.

'You said there had been a major breakthrough,' said Rabbi Aphron, directing his gaze towards Tom. 'Does that mean you are about to arrest someone?' He then added, almost as an aside, 'Because I hope so, otherwise this is just another of your wild goose chases. All you seem capable of is talking about this. We never seem to see any action.'

An hour or so earlier, Milner had called Rabbi Aphron to inform him that they had new information which he was sure the family would want to know about. Rabbi Aphron had, understandably, pressed Milner in an attempt to find out the details. Milner had, of course, resisted this, leaving Rabbi Aphron with little choice but to agree to this meeting.

The word had clearly spread because, in addition to Rabbi Aphron, Emmanuel and Ruth, also there were Rabbi Aphron's two other children, Sarah and David, as well Mrs Green's daughter, Rebecca, and son, Daniel. Now that Tom, Milner and DC Bennett had also arrived, there was standing room only.

'So, why don't you tell us why we are all here?' asked Daniel, the impatience in his voice very apparent.

Tom turned to face Milner and simply said, 'Detective Sergeant Milner.'

'Emmanuel Aphron,' Milner said, 'I'm arresting you for the murder of Benjamin Green, the attack on Simon Weiss and perverting the course of justice.'

Chapter 67

Even before Milner had finished reading him his rights, pandemonium had broken out. Everyone was shouting at once, but it was Ruth's voice which eventually made itself heard. Unsurprisingly her fury was directed at Tom.

'This is outrageous. How dare you accuse my husband of murder just because of your own incompetence? It's obvious what is going on here. You are out of your depth and under so much pressure to make an arrest, just to save your own career, you are now willing to accuse a totally innocent man.' She then seemed to remember something else. 'Have you forgotten how we were attacked, here in this house, less than twenty-four hours ago? How can you possibly explain that? Do you think we simply made it up?'

'I'll come on to that in a short while,' replied Tom, as calmly as the situation allowed.

Now it was Rabbi Aphron who spoke, although, surprisingly, without any hint of anger. 'You do know this will be the end of your career, Detective Chief Inspector Stone. Up until now we just wanted you removed from the investigation. But this is now something totally different. As you, no doubt, have already realised, I have powerful friends within the Metropolitan Police. I have already been told how you have a reputation amongst senior officers as a troublemaker and someone who has become obsessed with his own personal fame. Well, I suspect you are just about to become very famous, although certainly not in the way you might have had in mind.'

Tom chose not to respond to Rabbi Aphron's comments. Instead he turned to face Emmanuel. 'Where were you on the evening of the 23rd of May, between 9.45pm and 10.45 pm?'

Rabbi Aphron's earlier equanimity had now disappeared.

249

'This is totally scandalous. I will not accept it,' he almost shouted.

'Father,' said Emmanuel. 'I can easily answer that, and then perhaps we can stop all of this nonsense.'

His confident tone of voice, together with his positive body language, had the immediate effect of easing the tension and reducing the previously growing anger.

'I was here, at home. I'd arrived back from work at about 6.30pm and remained here,' Emmanuel said.

'Are you saying that my husband is lying?' asked Ruth, clearly exasperated by this line of questioning.

'It's just we have a witness who saw a black BMW driving away from the place where your father was murdered, at around ten past ten. I understand, Mr Aphron, that you own a black BMW. Is that correct?'

'I'm sure you already know the answer to that,' he answered, still exuding total confidence. 'Although I would point out that half of West London also seem to own black BMWs. Perhaps you should also question them.'

Milner, referring to his notes, then directed a question at Ruth. 'You've previously said how, on the evening of the 23rd of May, you were out, at your mum's house, and then went to collect your son from the train station, and didn't arrive home until almost midnight. That is correct, isn't it?'

'Yes,' she simply replied, although this time without any of her previous anger.

'Is that the sum total of your evidence?' asked Rabbi Aphron. 'That Manny owns a black BMW?'

'No. We have other evidence,' replied Tom. 'You just referred to your son as *Manny*. We now have reason to believe that is what Mr Green tried to say to the paramedics.'

Now Daniel decided to get involved. 'First you said it was *Hannah*, then *Mama*, and now you are saying Papa said *Manny*.' He began to laugh. 'This just gets more unbelievable by the minute.'

It was Ruth who asked the question that everyone had been thinking but no one, so far, had actually asked. 'Why on earth would Manny murder Papa?'

'It's all about his grandmother Ethel, but I'll get on to that shortly,' said Tom. 'I would agree with you that, so far, our evidence has been mainly circumstantial, but' – he paused just long enough to get everyone's attention – 'we also have other indisputable evidence which proves your husband murdered your father.'

He then turned to directly face Emmanuel. 'To begin with, there were things that you said which worried me.'

'Really?' replied Emmanuel, now in a sarcastic tone of voice.

'Yes. For example, you appeared to know that the person mentioned in your grandmother's letter to Jacob – that's Oskar – was German. As far as I know, no one had actually mentioned that to you. So either you knew – in which case, how was that? – or it was an educated guess.'

'Next, you'll be saying Manny wrote the threatening letter that I received,' said Rabbi Aphron, with a slight laugh that suggested his continued total disbelief.

'Well,' said Tom, 'that's exactly what I am saying.'

By now everyone was completely silent, so Tom continued. 'Just like your comment about Oskar being a German, you provided me with a clue when, later, you were discussing the letter. You used the words ...' Now it was Tom's turn to refer to his notebook. '*It wouldn't be a surprise if we were next.* These were close to some of the words contained in the letter. Once again, was this a mistake on your part or simply coincidental? At that stage I was willing to give you the benefit of the doubt, but that benefit soon disappeared when we received the DNA results. The letter and envelope both held quite a lot of fingerprints and so were partly compromised. But the other mistake you made was when you sealed the envelope. You must have licked the envelope to stick it down. Was it an old envelope or just force of habit? Anyway, whatever the reason, we now have some very clever people who can extract DNA from things such as that ... which they did. The DNA extracted from the letter sent to your father was yours, Mr Aphron.'

Mr Aphron didn't immediately answer, clearly thinking through all of his options. Finally, he admitted, 'Okay, I sent the letter. That hardly proves I murdered Benjamin. And, anyway, I sent the letter before then.'

'Why did you send it?' asked Rabbi Aphron, his earlier disbelief now replaced by outright shock.

'I wanted to help with the planning application, that's all. I thought it would generate sympathetic coverage and make it more likely that the application would get passed,' he replied.

'Or,' said Tom, 'you sent it as possible cover for yourself, as you knew it would add to the growing belief that all of the attacks were racially motivated.'

'That is pure speculation,' said Emmanuel. 'There's no way you are able to prove that.'

Tom didn't respond to Emmanuel's assertion. Instead he simply continued with his own explanation. 'By then you were beginning to worry about what might happen if Mr Green carried out his threat to inform your father about the necklace.'

'The necklace?' repeated Daniel. 'What has that got to do with all of this?'

'Actually, it's got everything to do with it,' answered Tom.

Chapter 68

The room, once again, fell silent as everyone waited for Tom to continue.

'Before I answer your question, first I'd like to answer Mrs Aphron's earlier one relating to last night's attack. No,' he said, 'I don't believe you made it up. I believe your husband did it.'

Ruth looked at her husband, almost pleading with him to deny what Tom was saying.

When he didn't, Tom continued. 'Once again, it was an attempt to add credibility to the "racially motivated" theory. I suspect, though,' he said whilst looking even more intently at Emmanuel, 'that it was also an attempt to discredit me and so finally get me removed from the investigation. After all,' he added, now switching his attention to Rabbi Aphron, 'there had already been quite a lot of that.'

Before anyone could comment, he carried on. 'But you made a couple of mistakes. Firstly, Mr Aphron, you said that, after hearing the noise, you switched the light on at the top of the stairs. In fact, you switched the light on at the foot of the stairs. Your fingerprints were on the bottom switch, but there were no recent prints on the top switch. Why is this important? It's important because it allowed time for you to be outside, graffiti your own car and then throw the brick through your front window. You then ran back into the house, took off the coat and trousers you had worn outside, switched on the light at the bottom of the stairs and called out as though you were shouting to any potential intruders. You then ran outside, now in your pyjamas and without anything on your feet, and claimed to have seen two young men running away. It was all done with split-second timing.'

'You said he'd made a couple of mistakes,' said Daniel. 'If his fingerprints being on the switch is one, what was the other?'

Tom kept his focus on Emmanuel. 'In your haste to take off your coat and trousers, you hadn't spotted a tiny bit of yellow paint which had got onto your clothes when you were spraying your car. I asked the forensics team who were here earlier to take a look in your utility room, and that's where they found your coat with the paint. It matches exactly the paint on the side of your car.'

'Manny?' said Ruth, once again pleading for him to refute Tom's allegation.

Even though the weight of evidence was stacking up against him, Emmanuel, impressively, still managed to maintain an air of confidence. 'I wanted to keep the racial story going. I shouldn't have done it, I know, but there's a big difference between wasting police time and committing murder.'

'Well, let's move on to the murder,' suggested Tom. 'There are quite a few things which put you, Mr Aphron, at the scene of the crime at a time when you said you were at home.'

Everyone in the room now stared at Emmanuel before Ruth suddenly began to sob. When Emmanuel did nothing to comfort her, the atmosphere in the room changed dramatically from the original outrage and anger to something now approaching apprehension and foreboding.

'Firstly, as you know, an imprint of fresh tyre marks was found in the lay-by where Mr Green's body lay. Our forensics team were able to match them with the tyres on your car.'

'There must be hundreds of cars whose tyres potentially match the marks. It's hardly incontrovertible evidence,' said Mr Aphron.

'Well, I tend to accept what our expert forensics team say,' answered Tom. 'I suspect a jury might do the same.'

By now Ruth was sobbing uncontrollably, unable to take in everything she was hearing.

But Tom wasn't finished yet. 'You mentioned incontrovertible evidence, Mr Aphron. Well, this is exactly that.'

Milner then passed him a large colour photograph of what looked like a decorated hairclip.

'This is yours, Mr Aphron,' Tom said. 'It was found not far from Mr Green's body. It must have fallen off, or, more likely, been pulled off, during the attack on Mr Green. It is exactly the same type and design of hairclip you use with your skull cap. What's more, there were a few hairs still attached to the

254

clip. Not only do they match the colour of your hair but, more importantly, forensics have been able to extract some DNA from the follicles.' Tom paused whilst he handed the photograph back to Milner. This had the effect of increasing the tension in the room to an even higher level. 'The DNA contained in the hair is a perfect match with yours.'

For the very first time, Emmanuel lost control and, raising his voice, said, 'That's a lie. How do you know it matches my DNA? You have made up all of this just to save your own skin.'

'We managed to extract your DNA from the coffee cup you drank from when you attended the media conference,' explained Tom. 'And, as for trying to save my own skin, I'm afraid I gave up on that quite a while ago.'

Suddenly Daniel lunged at Emmanuel. 'You bastard,' he said.

It was DC Bennett who was the first to react and, after a brief struggle, managed to extricate Emmanuel from Daniel's head lock.

Whilst DC Bennett continued to restrain Emmanuel, Ruth stopped crying and said, in a surprisingly calm voice, 'But why? What had Papa ever done to you?'

When Emmanuel remained silent, it was Tom who provided a clue as to the answer. 'It was because of what your father had found out.'

Chapter 69

'You see, Mrs Aphron,' said Tom, 'the necklace that your daughter, Hannah, wore at her wedding, as we now know for sure, originally belonged to your father's grandmother. If you remember, she was wearing it in the photograph taken at her own wedding.' At this stage, Milner passed him the photograph of Jacob's mother. 'This is the photograph,' Tom said, holding it up for everyone to see. 'But it was stolen from her, by the Nazis, when she arrived in Auschwitz, and it was that which upset your grandfather at Hannah's wedding and why he kept calling out *Mama*. He probably thought at the time that Hannah was, in fact, his own mother.

'After Jacob, your grandfather, died, your father went through all of his personal belongings and found the photograph. He quickly realised the necklace was the very same one which Hannah had been wearing. But he also knew how that necklace, together with all of her other family possessions, had been stolen from his grandmother as soon as she had arrived at Auschwitz. I suspect he then became quite obsessed with finding out how his grandmother's necklace, which he knew had been stolen in Auschwitz, was suddenly being worn by his own granddaughter, over seventy years later. I know I certainly would have. You will remember,' he said, 'your mother and sister mentioned how your father had suddenly become very preoccupied after his father died. This, I believe, was the reason why. I'm also sure he came across the letter which Ethel sent to Jacob, where she mentioned how someone named Oskar had helped her during their time in the camps. He possibly also came across other items which provided even more information, but, so far, there is no evidence to substantiate that.'

'But why would Manny murder Papa just for a necklace?' asked Daniel, with incomprehension and disbelief clearly in his voice. 'It just doesn't make sense.'

Everyone once again looked towards Emmanuel, but, as he continued to remain silent, Tom provided the answer.

'After Ethel died in 2014, Mr Aphron was the person who took charge of sorting through her possessions.' Tom now turned to face David and Sarah, Emmanuel's brother and sister. 'You did not get involved, did you? It was your brother who did it.'

Sarah simply nodded in agreement, whilst David said, 'At the time, Papa had lots of other things to see to and so Manny, as the oldest, volunteered to do it.'

'It was a fateful decision,' said Tom, once again turning his attention towards Emmanuel, 'because you found things which, no doubt, both shocked and worried you. Shocked because of what your grandmother had written, and worried because of what it might do to your family's reputation and honour if the information ever became public.'

'What did you find, Manny?' asked Rabbi Aphron, sounding almost reluctant to actually hear the answer.

The direct request from his father, however, had the desired effect and, finally, Emmanuel began to provide an explanation.

'Apart from the necklace, and all of the other pieces of jewellery, there was a diary which Grandmama had kept, giving details mainly of her earlier life, as well as her time in the camps,' he said. 'To begin with I was amazed to find all of the jewellery. After all, I had never seen her wearing any of it and you had never mentioned that she even had it. But then, as I read the diaries, I quickly realised why that was the case.'

It was Rabbi Aphron who responded first, as a dawning realisation of what was to follow entered his head. 'Oh my God. I can't believe it. Please, no,' he said, now almost pleading with his son.

For the very first time, Emmanuel showed genuine emotion. 'I'm so sorry, Papa,' he said, tears now starting to roll down his cheeks.

Just as Tom was about to carry on with the story, Emmanuel continued. 'In the diaries, Grandmama had written how all of the jewellery had been given to her by a German officer who had been assigned to supervise some of the prisoners in Auschwitz. Apparently he had given it to her after they had left Auschwitz and had arrived in Dachau.'

It was Daniel who then made the shocking connection. 'And the necklace was one of those items of jewellery. Something which was owned by my great-grandmama, but which had been stolen from her immediately before she was taken to the gas chamber, and her death, in Auschwitz.'

It was clear how no one in the room was able, or, more likely, willing, to fully take in what Daniel had just said, and so Tom decided to resume his own explanation.

'In the camp Ethel had been assigned to a place named Canada. It was here where all of the prisoners' possessions were sorted into clothes, shoes, money and items of jewellery. It was while she worked there that she met a young German SS officer. His name was Oskar Lang. They became close and during those terrible last few months of the war he helped her to remain safe. It was also then, along, no doubt, with many others, that he helped himself to some of the more portable items of jewellery. It was probably when the American army liberated Dachau, and just before he was arrested, that he gave them to Ethel. But it's also clear that she had developed a terrible sense of guilt and this was the reason why she never wore them, sold them or even told anyone else about them.'

'Are you saying a Nazi SS man, who had stolen the jewellery from Jews arriving at Auschwitz, then gave them to Grandmama?' asked a disbelieving Sarah.

'That's exactly what I'm saying,' answered Tom.

'And that's why I couldn't allow Benjamin to tell anyone,' said Emmanuel suddenly. 'I had hoped, after Grandmama had died, the story would be forgotten. That's why I gave the necklace to Hannah for her wedding. What I didn't know ... how could I? ... was that Jacob would recognise it as his mama's necklace. After that, and once I started trying to prevent it all coming out, I was committed. It was almost as if I couldn't help myself.'

'So you *did* murder Papa,' said Ruth, finding it hard to get the words out between her rhythmic sobs.

'Ruth, I'm sorry,' he replied. 'I didn't start with the intention of harming Benjamin. We had spoken a couple of times previously and each time he had threatened to tell Papa. I pleaded with him not to as it would destroy Papa and all of the work he had done trying to ensure the events of the Holocaust would never be forgotten. It would forever be a stain on the honour of our family. But he wouldn't agree to it. He kept saying how his own family's memory was just as important to him. On that particular day, Papa mentioned to me how Benjamin had called to say he urgently needed to speak with him and how he had sounded very agitated. So Papa had agreed to meet with him, after the meeting, at the synagogue. I decided to talk to Benjamin, one last time, and try and persuade him not to do it. I waited for him to leave his house and followed him for a while. I was in my car and stopped alongside and offered to drive him to the synagogue. When we got to the lay-by, I pulled in. That's when I tried to convince him not to do it. But he suddenly became very angry and got out of the car. I also got out and ran after him. I grabbed him, so that he was facing me. I was pleading with him not to do it, but he just ignored me and then tried to push me away. That's when I hit him.

'Ruth,' he said, now looking pleadingly at her, 'you must believe me. That had never been my intention, but a sort of red mist came over me and I just couldn't help it.'

But Ruth was now totally inconsolable and couldn't even bring herself to look at her husband. An eerie silence followed, broken only by Ruth's continued sobbing.

Tom took the opportunity to get him to confirm more of the details. 'After you hit him, what happened next?'

'He grabbed hold of my head. That must have been when my clip fell off. I hit him again and he fell down. I could see he was in a bad way but I never thought he would die. It was then I thought I heard something and I just panicked and drove away.'

'Driving very fast in your black BMW,' added Tom, making his point but then resisting the temptation to labour it any further.

'Yes,' answered Emmanuel. 'I was in shock, not knowing what to do next.'

'But you soon did decide, though, didn't you?' suggested Tom. 'Because you later also attacked Mr Weiss, a totally innocent man, for no other reason than to try and cover your tracks.'

Emmanuel didn't immediately reply, and so Tom continued. 'This was all part of your plan to make it appear as though the attacks were aimed at the local Jewish community. When would it have ended? After someone else had been murdered?'

'I thought that would be enough, especially as we had been told you were about to be removed from the investigation. But you and your team kept asking awkward questions, and I was worried you were starting to get close to the truth.'

'If you had waited a little longer I would have been removed,' Tom said. 'In fact, tomorrow morning there was ... well, actually, there still is planned to be an announcement to that effect.' He paused, allowing what he had just said to sink in. 'But, somehow, I doubt that will now be happening.'

'All of this,' said Rabbi Aphron, clearly now very emotional, 'just because of a necklace. Why didn't you tell me?'

'And what would you have done then?' asked Emmanuel, a hint of anger now in his voice. 'You have made it your life's work to remind people about the Holocaust. How would it have looked if this had become public knowledge? Could you really have come to terms with the fact that your mama had accepted jewellery from a Nazi SS prison officer? Jewellery which had been stolen from Jewish families just before they were murdered. Imagine what it would have done to our family's honour.'

It was Tom who answered that particular question. 'Perhaps he would have come to terms with it if he had known that Oskar Lang was, in fact, his father.'

Chapter 70

All eyes were now on Tom. 'What did you say?' asked Rabbi Aphron, a combination of shock and utter disbelief now in his voice.

'I said Oskar Lang was your real father,' repeated Tom.

'How ... how do you possibly know that?' asked David.

'I have the DNA evidence to prove it,' said Tom.

'So, this Oskar Lang is still alive, then,' suggested David.

'No, he isn't. He died some time ago, but his son, Jurgen, is. He lives in Stuttgart, and I met with him a few days ago and took some of his DNA whilst I was there. Our forensics team were then able to match it with your father's.' Tom turned to face Rabbi Aphron. 'We took samples from the cup that you had been drinking from when, like your son, you attended the media conference. It's relatively easy now to match the DNA belonging to half-brothers.'

'Did you tell this Jurgen Lang about your suspicions?' asked David.

'I did, but that's all they were at the time ... just suspicions. I have yet to confirm to him those suspicions turned out to be accurate. I'm planning to call him tomorrow morning,' explained Tom.

By now, Rabbi Aphron had his head in his hands as the full implications of everything he had heard over the past few minutes became clearer.

'Was Grandmama raped, whilst she was in the camps?' asked Sarah. 'Is that how she got pregnant?'

'I don't believe so,' answered Tom. 'I suspect, however, like lots of other women who were there at the time, she did everything she could just to stay alive.'

'How dare you,' said Sarah, her sudden anger very evident. 'Now you are saying that Grandmama was a common prostitute.'

Her brother David put a consoling arm around her shoulders.

'I don't believe I said that at all,' answered Tom, as calmly as possible. 'In fact, I have the utmost respect and admiration for your grandmother. She only did what I'm sure most of us here would have done if we had been there at the time. The instinct to stay alive is, after all, one of *the* most basic human instincts. For what it's worth, I do believe she and Oskar did fall in love. There is some evidence to suggest she spoke up for him after his arrest in Dachau. It appears as though her support had some effect because, although he was sentenced to five years' imprisonment, other contemporaries of his received longer sentences. Anyway, we will never know for sure. What is quite clear, however, is that without Oskar's help, your grandmother would not have survived her time in Auschwitz and later Dachau. But please don't take my word for that. I suggest you speak with Yitzhak Sax, who is still able to graphically describe what it was like during those dreadful times.'

Tom then took, from his pocket, a small black-and-white photograph, and handed it to Rabbi Aphron. 'This is your father, Oskar Lang.'

Chapter 71

It was late by the time Tom, Milner and DC Bennett returned to the station. Emmanuel Aphron had now been formally charged and was currently being held in one of the station's cells.

'Sir, that was a masterpiece,' said DC Bennett. 'Just amazing.'

'Well, we got lucky,' said Tom. 'If it hadn't been for the DNA taken from the hair strands caught on his skull cap clip, then it would have been almost impossible to prove he had killed Mr Green.'

'When did you suspect it was his?' asked Milner.

'When we first met him, I noticed he had odd clips holding his skull cap in place. One of them looked like the one found close to Mr Green's body. That was our real breakthrough. Sometimes you need a bit of luck.'

'And what about Oskar Lang being Rabbi Aphron's father?' asked Milner.

'That was more of a hunch, as a result of our conversation with Mr Sax. It was clear that his father wasn't necessarily Josef. Ethel's letter, when she mentioned Oskar, just added to my suspicion.'

'What do you think will happen now, with the Aphron family?' asked DC Bennett.

'I honestly don't know. They have so much to come to terms with at the moment. I do hope, though, at some point, they make contact with Jurgen Lang. But maybe that's me just being a bit of an idealist.'

Both Milner and DC Bennett started to laugh. 'I've never heard anyone describe you as an idealist, sir,' said Milner.

*

It was almost midnight when Tom arrived home. After all the tension and excitement of the preceding twenty-four hours, he suddenly felt very tired.

This was confirmed when Mary saw him. 'You look exhausted,' she said. 'Has it been a bad day?'

'Actually it's been a very positive one. Well, at least the end part was positive. The early part started badly and then just got worse. But, as they say, it was all right in the end.'

'Do you want to talk about it,' asked Mary, 'or do you just want to go to bed?'

'I might look tired and I'm sure I am, but at the moment my head is still spinning. I doubt very much whether I could sleep anyway.'

So Tom told her everything which had happened, including the call he had received from DCS Small informing him about being replaced by a new investigative team. He told her about the DNA results and the subsequent arrest of Emmanuel Aphron. But it was the revelation concerning Oskar Lang and Rabbi Aphron which intrigued her the most.

'That's just incredible. And what was Rabbi Aphron's reaction?'

'Shock. Disbelief. Incredulity. Every emotion you would expect,' answered Tom. 'Not surprising, really. Especially considering he had also just found out how his son had murdered one of his friends and attacked another one. I defy anyone not to experience those emotions in such circumstances.'

*

Next morning, as Tom was eating his breakfast, his mobile rang. It was DCS Small.

'Tom,' he said. 'I have just heard. Many congratulations. You must fill me in on the details. I've only heard bits and pieces, but it sounds simply incredible.'

'Well, sometimes, sir, you just have to trust the evidence,' Tom answered, before adding, 'especially when that trust is being thrown into question.'

Tom's response was not lost on DCS Small. 'You have every right to feel as you do. It's clear that some of the top brass wanted you off the investigation. We can only speculate as to why that should be.'

'I don't think we need to spend too much time speculating, sir. We both know why that is. Being bounced off an investigation is one thing, but having your integrity and professional reputation deliberately trashed is another thing entirely.'

DCS Small didn't immediately respond, leaving an uncomfortable silence. Eventually, though, he said, 'So, what will you do now?'

'That's a very good question, sir,' he answered. 'The one good thing which has come out of all of this is that I am now clear as to what I intend to do. I don't really know why I didn't do it months ago.'

'And what is that?' asked a hesitant DCS Small.

'I think you know already what it is,' Tom said.

After the telephone call had ended, Mary, having clearly heard Tom's part of the conversation, said, 'Are you saying what I think you are saying?'

Tom nodded. 'You know, some time ago, you said you would support me whatever I decided.'

'I remember,' she answered hesitantly.

'Well, I think I'm going to need it because, I suspect, it's the only support I'm likely to receive.'

Chapter 72

It was later that same morning and both Tom and Milner were standing in Commander Jenkins' outer office, waiting to see him.

'Are you sure you want to get involved in this?' asked Tom.

After his conversation with DCS Small, Tom had immediately called Milner and asked him to bring with him, to the station, the file which Tom had asked him to look after. When they were both at the station Milner, not for the first time, had asked Tom what the file contained. So Tom had finally told him.

Unsurprisingly, Milner initially couldn't quite take in everything he was hearing and, after Tom had finished, remained speechless for what seemed like an age. Even then there was still sheer disbelief in his voice when he did speak, and it wasn't until Tom had played the covert tape of his conversation with Commander Jenkins that Milner's disbelief began to evaporate, quickly being replaced with outright anger.

'We've had this discussion already, sir,' said Milner. 'Why wouldn't I want to get involved?'

'Because, no doubt, you are feeling emotional about it. There's a danger you are being led by your heart and not your head. Also,' Tom added, now looking directly at Milner, 'you have to consider your future career prospects. As I've told you previously, my own career is coming to an end, but yours is all still ahead. You have the talent to go all of the way to the very top. Remember what Mr Sax said to you about becoming a very senior police officer? Well, he was right. This will almost certainly be career-ending. You don't have to do this just because you feel that you have to show loyalty to me.'

Now it was Milner's turn to look directly at Tom, and say, in as serious a tone of voice as Tom had ever heard from Milner, 'I didn't join the force to apply the law just to one group of people. It's not original, I know, but the law is the

266

law and should be applied to everyone, irrespective of their position in society. Otherwise, what's the point?'

Tom couldn't help smiling, at least inwardly, as he was sure that he must have, at some point, used those exact words.

'And also, incidentally,' added Milner, 'what is wrong with showing loyalty?'

Before Tom could respond, Commander Jenkins' PA suddenly said, 'Commander Jenkins is ready to see you now.'

When they entered the office, Commander Jenkins was seated at his desk, his body language clearly suggesting an air of suspicion. He didn't get up. 'I'm assuming this is not a social visit.'

If he had been expecting some sort of preliminary discussion, then he was immediately disappointed.

Without any preamble Tom said, 'Michael James Jenkins, I am arresting you for perverting the course of justice as well as encouraging a third party, or parties, to commit a crime.' Without taking his eyes away from him he then said, 'DS Milner. Could you please read Commander Jenkins his rights?'

Even whilst Milner was doing this, Commander Jenkins, returning Tom's stare, said, 'You have just made the biggest mistake of your life.'

Lightning Source UK Ltd.
Milton Keynes UK
UKOW05f0403050717
304662UK00001B/34/P